Johnny Goes Loco

STEELTOWN CHRONICLES, Volume 3

Dave Walker

Published by Dave Walker, 2025.

This is a work of fiction. Similarities to real people, places, or events are entirely coincidental.

JOHNNY GOES LOCO

First edition. July 23, 2025.

ISBN: 978-1069682826

Written by Dave Walker.

Also by Dave Walker

STEELTOWN CHRONICLES
Making Steven Famous
Norbie Gets Screwed
Johnny Goes Loco
Tony Needs Speed

Watch for more at www.davewalkerauthor.com.

"The girl I used to love lives in this yellow house

Yesterday she passed me by, she doesn't want to know me now."

--The Who, "The Real Me'

"But I won't cry for yesterday, there's an ordinary world
somehow I have to find"

—Duran Duran, "Ordinary World"

Chapter 1

Is it normal to want to kill your friends?

"Open up, John!" Donny cried, banging on my front door. "It's been three days. And this time we're not friggin' leaving!"

He'd been banging on and off for an hour. Persistent and crazy and caring, that was Donny Love in a nutshell. The only reason he and Norb and Tony knew I was home was because they'd seen me peering through a crack in the living room drapes. Yesterday, I'd made the same stupid mistake.

I really did want to kill these guys, but only temporarily, just long enough so I could fix my shit, uninterrupted. I sank back into my living room couch. I kicked an empty beer can and watched it roll along the carpet and join the pile of Lay's sour cream and onion chip bags, empty Haagen Daz ice cream cartons, and greasy Aurora Pizzeria boxes. The pile of crap reminded me of a funeral pyre, one I couldn't wait to set on fire and dive right into.

I swigged hard from a bottle of Ouzo.

I should have been grateful my friends were trying to help me, but I wasn't. That had never been our deal. They knew I was a lone wolf. Besides, and I don't mean to sound arrogant, but they couldn't fix me—I was way smarter and more well-read. And, no, Norb's comic-book reading didn't count as real reading, and Donny had grown bored with books and hadn't finished one in years, and Tony only read *Hot Rod* Magazine, whereas I read psychology texts and serious literature, and could easily have gone to university if I'd wanted, so, yeah, I was definitely the only one smart enough to fix me. Over the years, I'd done just that, and sometimes with great success.

I'm also a lot like my dad—stubborn and resourceful. That's how he turned a hole-in-the-wall shit box into a successful Greek restaurant.

I'm also complicated. So, yeah, my friends had zero chance of fixing me. And what they didn't understand is that a real man fixes his own shit, alone. Of all people, Tony should understand that.

I breathed deeply, trying to shake off my pride, which, as always, was wasted effort.

Against my better judgement, I crept into the dining room at the back of the house and peered through the gap in the curtains. I half-expected eagle-eye Donny to be peering back at me, but he wasn't there.

Instead, there was good ol' Norb, his breath misting the cold air like steam off a boiled egg. Behind him was the snow-laden shopping cart I hadn't bothered to return.

My insides cinched—it really touched me that Norb was so concerned for me, that any of my friends were. They were missing work to come check up on me.

Shame burned inside my chest. This was all my fault. My out-of-character behaviour had ripped them away from their responsibilities.

"Go home, Norb, I work alone!"

"John, we know you work alone," he peeped. "Just please open up so we can see you're okay. Then we'll go, I promise. Scout's honour!" The fool even saluted. *What the hell?*

"I'm fine!" I roared, my voice rattling the glasses in the kitchen sink. "Now hit the road or I'll call the cops!"

I backed away from the drapes and crossed my arms in determination.

Norb was mumbling something, but I stood my ground. I could outwait them all. The benefit of living alone was that no one could come in, if I didn't let them. But I hadn't always been alone.

Seventeen years earlier, a year into marital bliss, my wife Sophia had suddenly walked out on me, without a word of explanation. The next day, her lawyer had couriered me divorce papers. To say I was in a total state of shock would be the understatement of the century.

I'd tried to call her cell phone but it was no longer in service. Apparently, she'd planned it that way. I was devastated.

The worst part was not knowing why she'd left. I'd spent days doing a forensic analysis of our lives together. Other than the occasional argument over me leaving a mess in the kitchen, I'd thought we were golden. The sex had been great, too, and we'd laughed a lot.

So, basically, no warning. And zero chance for me to make things right, whatever those things were. I'd begged her parents and brother for her contact info, but, out of loyalty, they wouldn't give it to me. I loved the Andonis family. They'd treated me like a son. So, I'd not only lost the love of my life, but my second family, too.

A week after Sophia dumped me, rage set fire to my heartbreak, and I found myself hiring a lawyer. We asked for the house and Sophia just let me have it. Guilt? I fucking hoped so! For the sake of my mental health, I should have sold the house and started over. But I didn't, because I wanted to punish her for leaving me. Sick, right? And the really sick part chose to live with the ghosts of *us*, flitting around in our marital home.

Obviously, I never got over Sophia. I never stopped loving her, despite my bitterness. So, the big question is this: How sick is a guy who keeps loving someone who ripped out his heart a lifetime ago?

Now, at the thought of my ex-wife, hot flames grew inside my skull. I fell into a familiar pattern of ruminating. Thinking of all the Wayne Dyer books I'd read over the years, I stood outside myself and *witnessed* myself having Sophia thoughts, then I sent myself all the love I could muster in my depressed state. Slowly, some of my pride and anger dissipated. I focused on my breathing. For the moment, I felt peaceful.

Just two days earlier, I'd dug up the "Just Married" sign that we'd taped to our car and strung it across the front window of my house, hoping that Sophia or someone she knew would drive by and see it. Then she'd realize just how much she'd screwed me up.

Putting up the sign was ludicrous, I know, but I was hurting, my house was haunted, and I was the stunted, idiot monster brooding inside it.

"Open up, John!" Tony growled, hammering on the basement window. "Or I'll huff and I'll puff and I'll blow your frickin' house down!"

I whipped open the drapes and shouted, "Everyone go the fuck home and leave me alone! I'm fine!" The guys were gawping at me, like they'd never seen a guy hanging out in his underwear. I gave them the finger, then went back to the couch and swigged some more Ouzo.

"Fuck the self-help bullshit!" I shrieked, kicking Your Sacred Self to the floor. I guzzled the rest of the booze and gasped as it burned my throat. "Witness that, Wayne Dyer!"

Just because I struggled with my own emotions didn't mean I didn't have any for anybody else. I sure as hell did. Case in point, the time Donny slunk back to Hamilton and visited me at the restaurant. He'd wanted to see if I was content running the family business instead of chasing my dreams, like he had. I'd invited him to my house and showed him my basement dance studio, so he'd know a man can still dream and also lead a normal life. Also, lately, I'd been kinder to Norb. I rarely called him Eggie anymore. He'd earned my respect when he'd bravely swung off the bowling alley roof and defeated The Screw. Plus, he was now married with a child. The urge to be sarcastic was still there, but I'd found a way to heave back on it before I said something stupid. It was exhausting work, but so far, so good.

After the divorce, my sarcasm sank to new depths. No one was safe from my digs. And, worse, I'd pasted a smile on my face, and bought only the most stylish of clothes, as if that would distract everyone from my damaged state. I couldn't remember the last time I'd worn jeans.

"What's with the fancy duds?" Donny often said. "You're obviously over-compensating for what Sophia did to you. You should get some help with that, brother." And I'd snap back with,

"How's the music career coming, Donny?" Or, "Still married, bud?" Or "You're a psychologist now? Congrats, man." But Donny was right—I just couldn't stop.

I'd always been proud, but after my divorce my pride became toxic.

Two years after Sophia dumped me, desperate to escape and understand my pain, I'd enrolled in Psychology 101 at McMaster University. Although I'd found the concepts fascinating, they'd given me no relief from the memories of the woman I'd loved so deeply and openly and profoundly—the books hadn't taught me how to apply the concepts to real life. Total waste of time and money.

Fortunately, Norb's wife Morag had turned me on to self-help books, especially by Wayne Dyer, and I'd borrow all his books and devour them. Finally, I'd found practical psychological techniques to help me cope.

But once they started working, I'd stop reading, and inevitably Sophia would show up in my head and I'd hit the books again to flush her out. But sometimes I let her stay because it was better than being alone. Sick, sick, sick.

This latest crisis of mine had started three days earlier, when I'd done something shocking. Like a zombie, I'd found myself walking out of the family restaurant during a busy dinner shift. I'd bunkered down like a slob inside my normally immaculate home, determined to once-and-for-all find a way to kick Sophia out of my head. I'd cranked the thermostat and stripped down to my underwear.

Now, I went to the fridge, grabbed a five-litre tub of Death by Chocolate ice cream and flopped back on the couch. Depression was the greatest excuse to binge eat. Since nothing else mattered, why not kill yourself with ice cream?

I hadn't shaved in ages. I didn't care. I stunk. I hadn't brushed my teeth. Again, didn't care. And I didn't care that I didn't care. At the last minute, I'd cancelled today's salsa class at Lyle's Academy, and I never did that, unless I was sick, and I was rarely sick.

My cell phone rang, startling me. It was Donny. He'd already called me three times that morning. Once again, I let it go to voice mail. I knew I'd pick up next time to let him know I was still alive. Ma and my sister Amara had dropped off a pamphlet with a bunch of crisis hotline phone numbers. I'd done my best to reassure them, through the front door, that I didn't need to go to the hospital.

This morning, pissed off, I group-emailed my family and friends and ordered them to leave me the fuck alone, because if they didn't, I'd burn down my house with me in it. Then, I'd added a smiley face, so they'd think I was only kidding, which I sure as hell wasn't.

Then I'd added a P.S., saying I was a big boy capable of handling his own problems, and so not to worry, I'd explain everything later. It was a real crap email, I know, but the last thing I wanted around me was people who loved me.

On the tv, an infomercial salesman who bore an uncanny resemblance to Donny was trying to sell me diamonds. Anything to do with diamonds reminded me of Sophia—she'd loved jewelry.

I tried to forget her by stuffing a huge spoonful of ice cream in my mouth, praying for a diabetic coma and a quick death. Instead, I got brain freeze.

I'd just scarfed some potato chips when a bizarre sight bumped me up off the couch. The chips flew out of my mouth as I cried, "What the fuck, Love? Are you shitting me?"

Up through an ancient heating grate, he'd popped his head like a jack-in-the box.

Melting snow drizzled through his thick, reddish-brown hair. Weirdly, he was wearing Allison's pink ski jacket, a Santa hat and a thick green scarf. He was a demented Christmas elf!

"Love, you broke into my house? What the hell, man!"

"Thong underwear, Johnny?" Donny started to laugh. "Super sexy!"

I tried to whack-a-mole his head with my fist but he flinched back down into the safety of the basement and smirked up at me like an imp.

"Johnny, brother, we're worried about you. Seriously."

I shoved the grate back into place. "I told you and everybody else to leave me alone and I meant it! Show up here again and I'll call the cops. Now get out!"

Before I knew it, he'd jackrabbited up the basement stairs into my living room. "Norb's trying to jimmy your back door. You should probably just let him in, before he breaks it."

"Are you shitting me?"

Just in case Donny was actually telling the truth for a change, I raced through the kitchen to the back door, hoping to stop Norb. The *front* door opened. I could hear Norb talking to Tony.

Assholes! They'd faked me out!

I found Tony, John, and Donny huddled in the front hall.

Norb couldn't meet my gaze. His face was red from exertion, and he was panting as if he'd just finished one of his heroic hundred-metre dashes. He wore a black Steeltown Avenger t-shirt, but no winter coat, and his purple Converses were caked with snow. Tony looked exhausted—black bags hung under his eyes. He wore a nylon Canadian Tire winter jacket over a pair of greasy coveralls. Obviously, both Tony and Norb had come from work.

"How did you open the door?"

Sheepishly, Norb held up a key. "Your Ma had a spare."

"You called my—"

"Don't get mad, John!" Norb wheezed. "We're just trying to help you. We're your friends."

Tony winced at my thong. "Put some clothes on, would ya?" He crinkled his nose. "And when was the last time you had a shower? You stink, man."

"Dammit!" I cried, shrugging on my crumpled house coat. "You're all lucky I don't call the cops and press charges!"

Donny slapped his hands to his cheeks, feigning fear.

I raised my fist.

"Tsk, tsk," he said, wagging his index finger at me.

Tony was impatiently tapping his foot, and Norb was mesmerized by the infomercial.

"Fine," I scowled. "Whatever. Make it quick."

I sank into the blue chair beside the tv and crossed my arms.

Norb and Donny crashed onto the couch like eight-year-olds psyched to watch Saturday morning cartoons. Why were these idiots still in my life? I should have ditched them years ago!

"What's with the pipe?" Donny asked, eyeing the table beside me. "Are you a *real* psychologist now?" He stroked a pretend goatee. "Hello, I'm Dr. John Pappas, the Tim Hortons headshrinker, how can I help you today?" He laughed at his own joke, in typical style. He stuck my pipe in his mouth, arched an eyebrow and pretended to read my Psychology 101 text book.

I gave him a fuck-you glare but he pretended not to notice.

Tony grimaced. He wasn't a fan of psychology—he shot from the hip.

I was desperate to get these idiots out of here before I unravelled, and I almost told them to hit the road again when I saw Norb staring at me with Mother Theresa-level compassion. That broke me. I tried to wipe away my tears fast but the guys had eyes on me. How humiliating. They'd never seen me like this.

"Stop it, Norb," I blubbered.

"Stop what?" He cocked his head like a dopey puppy dog.

"Stop looking at me like that! You're trying to break me." I pawed away at the tears on my cheeks but they kept coming.

He was dumfounded. "Sorry John, I'm just concerned about you, that's all. Scout's honour."

"Again with the Scout's honour?" I scoffed, and that was enough to jolt me back to feeling like myself. Sarcasm was my go-to energy booster, and although that wasn't a good thing, it was all I had. "Norb, you never even went to Cubs, much less Scouts. Give it up!"

I focused on slowing my breath and found a way to regain my composure.

My friends were still stunned.

"Sorry," I snuffled. "I'm not normally like this."

"We know," Norb said. "What the heck's wrong?"

Tony raised an eyebrow at me.

"I'm not ready to talk, guys. Please just leave."

I was about to get up and open the door for them, when Tony leaned forward, intense, his foot still tapping.

"Listen, Howard frickin' Hughes, you've been clammed up in this pigsty for three days and you look like a bag of shit. You're sick in the head, and I know that because you're acting just like my Aunt Beatrice did when she lost her nut. She hid in the attic for a month and lived off of canned sardines before anyone found her. Then she spent the rest of her sad life in the psych ward. Is that what you want? Do you really think you can fix yourself, John? You've been trying for years and look where it's gotten you. Frickin' nowhere. And now you're a frickin' mess."

Tony, Mr. Compassionate. But in his own way, he totally was.

"I'm not sick, Tony, I'm just depressed, okay. It looks bad, I'll give you that, but I'll get through it. I always do."

Tony eyed the garbage piled in the middle of the room and winced. "You're in deep trouble, John, and I'm seriously concerned about you."

I felt the tears welling up again, but I plunged them back down. "Shouldn't you guys be at work?"

"Don't worry about that," Tony said. "And don't change the subject."

"Self-employed," Norb said, "Tank's running the show today. All cool on my end."

"Working from home," Donny said, triumphantly, scratching his crotch. "Column's not due for a couple of days."

I felt something relax inside me. "Okay, fellas," I said. "I'll tell you what's going on, but then you have to leave."

They looked at each other and nodded.

"Promise?

Tony looked exasperated. "Talk, Pappas."

"Okay, so I was at the restaurant on Friday, cleaning out the espresso machine. Suddenly, something inside my brain just kind of folded, like a house of cards, and I found myself walking out the door, without my winter coat. And I felt such despair. I remember walking up the escarpment stairs and not caring that I was freezing and the snow was blinding me. Then I went to Price Chopper and stuffed my shopping cart with junk food. I didn't take a cab, I just pushed the cart through the slush." I'd gotten a bit of frostbite on my nose. I touched it carefully to see how the scab was healing up.

Donny eyed it. I could tell he was considering a smart remark.

"Why is it so friggin' hot in here?" Tony complained, rolling up his sleeves. Sweat was beading on his forehead. I should have turned down the thermostat for him, but at that moment moving seemed impossible.

I cast my gaze downward. I felt so guilty and ashamed for abandoning the restaurant like that. "I let down my folks, big time."

"That's so heavy," said Norb. "Really, really heavy. It's like you're Superman, hiding out in your Fortress of Solitude, or something."

Tony narrowed his eyes.

Donny was drumming his thighs with his hands. "Is this about never taking a shot at Broadway?"

"Broadway?" Tony said, "What does that have to do with anything?"

Norb was stroking his beardless chin, deep in thought. "Broadway, that sounds so epic."

I shifted uncomfortably. I couldn't seem to stop this odd flow of confession.

"Maybe that's a part of it, Donny," I sighed. "For the first time in my life, I feel I'm at a crossroads, but I just didn't see it coming. I never gave it a shot. Let's be honest, OK? I'm a coward. Not like Norb. Norb had the balls to write a comic book that should have failed but didn't, and he faced a psychotic little freak and actually beat him."

Norb's face was suddenly still. I hoped I hadn't damaged our friendship by criticizing his comic book. *Say something nice, dammit!*

"You really do have guts, Norb. You're smarter than me when it comes to make-believe, way smarter. And your comics are published by a real publisher. And you're a real, in-the-flesh comic book hero."

He brightened.

I shifted my gaze to Donny.

He looked...skeptical.

"And you, Donny," I said, "fail at everything but you keep trying. And that makes you a courageous failure, whereas I'm just a cowardly failure, and you absolutely succeeded when you married Allison, who we all know is way too good for you, right?"

Norb and Donny were trying really hard to smile, despite my backhanded compliments.

"Sorry," I stammered, "none of that came out right."

Tony pointed an accusatory finger at me. "Johnny, I might be a grease monkey wop but I'm smart enough to know you're not telling us the whole story. Spill, Lamb Chop, or I'll spill for you."

If it had been the other two pressuring me, I would have cleverly deflected. But tough, big-hearted Tony had cornered me. And when he had that angry look on his face, he actually scared me. I had no choice. I spilled.

"Fine. I've never got over Sophia. Not really. Not ever."

I pointed at the stack of books on the coffee table. "Those don't work anymore. They're fucking useless." I'd never said that out loud before. I held my breath and wrapped the usual steel wall around my heart.

Tony was nodding, making full eye contact with me, a rarity.

"You need to make things right with her," Norb peeped.

"Wow, I never thought of that," I said sarcastically. Shit, I'd gone back to old habits. "Sorry," I grumbled.

"Norb's right," Donny said. "You need to make things right with Sophia for your own sake. Maybe write her a letter and tell her how much pain she's caused you." He leaned forward, his eyes widening. "Or maybe give professional dancing a real shot before you get too old. Maybe *that's* the real issue here. Maybe it's all about regret, with bits of Sophia and dancing tangled together."

"Give dancing a real shot? At forty-one?" I laughed sardonically. "Yeah, right. That shipped has sailed." I thought about what Donny had said. "But I *was* content teaching a dance class and working at the Olympia."

"Maybe deep down you feel like a coward," Norb offered. "That's how I felt all the time around Morag. But then I became the Steeltown Avenger and battled The Screw. After that, I knew I was brave. And it was easier to look at myself in the mirror. I'm a better husband for it and a better father, too."

Norb's words made me bristle. No man wants to be called a coward. Tony avoided my gaze, which was pretty telling.

For once, I didn't have a sarcastic come-back—dammit, Norb was right. And it bothered me that he'd shown real courage in his life but I never had. I'd always thought of Norb as a total geek, and myself more like a Greek James Bond. Obviously, I was deluded. So, what was my problem? What was I *really* afraid of?

I stared down at my bare feet—it was easier than looking my friends in the eye.

"On second thought," Donny piped up, "writing Sophia a letter might be a really bad idea. Those things rarely go well. A guy at the paper sent his ex a letter and she took out a restraining order on him. He went into a major depression and tried to kill himself."

"Now, *why* did you have to say that?" Tony glared at Donny.

Donny ignored him. "John, Sophia divorced you seventeen years ago. Think about it. She moved on, but *you* haven't even started."

My stomach curdled hearing that.

Donny sat back hard against the couch. "And by the way, I recognize that I'm a total hypocrite. We all know I'm terrible at moving forward in life, so I guess I'm an expert at this stuff."

"Look, why did Sophia leave you?" Tony asked. "You never did give us a straight answer." He was staring at me like a moody bulldog.

To be honest, I was glad he was pressuring me. It was a relief to finally be opening up. "I have told you. No fucking idea. She never said. But what you don't know is that I sent her at least fifty letters, begging her for some kind of explanation, but she never responded. I think her family was intercepting them, or maybe everyone was advising her to ignore me, including her lawyer. Either way, she didn't have the fucking decency to respond."

I swallowed against the growing lump in my throat. "Nope, no closure for you, Johnny Pappas. You get sweet fuck-all!" I was shaking now. "All I ever got was her parents telling mine that she was happy in her new life and to respect her privacy."

I jerked to my feet. "What about respect for *me*? Huh? What kind of sadist doesn't give a reason for divorcing you!"

I kicked the side table, upending my stupid books and pipe onto the floor. Then I buried my face in my hands and wept, doubled over.

Donny shawled me with his scarf. Norb patted me awkwardly on the shoulder. And Tony, well Tony just nodded empathetically. "I'm friggin' sorry, John. I had no friggin' idea she'd done such a number on you."

"Thanks," I snuffled.

The phone rang. It was a welcome diversion. I went into the kitchen, and for some reason, I hit the speaker button. "Hey, Ma."

She was in a panic.

"Uncle George fainted and smacked his head on a table! An ambulance took him to the hospital, and we had to clear out the restaurant so we could clean up all the blood. It was awful. Please come and help out, Johnny. George is going to be in the hospital for at least a day or two. Please. Just for a while."

Guilt and shame ironed my chest. "I'm sorry, Ma. That's terrible news."

"So you'll come and help out?"

My arms went numb. I hung up.

Tony was jabbing his index finger at me. "Johnny, you gotta help your parents!"

But I was paralyzed. I couldn't help them. I couldn't even help myself.

I went to the front door and swung it open. This time I wasn't taking no for an answer.

They all eyed each other, shrugged and shuffled out.

Five minutes after they left, Donny returned to pressure me into going out for dinner. I agreed right away so he'd leave me alone. I needed to get back to my drinking. I had zero intention of socializing.

After the door closed behind him, I slid another bottle of Ouzo out from under the couch and took a long, hard swig. Then another, and another...

Chapter 2

SO, WHEN DONNY SHOWED up, I'd planned to be out diving in front of cars or playfully leaping off the escarpment. But then I realized that drinking myself into oblivion with Donny at the Blue Ball would be way more fun.

Jacketless, I'd stumbled down my front steps wearing the same ripped jeans and black t-shirt and running shoes I wore grass-cutting. I didn't give a royal fuck how I looked, or that I hadn't showered in ages.

I hadn't stepped foot inside this low-life dive bar at the corner of Flux Road and Steel Street since high school. Bad things happened there, so Donny was always telling us. He prided himself on going there, proclaiming he drank with *real* Hamiltonians, or "the salt of the earth", as he liked to call them. No doubt he'd seen some pretty scary stuff there, and some of it had even found its way into *The Gazette*.

At least it was early on a weeknight, so hopefully the really nasty people hadn't arrived, other than the three bikers glued to the end of the bar.

"They're on their way!" Donny hollered above the loud music. *My friends are always on their way*, I thought. *Story of my fucking life!* We sat at a sticky table next to the dance floor.

The DJ was playing Michael Jackson's "Billie Jean". Like the music, the Blue Ball was pure time-warp. Against a black wall was a badly scuffed stage. In front of it, a sunken dance floor. Hanging from the ceiling was a disco ball, the same size as the one in my basement studio. It was actually half-way decent.

The place reeked of stale beer. Behind the bar, surrounded by gleaming liquor bottles, a massive blue bowling ball jutted out of the wall. It was garish but eye-catching. Donny was a house league bowler and had once told us it was common for bowlers to drop in for a post-game nightcap. But not on weekends, when, by eleven pm, the bar was Biker Central. Whenever you heard a siren in the neighbourhood, you knew the cops were on their way to break up a fight or deal with a stabbing. Donny's Dad, Archie Love, was right when he'd said, "Nothing good happens in a bar after eleven p.m."

"Now they're definitely on their way," Donny said, snapping his phone shut. "Fun will be had!" He raised his pint glass and we clinked. And drank. And drank some more. I'd sobered up earlier in the day, but now I was loosening up again.

Fun with Tony and Norb? I thought. *In this dump? Gee, can't fucking wait!* But I knew Donny was simply trying to put a positive spin on things and cheer me up. "Thanks, Donny," I slurred. "You're a good friend."

A grin cracked his face. He was clearly enjoying seeing me get drunk. Well, it would be his last chance, because I was intending to drink myself to death.

I finished off my double martini and ordered another from waitress Trish, whose hair had frizzed from too many bleachings. I ordered Donny another beer.

"Lucky for you, bud, Lynn's working tonight," Trish said. "She's the only one willing to make the fancy stuff. Last guy ordered a martini ended up dead in a dumpster." She winked at me and took our empties.

I eyed the bikers. One of them was squinting back at me so I nervously looked away. I told myself to just order a beer next time.

I focused on the glitter ball. Discoing here would be as suicidal as it would have been back in high school. But maybe I would, I thought, soon, just to piss off those fucking bikers. Hopefully, they'd kill me. If I drank enough, I might not even feel it.

"Oh yeah, we're going to have a blast!" Donny said. The beers were kicking in.

"A blast?" I said, "Why, is Tony bringing a rocket launcher?" I guffawed. "I hope Norb brings an Invisiblator! I could really use one of *those* right now."

Trish returned with our drinks. I downed mine before she left. "Another round!"

"Slow down, champ," Donny said, looking toward the doorway. "You don't want to pass out and miss all the fun."

Trish's departure was like a curtain had swept aside.

Two outlandish-looking women dragging suitcases rushed towards our table. Between the big hair and the '80s-style get-ups, they would've given Cyndi Lauper a run for her money.

"Donny!"

Donny jumped up from his chair. "Sheena! Oh my God, so good to see you!"

They embraced. Sheena's hair was blonde and practically electrostatic, as if she had her hand on a Van de Graaff generator ball. Her hair may have looked batshit crazy, but the rest of her seemed less so. White knee-high platform boots hugged solid, shapely legs, and she was wearing a turquoise wet-look mini-skirt and a cropped jean jacket frayed at the cuffs and decorated with sequins.

Donny turned to the second woman. "Agnes! Oh my God, so good to meet you." They shared a quick hug.

Agnes's clothes were almost identical to Sheena's. Her auburn hair poofed out to great heights and spilled onto her shoulders. Her round face was open and welcoming, and she wore bright red lipstick.

"John, this is Agnes."

She flung out her hand, beaming at me.

"Who are you ladies?" I half-slurred, shaking her hand.

Agnes cackled. "Strangers from a strange land," she said in a thick Scottish brogue.

"Oh, aye," laughed Sheena, "that's us, right enough."

"I'm Agnes MacDonald, and this is Donny's cousin and my best pal, Sheena Stirling. We've just arrived from Glasgow. Sheena has told me much so about you, Donny," Agnes said. "She says you're quite a character."

"Oh, you have no idea," I grumbled.

Donny just laughed.

Sheena stuck out her hand to me. I half-expected it to be sticky with pink gum or rock candy, but it wasn't. Instead, it was warm and soft and gentle and smooth, like her sing-song voice.

My inner snob was all ready to write these girls off as trampy. But then Sheena looked into my eyes and took my breath away. *You're drunk, Pappas! You want her to have nice eyes. Stop that, you idiot!*

Donny elbowed me in the ribs, breaking my trance. I let go of Sheena's hand.

"Whoops. Nice to meet you."

"Eh, um, you too, John," she said politely. "I've heard so much about you." She looked to Donny for help.

"You have?" I glared at Donny, but he shrugged me off. I knew that bullshit innocent look on his face. He was up to something! Was he trying to set me up? With Agnes? Sheena? He had no right to set me up! I was fucking depressed. A relationship was the last thing I wanted or needed.

As we all took a seat, I whispered into Donny's ear. "Don't think I don't know what you're doing here. You lied to me, man. You said Norb and Tony were coming."

Donny feigned shock. "I said *they're* on their way. I didn't say *who* they were. So technically, that's not lying."

He had a point. I hated when that happened. "Fine," I said, letting it go. "Whatever."

Trish re-appeared. Agnes ordered a beer and Sheena a Scotch.

"Did you two just come from the airport?" I asked, eyeing their luggage.

"Aye," said Agnes. "Our plane arrived late. So Donny paid for us to cab it straight here and celebrate." She smiled at Donny and he smiled sheepishly back.

"Celebrate?" I said, over-enunciating to prove I wasn't *that* drunk. "As in celebrate your vacation?"

Sheena traded a jolly look with Agnes, and they both laughed. "Och, we're not on vacation, John," Sheena piped. "We've just immigrated! Hamilton's our new home!"

I was dumbstruck.

"Welcome to Canada!" Donny cried and raised his beer. "Trish! Sixteen B-52's!"

He kicked me under the table.

"Yes," I stammered, "welcome to Canada!"

We clinked glasses.

I leaned into Donny and tried to whisper over the blare of Bryan Adams singing "Cuts Like a Knife" through the overhead speakers. "Sorry, buddy, but this is all a little too cheerful and social. I'll just bring everyone down. I'm leaving."

I was about to get up when Donny, who was on a first-name business with the deejay and every other guy in The Village, yelled, "Right Brucie, crank it up, brother!"

On cue, the deejay (who looked way too much like Uncle Bobby from the old kids' television show) spun Iggy Pop's "Lust for Life". He and Donny saluted each other.

"Ach, Iggy Pop!" Sheena cried. "I love Iggy!"

Trish returned with our drinks.

Sheena downed her Scotch, chased it with a healthy swig of Agnes' beer, then leapt out of her seat, her hair shifting like a giant red dandelion clock. Before I knew it, she'd grabbed my hand and hauled me down the two steps to the dance floor.

Donny signalled Bruce, and with a flick of a switch he started the disco ball spinning. Donny and Agnes leapt onto the dance floor after us.

Sheena hunched over and began pumping her leg against the dance floor, pretending to dig something out of the floor in rhythm to the music. She looked like she'd learned to dance by watching the *Beverly Hillbillies*. Was this some kind of popular dance in the wilds of Scotland? I wondered. What was it called—the tattie digger?

I wasn't a fan of Iggy Pop, but I couldn't resist a glitter ball spinning above a dance floor. Possessed by the ball and drunk as a skunk, I had an insane urge to antagonize the bikers.

I busted out my finest basement disco moves, straight out of *Saturday Night Fever*, in the sleazy Blue Ball of all places, with two freshly immigrated Scottish lassies doing the tattie digger, and some scary-looking bikers staring daggers at me. Without missing a beat, the girls lifted B-52 shots off our table, tossed them back, and kept dancing.

"I'm so glad you moved to Canada!" Donny cried. "That's so awesome!" He downed another shot and slammed the glass down on our table, then lunged back to the dance floor.

"Thanks, Donny," Agnes cried above the music, "and thanks so much for sponsoring us."

Sheena was eyeing me as I did the Hustle. She was impressed, despite the sloppiness of it, me being hammered and all.

Half-way through the song, Donny cried, "Hey! Let's go drunk bowling!" His eyes were popping.

"Naw," I slurred. "Naw, let's just stay here. Dancing's the thing, man."

"C'mon. It's on me," he said. "I know a *guy* who works there. It's rock'n'roll night. You can drink and dance and bowl. A triumvirate of fun!"

"Ach, that sounds great," Agnes said, and Sheena politely agreed.

"Besides," Donny said to me, eyeing the bad boys at the bar, "This place is filling up with regulars, and I know how you feel about those guys."

Two more dirt bags entered the bar. One had a face like a tombstone and was scanning the room for a threat, or maybe someone to fight. His buddy reminded me of a rat, and kept thumbing his nose as if he'd hit the coke too hard. They joined the other bikers at the bar who clapped them on the back like old buds.

Even as drunk as I was, I knew a bad situation when I saw one.

"Drinking and bowling," I shouted. "I'm in! But after Iggy."

I spun away in a perfect pirouette.

"Oooh," Sheena cooed, "you're quite the dancer, John!"

I bristled but forced a smile. Compliments made me uncomfortable. I didn't trust them after what Sophia had done to me.

Like some 14-year-old trying to impress his date, I transitioned into the Funky Chicken. I knew I ought to be embarrassed by my showboating but I was having too much fun to care.

The booze and the music had beautifully banished my dark mood, and so had a couple of nutty Scottish lassies. Once again, Donny had stuck his nose where it didn't belong, but, for the moment, I was kind of glad.

Next thing I knew we were careening into Irondale Bowling Lanes, dragging the girls' suitcases.

We passed the long snack bar, the same one that had been there since my childhood. The whiff of hotdogs and French fries made my stomach gurgle. We picked up shoes at the hub and settled into our lane. Donny hit the bar for more drinks.

Naked Eyes was singing, "Always Something There to Remind Me" through the ceiling speakers. That 80's classic always reminded me of Sophia, but tonight there was a lot to distract me from gloom.

The place was packed. Balls thunked and whirred along the wooden lanes. Soft purple and pink neon light glowed, and people were laughing and cheering each other on. I started to think that maybe this was going to be okay, after all.

Like the Blue Ball, I'd rarely set foot here. I figured the last time had been Tony's tenth birthday in the banquet hall downstairs. Five pin bowling wasn't my thing, nor was the blue-collar crowd.

Agnes and Donny drank beer and chatted. Sheena was unselfconsciously dancing with herself, as Billy Idol rocked the alley. She somehow managed to pogo without spilling a drop of beer. She even tripped over her suitcase without missing a beat. Impressive!

It was my turn. I slid pass the foul line and threw a gutter ball. "Strike!" I cried, laughing.

I found myself busting out some MC Hammer moves. The bowlers in the next lane weren't impressed. A crusty old guy sneered at me. I flipped him the bird, and he returned the gesture, with interest.

But I wasn't deterred. I felt good, *really* good, booze-fueled good. I was no longer a depressed shut-in! Oh, the healing power of booze, bowling, and babes!

I watched Sheena dance beside the ball rack, full of joy and giving no effs about what anyone else thought. A powerful urge overtook me. I slid toward her, planning to pull Sheena into my arms for a dip, tango-style, but I miscalculated. I pulled way too hard and her head jerked towards mine. Her spiky hair made landing on my face.

"Oh, fuck!" I cried, clamping my hand over my eye, staggering back. I tripped over her suitcase and crashed onto a seat. Stinging pain drilled my watering eye.

"Sorry," I slurred.

"You missed," she said, plunking down beside me. She gently pulled my hand away from my face and examined my eye.

"I did?"

I looked into her eyes, a clear blue, lovely and pure. My heart melted.

She leaned into me, and we kissed, long and deeply. I felt a wave of nuclear heat in my chest. I'd only ever felt that way kissing Sophia. Panicking, panting, I jerked away from Sheena.

"Uh, I need to pee, I'll be right back!"

But instead of heading to the washroom, I escaped out the back entrance.

Chapter 3

"ARE YOU OKAY, JOHNNY?" Ma said softly.

I twitched into a sitting position, wondering how the hell I'd ended up on her couch. Then the Main Event from the previous night screeched into memory. I'd kissed Sheena! Fuck me! I groaned with regret and humiliation. Booze and bad judgement, I thought. But worst of all was that I'd misled her. I didn't want a relationship with her or anyone else! First chance I got, I'd apologize.

I was back in the living room of my childhood home on Rebar Avenue, one street north of Donny's on Limestone Avenue, and two streets north of Tony's on Iron Oak Way. Ma's house was basically a shrine to all things Greek. Three brick arches fronted the house, concrete lions guarded the door, and white Doric columns framed the fireplace. On the wall, there was a wooden crucifix, surrounded by framed family photos: my sister Amara and me as kids, clutching dance trophies, family vacations down in Myrtle Beach, and black and whites of Ma and Pops, young and freshly arrived in Canada. In one photo, they were proudly standing in front of their hole-in-the-wall restaurant, before they'd fixed it up and started their family.

My stomach roiled. The room was spinning and my head pounded. I was so hungover and ashamed, I wished I had a hole to crawl into.

Worse, I was a forty-one-year-old man needing to be mothered. How else could I explain that I'd instinctively come home? *Pathetic!*

"Sorry, Ma, I had a rough night. I need to go home now." But as I got up, a wave of nausea pinned me to the couch.

Ma was still strikingly beautiful. She looked far younger than sixty-nine. She often laughingly said she owed her good fortune to olive oil and Jesus Christ. I couldn't disagree, being a believer myself.

She'd dressed for work in a brown pant suit, and done up her hair in a sensible bun. As usual, she carried herself with grace and humility.

"Is Pops at the restaurant?" I croaked. It was bad enough that my mother had to witness me in this state. I sure as hell didn't want my father to see me like this. My gorge rose.

"You know he is." He was always early.

Ma was more calm and collected than usual, and that worried me. She had something to say.

"What time is it?"

"Nine-thirty." A look came over her face. The last time I'd seen it had been the time I'd really disappointed her at age nine, when a neighbour had caught Donny and me stealing peaches off his prized tree—all Donny's idea, of course.

I hated disappointing Ma and Pops. And mostly I hadn't, not in any life-shattering way. I wasn't built to disappoint. I knew that about myself. In a way, I'd always been their golden boy.

I dreaded Pop's reaction to me going AWOL from the Olympia four days earlier. It wasn't something I was ready to deal with, especially this hungover.

"You look terrible, Johnny," Ma said.

I was so upset with myself, all I could do was nod.

A broken vase lay on the carpet. The flowers were wilted, like me.

I was still wearing my running shoes. Dirty footprints tracked the carpet.

"I'm so sorry, Ma, your vase. And your carpet! I'll pay to have it cleaned." I felt such shame.

"Don't worry about that now. Drink some water, you'll feel better." She pointed.

On the coffee table, beside my cousin Zoe's wedding invitation—no way was I attending hers or any Greek wedding, ever again—she'd set a glass.

Hands trembling, I picked it up and guzzled the icy water. I'd no idea how parched I was until the liquid hit my throat.

"Slow down, Johnny. You'll make yourself sick."

But I'd already downed it. Now I had brain freeze, on top of everything else.

I hadn't been this hungover since the morning after the Grade Twelve graduation dance. Now I remembered why I rarely drank. My current four-day bender had just about killed me.

"Johnny, I want to talk to you about something."

"I know, Ma, but not now, please. Tomorrow, okay?"

Ma nodded. I knew that nod. There was a subtle willfulness to it, the same nod she used on my Dad when she didn't agree with anything he was saying. Ma was the master of the nod, and the queen of persuasion.

I hung my head.

"Okay, Ma, fine. But before you lay into me, you need to know how sorry I am for walking out on you and Pop. I had a kind of crisis. I didn't see it coming. It just happened. And that's the God's honest truth." I buckled down against another round of nausea. "It was never my intention to hurt either of you. How's Uncle George managing?" Ma's older brother was probably barely keeping the customers served.

"He got four stitches in his head, but it will heal. He comes home today, but the problem is he's no spring chicken. His arthritis is killing him, and his memory's slipping. You know, when he was young, he was the best waiter. Customers loved him. He always remembered their names, too, and people came back for our service, all the time. He was that good. A Hamilton legend."

"I'm sorry, Ma. I'll be back soon, okay, I promise. I just need a little more time." *Don't make a promise you can't keep.*

"Amara has agreed to help out on the weekends while Greg looks after the kids. And your father helps where he can, so in the short term we'll survive."

"Thanks, Ma, I really appreciate it. You have no idea."

"When you come back, I want you to take over the bookkeeping. Your father's getting a bit forgetful and he makes mistakes, costly mistakes. I'd do it, but I have my hands full with the ordering and the cleaning. And I'm not getting any younger."

"Bookkeeping?" I said, feeling dubious. "Sure." The thought of book-keeping was repulsive to me. I was a people pleaser, a waiter, not a numbers guy. But I also knew the family business was about teaming up and making it work, for everyone's sake, even if that meant doing things I hated.

My heart fell. All of a sudden, I really understood that my parents were old. Before I knew it, they'd be retiring and I'd be stuck running the business, waiting for my turn to get old and burned out.

Is that all there is to life?

Ma narrowed her eyes. There was something else on her mind. "I want you to go see Sophia."

First, I was stunned. But then, fiery anger erupted inside me. "What's she got to do with anything?" Ma knew her name was never to be mentioned. I'd made that very clear years ago. Hell, *everyone* knew not to talk about her, not around me.

"Because you've never forgiven her. That's why you're sick and hungover on your mother's couch."

I began to squirm. *Leave before this gets worse.*

Ma was nodding very slowly. "You need to see her, Johnny, express your feelings, your hurts, your pain, and forgive her with all your heart, so you can move on with your life."

"*Forgive* her! You can't be serious! She ruined my life, Ma!" My heart was painfully racing. I staggered to my feet.

"Stop! Stay here and listen to your mother."

When your Ma uses that tone, you stop, even when you're over forty.

"The day Sophia left you, you shut down. No girlfriends. No dates. The only thing you do is play road hockey and go to Tim Hortons with your friends. You teach one dance class every week, then the rest of the time you hide in your house like a hermit. Anyone mentions Sophia's name and you go crazy. And you've become so smug and distant, your father and I barely know you anymore." Tears welled up into her eyes. "I do understand why you've shut down, Johnny, I really do, but it's been too long and..." She swallowed. "It's all very sick."

I crossed my arms and dug my fingers into my biceps.

"It was so traumatic, Ma, you know that." My jaw tightened. "Heartbreak ruins a man. And Sophia ruined me. She *made* me sick when she walked out on me."

"No, son, you have made yourself sick. And it was so, so long ago, Johnny."

"Fuck Sophia! I hope she rots in Hell. She fucking deserves it!"

My mother glared. "*Stamato!* Watch your language! You're too proud, Johnny Pappas. Ever since you were a little boy, you never admitted when you were wrong. You keep all the customer orders inside your head, same place you keep your pride, and you say you never make mistakes, but I see them, and *I* fix them."

"You do?" I huffed. "Well, I didn't ask you to."

"Your father makes lists to help himself. That's how he's always gotten things done. Sure, it's old-fashioned. But you should try that, Johnny. Make a list of things to help you forgive and forget. It might help you finally heal."

"I'm not Pa," I said. "I don't need to make lists. And I rarely get anything wrong. I'm—"

"Except for Sophia."

That hit really close to the bone. Not knowing why my wife had left me had been hard enough, but if I was being honest, the sneaking dread that it had all been my fault haunted me.

I rushed to the door.

Ma stood up. "Make things right with Sophia so you can move on with your life."

I held the doorknob, ready to bolt. I couldn't bear to turn around and face my mother.

"I tried that, okay? After the break-up, I wrote her letters and she didn't respond. Not once! I sent emails. Nothing. She's fucking evil, Ma." I sighed deeply. "Sorry for swearing. Again."

"I think you still love her."

She'd hit the nail on the head with a fifty-pound hammer. Ma was looking right through me. I found myself slouching back to the couch.

"This is none of your business, Ma," I muttered. "And I *don't* love Sophia. I hate her, and I have every right to after what she did to me."

"I'm still on very good terms with the Andonises. Maybe we could arrange a private meeting between you and Sophia." She came over and put her hand on my shoulder. "Son, you can't continue the way you have been. You're sick with her memory. It's ruining you. You're drunk. You're sarcastic and bitter. You're even getting wrinkles. You need closure."

"Closure? You know, Ma, if Sophia had given a shit about me, *she* would have given *me* closure the day she walked out. But she didn't." I put my head in my hands and groaned. "Look, I'm afraid of what I'd say if I saw her again. OK? I'm afraid I'd lose control, make things worse, if that's even possible."

"So, in other words, you have nothing to lose," Ma said.

I couldn't disagree.

"No good or decent person walks out on their spouse without an explanation." I wiped away a fresh tear.

"Forgiveness, Johnny. Like Christ taught us."

At that particular moment, I didn't care what Jesus had to say. To the best of my knowledge, he'd never been divorced!

I made for the door again, sweaty and trembling.

Ma hooked her arm around mine to steady me. "Don't be such a prideful man, Johnny. Pride goes before a fall."

I pulled out of her grasp and lurched to the bathroom. I puked long and hard into the toilet, until there was nothing left but the bitter taste of bile. And regret.

Chapter 4

EVERY GUY VOWS TO BE his own man, but sometimes, regrettably, he finds himself doing something his Dad would do.

Like making a stupid list.

I was *that* desperate.

I'd pushed through and written the list.

Like Ma had said, Pop had built a solid business using to-do lists. They worked for him. He got things done. He was successful. And I respected that. But sometimes I felt defiant.

Even as a kid, the urge to escape had struck me from time to time, when I'd worked at the Olympia, bussing tables. When your folks own a restaurant, you get put to work at a young age. Generally, I was happy enough working with my parents, but sometimes I became restless.

I couldn't shake the thought that if I stayed at the restaurant, I'd end up stunted and trapped, like Norb had been for so many years.

At first, Pops hated that I didn't make lists. But eventually he relaxed when he realized I never made a mistake, although Ma had just said differently. Maybe my self-image wasn't entirely accurate?

These days, outside of my serving duties, I was in charge of managing and scheduling the wait and kitchen staff, as well as the busboys and dishwashers.

Early on, I realized I could be my own man *and* also work the family biz, and so for the most part I was content to teach a once-a-week dance class and wait tables full-time. The tips were good, and I'd been doing it so long now that it was practically second nature to me.

Now, at my kitchen table, I looked at my handwriting. Sophia had always said I had beautiful handwriting. Today, it looked like chicken scratch. It was a painful metaphor.

Slowly, a strange list had grown on the notepad. All those years spent studying self-help and psychology books had paid off. Either that, or I was full of shit.

My phone rang, startling me so badly that I almost launched through the ceiling.

It was Norb. He didn't often call. Donny was usually the one calling for a guys' meet-up.

But today I knew exactly why he was calling. No doubt, he wanted to make sure I wasn't going to kill myself.

"Hey, Norb.

"It's Norb," he said.

"Yeah, I know it's you, Norb."

"Okay if I swing by in about twenty minutes?"

"Why?"

"We should hang out."

"No, E—" I caught myself before I called him Eggie. I had to give myself credit. I was really trying. "Norb, I need some alone time. Try me again tomorrow, okay? Thanks, buddy." I hung up before he could object.

Donny had called earlier and left a message, pumped and excited that we'd all had such a blast last night. According to him, Sheena had said I was an amazing dancer and wanted the four of us to go out again. *Yeah, right.* Considering how drunk we'd all been, I was surprised she even remembered me.

But maybe Donny wasn't just being kind? Other than sticking my tongue down Sheena's throat, maybe I hadn't acted like such an ass, after all. Maybe Sheena and Agnes were the forgiving types, unlike me, the Hamilton grudge king.

Then I got cranky again. Obviously, Donny had been trying to set me up with Sheena. *Fuck off, Donny!* Sheena was nice and sweet, but she definitely wasn't my type. I preferred sophisticated women with class and style, like Sophia. Sheena would do better dating a young Rod Stewart, or even a middle-aged Johnny Rotten.

Then I remembered her eyes. They were so clear, the kind of eyes that could look past all your bullshit, see right into your soul. Blue like the purest water. And her smile was the opening note of the happiest eighties tune ever written.

Dazed, I read over my to-do list:

1. Develop greater self-awareness
2. Find your courage, like Norb and Donny did
3. Cultivate your gentleness
4. Move forward, leave the past behind
5. Find joy in life
6. Resolve issues with Sophia so you can fall
in love again.

Number six made me cringe. I never wanted to fall in love again. Too painful.

My first instinct was to crumple up the list and toss it in the garbage can. It landed behind the stove, out of sight. Grumbling, I thrust my arm into the dust bunnies there to retrieve it. I sat down and smoothed it out. It was an impossible list, straight out of all the self-help books I'd ever read, more or less. Maybe someone else could do those things, but not me. Not a chance. Still, just for the hell of it, I stuck it to the fridge with a Steeltown Avenger magnet that Norb had given me.

I stared at the list, perplexed. Whether I liked it or not, I was the author of that list.

I guessed that was how a fiction writer might feel when he finally discovered his voice, but instead of feeling exhilarated, I felt incapable of the task I'd set out for myself.

Although Pops would have been proud of me for writing a list, he'd never know. Neither would Ma, or my friends. I'd make certain of that.

I sat on the couch and chewed on the last slice of cold pizza, surrounded by the rubble of the past few days. Making the list should have made me feel better. But, like most things, it only reminded me of Sophia.

I tried to focus on the pizza, trying to live in the moment. But instead, I found myself kidnapped by a vivid memory of the first time Sophia and I had shared pizza at what became *our* little table inside Aurora Pizzeria. Back then, we were always laughing, deeply in love. Young and beautiful, she'd made my heart bump. My body *remembered*.

Stop! You're doing it again! Desperate to brighten the blackness spreading through my heart, I took three deep breaths and tried to relax. I sat quietly, being mindful, until Sophia's image dissolved, along with the hurt in my heart and belly.

Finally, I found myself back in the present moment and able to function.

I used to wonder how long it would take before I wouldn't need self-help techniques anymore. After years of using them, I'd realized I would always have to use them. Was that normal? Did heartbreak mess up other people for a lifetime? Or just sick, pathetic idiots like me?

I should have moved away years earlier. Instead, I'd stayed put in the Village and subjected myself to Sophia triggers, and being the overly-sensitive type, I was easily triggered: a storefront, a house, the angle of the sun against a brick wall, a beige Honda Civic, a hot teenage brunette giggling as her boyfriend kissed her neck while they waited for the Steel Street bus.

There's a movie, *Eternal Sunshine of the Spotless Mind*, where a couple who've had a bitter relationship get their memories erased. When I saw that movie, I was stoked, until I realized that the point of the movie was that they belonged together, unhappy or not, and that they could never really forget each other. I sank pretty deep at that point.

Once again, and to no fucking surprise let me tell you, the Aurora Pizzeria memory resurfaced! Sophia's voice was clear in my head! Until now, I'd forgotten exactly how she sounded.

"Leave me the fuck alone!" I screeched.

I needed something way stronger than self-help and psychology and well-intentioned friends.

I dropped an album on the turntable and cranked up "Dazed and Confused".

Norb would have been proud—he loved Zeppelin.

When the song rocked hard, and guitarist Jimmy Page tore it up with his blistering guitar solo, I indulged in therapeutic air-guitaring and head-banging.

Back in high school, I was too proud for such antics. When Donny and Norb would flail about to Van Halen in the cafeteria, I'd shake my head at their immature behaviour. Tony couldn't stand it when they acted up like that. Sometimes, utterly disgusted, he'd leave, on the way out throwing them his infamous "Italian salute."

But now, with one foot firmly planted on the first step of the psych ward, I finally got why people did this. It was cathartic! Music therapy! Rock the negativity out of your soul! Why had I waited so long?

I was about to make a phenomenal leap off the sofa, arms swinging, when I caught movement out of the corner of my eye.

I scrambled off the couch, angry and humiliated. "What the fuck, Norb? What are you doing here again?"

Norb was holding what looked suspiciously like my sour cream and onion chips from the kitchen.

"Don't you ever knock?"

Norb was grinning at me. I was still trying to get used to his new moustache. It was thick and bushy, and totally Magnum P.I., but at least it wasn't as weird as that Gimli beard he'd had for years.

"I did knock but the music was so loud you couldn't hear me. So I let myself in." He wheezed out a chuckle. "Awesome air-guitar, man."

He was starting to bounce around to the music, so I glared at him and turned it off, just out of spite.

"I don't know what you think you saw, but I was *not* air-guitaring."

"Why not? It's fun, right? Maybe you should do it more often."

Cultivate your gentleness, a voice said inside me. *Shit, right, the list.*

"Norb," I said, trying not to sound exasperated. "Take a seat or something. Don't just stand there."

"No way, Johnny, I'm taking you out. It's not good for you to be cooped up by yourself, brooding all the time. We need to get you back out there. It's like when Captain America got framed by the President and got all bitter and renounced his identity and then became Nomad. You're becoming Nomad, Johnny."

Shit, this wasn't going to be easy. *Cultivate. Your. Gentleness.* I breathed deeply and slowly. "Yeah, okay, sure, I'll work on that. So where are you taking me?"

"Wing Man. My treat!"

Suddenly, I was furious, but it wasn't his generous offer that had pissed me off.

"Norb, what the hell is that in your hand?"

"Oh, I found it on the fridge. I was going to ask you about it." He was holding my list. And then he was reading it!

"Norb! That's none of your goddamned business!"

I lunged and ripped it out of his hand, crumpling it up and jamming it into my pocket.

"Just get the fuck out my house!"

"Okay," he squeaked. "I'm sorry, Johnny! Okay?" He looked grief-stricken.

"And don't ever let yourself in again! Understood?"

Nodding, he quietly let himself out the front door. Just before he closed it, he whispered "sorry" again.

Now I was the one feeling guilty. I was an asshole.

Chapter 5

I'D BURST OUT MY FRONT door and apologized to Norb for kicking him out. Afterwards, we'd gone out in his "new" 1985 Chevette, which was yellow and rusted out.

Be good to Norb, I told myself. *He's still hurting from his mom's death, and keep the outing short before you hurt him again.*

Seeing him so broken at his mom's funeral back in December had unscrewed something deep inside me. I'd found myself giving him a long, hard hug. He'd wept on my shoulder. But I couldn't bring myself to tell him I cared about him. That was always too hard to do. Giving a hug was tough enough.

I'd half-expected Tony to roll his eyes at me and Donny raise his eyebrows, but instead, they'd nodded solemnly. At that moment, I realized we'd all grown up a little more.

There's nothing like the death of a parent. It changes you.

But, for me, to stop pushing Norb's buttons was like Donny not doing dumb, attention-seeking shit. It was almost impossible. And Norb had always been such an easy target.

And who was I, if I couldn't bug Norb? Who was he, if he didn't react? Bugging Norb was a bad habit I'd carried over since high school. It was now way past its due date, like sour cafeteria milk.

If I stopped razzing him, what would hold our friendship together? How much did a snobby middle-aged dancer and a dopey comic-book writer really have in common? "Ach, nae much," as Archie Love used to say when I'd ask him what was new.

Shut up, I snapped at myself. *Norb's a great guy. That's more than enough reason to stay friends. And, despite his dopey appearance and his weird voice, he's got more courage in his baby toe than you do in your entire health-nut body. He found the balls to be the Steeltown Avenger and swing from the bowling alley rooftop and face a bunch of gun-toting thugs. He had the balls to marry and start a family with Morag. What the frig have you done? Huh? You quit the family business and left your aging parents in the lurch, that's what! Be like Norb, asshole! For once in your life, be a fucking hero!*

Our thirty-something waitress startled me out of my trance when she arrived with our order. She narrowed her eyes at Norb. I could tell she was trying to decide if he was the same Village Vigilante she'd seen on television and YouTube. Then she blinked and went off to wait another table. Norb looked relaxed.

Thank God Donny's Village Vigilante and Humpty Dumpty bullshit had ended. If it had gone on any longer, I'm sure Norb would have cracked under the pressure. He really was a guy who needed to live a quiet, humble life.

After the media had nicknamed him Humpty Dumpty, I'd finally stopped making jokes about his head size because Norb actually *did* resemble the character from the iconic chip bag. But even I couldn't be that cruel.

One day, during our lunch at the mall, a group of teens from the other side of the food court had pointed at Norb and cried, "Humpty Dumpty!" Norb's brilliant retort? "Sticks and stones will break my bones but names will never hurt me!" Bizarrely, that had gotten him a round of applause from the oldsters sitting nearby. He gave everyone a big smile and then took another hearty bite of his Boston Cream donut, a glob of filling landing on his chin. Personally, I would have lost it on those punks. But there wasn't an unforgiving bone in Norb's body. He'd already forgotten about it and moved on to telling me about an idea he had for his comic book.

Now, half-way through helping Norb devour four pounds of wings and guzzle a jug of cold draft beer, I said, "Thanks for taking me out, Norb. These wings are excellent."

"Anything for you, bud." There was a smear of BBQ sauce on his chin, which I was trying not to glare at.

"Thanks, man."

The joint was the size of a shoebox with six tables and red checkered table cloths. "Small and quaint," I said. "I like this place. Cool vibe." From behind an orange formica counter, the owner was on the phone taking an order.

"Once, Morag and I ate eight pounds of wings here. A restaurant record."

"Wow, that's an obscene amount of food."

Norb always did have a healthy appetite. And although the sauce on his face was really bugging me, I didn't say a word. *Good job, John. Keep it up!*

Beyond the front window, I saw a group of twenty-somethings crowding into the Blue Ball across the street, about to enjoy a night of partying. *Man, that was us twenty years ago*, I thought. *Scary how time flies.*

"So, John," Norb said, finally wiping his face with a napkin. "How are you, anyway? How can I help fix you?"

My cheeks flushed with embarrassment. "Fix me?" I said, trying not to grit my teeth. "Uh, Norb, no offence, but *you* can't fix me. That's on me. Anyway, who says I need to be fixed? I'll be fine. I've been down before, but I always get back on my feet, you know that."

He looked politely unconvinced. And so was I, if I was being truthful.

I re-calibrated so I could force some kind words out of my mouth. "It was nice of you to invite me here. Really, thank you. I appreciate it." Being kind wasn't as hard as I thought it would be. And it felt just as good as being sarcastic did, so that was a win-win. I felt lighter.

But how long could I keep up my nice guy act? Something about Norb had always *made* me sarcastic. Did I really believe I was better than Norb? Not really. Maybe I sensed that putting him down in front of other people would make people focus on *his* shortcomings, rather than mine? It was a painful revelation. Stung with shame, I immediately felt awful for all the years I'd used Norb as a means to pump up my own fragile ego. What a shitty friend I'd been! He should have dumped me years ago.

"You're very welcome," Norb said, finally, through a mouthful of wings. Fresh sauce clung to his moustache. I handed him a napkin, but I had to look away. What was helping to keep me in check was Norb generously offering to pay for my meal, and his deep concern for me. More than that, I knew he wouldn't or couldn't change his Norb-ness.

Sitting at a table next to the wall were two guys in their early thirties. *Shit*. Norb's bearded face was emblazoned on one of the men's t-shirts. He was gawking at Norb, obviously wondering if Norb was the Village Vigilante. Was he going to ask him for an autograph? I sighed in relief when the guy went back to eating his wings. Norb was oblivious to the whole near-disaster.

"So, John, are you quitting the Olympia for good?" He swigged his beer.

Ouch. The thing I'd been trying very hard *not* to think about. "Not really sure yet. I'm just, you know, trying to live in the moment." I concentrated on breathing. My anxiety was ratcheting up again.

"How about a dancing career? Have—?"

"Norb!" I thought I was going to bawl him out, but then I totally surprised us both. "I'm really sorry I wasn't there for you after your mom passed. I should have been a better friend. I was selfish. Shit, I've always been selfish. I'm sorry, Norb, I really am." Hot blood burned my cheeks.

Norb held his gooey wing in mid-air, eyes wide. He'd never heard a real apology from me. Poor guy, I literally thought he was going to pass out.

"Don't worry, Norb. I'm not having a stroke. I'm still a total jerk, but I'm trying to do better, that's all."

He was still in a state of mild shock.

I shifted uncomfortably in my seat.

He carefully set his half-eaten wing back down in its basket. "Thanks, John," he said. "I really appreciate that." Tears welled up in his eyes. "I miss Mutti so much. If it wasn't for Morag and the baby that's coming, I think I'd be super depressed. I'd probably go on medication."

"Thank God for Morag, right? And once again, congrats on Morag's pregnancy. That really is great news. When's the baby due?"

"Four weeks."

"Four weeks? Shit. Where is the time going? Man, you're going to be someone's dad, Norb! Unbelievable, right? Do you know if it's a boy or girl?"

"Nope, we've decided to keep it a surprise." A big smile lit up his face. "I can't wait to be a dad. It's going to be awesome."

I managed a smile and took a long, hard gulp of beer.

Step Number 4: Move forward, leave the past behind.

I swallowed the knot of pride tightening my throat. This wasn't going to be easy, but I knew I had to try. "Norb, moving forward, I'm going to try really hard not to push your buttons." This hurt to say, but I forced myself. "To be honest, buddy, I'm surprised you didn't dump me years ago. I've treated you like crap."

His eyes lit up. "Wow, is this really happening? It's like Wonder Woman captured you with the Lasso of Truth and now your real self is emerging." He chuckled. "Man, this is great, John. Although, I must say, part of me is afraid you're just setting me up for the King-er of sarcastic jabs." He jabbed his chest with his greasy thumb. "But, hey, I can take it. After all I *am* the Steeltown Avenger." He laughed at his own joke, the way Donny would, then blinked back a rush of tears and rubbed his eyes with his palms, leaving a faint smear of BBQ sauce.

"Anyways, you know, you haven't treated me so bad. And you can still give me the odd put-down, if you want," he generously offered. "I mean you wouldn't be John Pappas without a little sarcasm, right?"

"Right." I felt like crying, as it dawned on me that maybe Norb was actually fixing me by being his sweet self. In that moment I knew I didn't deserve him. He was so much better than me. So much.

"Well, now that you're under the lasso's spell, what else do you need to get off your chest?" Norb's eyes were shining now, and he was rubbing his hands in delight.

Instead of being cross with him, I was shocked to find myself saying what I'd *felt* for some time now.

"You're courageous, Norb. You're a brave, courageous, frickin' hero. You know that, right?"

He thought about that for a moment. "I guess I am," he said, sheepishly. "Well, thanks to The Screw. I mean, without him showing up and threatening to kill everyone I love, I wouldn't have found out I was courageous."

I suddenly realized I was sitting ramrod straight, tensed up so hard my shoulders hurt. Despite my best intentions, my face was frozen in a tight, smug grin. I secretly hoped Norb would do a friend a favour and punch it the fuck off my face. I felt disgusted with myself. Was I always like this around people? Oh God, I hoped not!

Step Number 1: Develop greater self-awareness. I consciously relaxed my face. *What a smug dick you are, John!* I considered stabbing myself in the eye with a butter knife.

"Geez, John, are you okay?" Norb said.

I stared at my hands, clenched in front of me on the table. "To be honest, Norb, I'm not okay. I'm a disaster. I have been since Sophia dumped me." I drank some beer. "Seventeen years is too damn long for anyone to be depressed."

"Depression's a real curse," Norb said, nodding. "My Uncle Felix had it so bad he couldn't work. He just sat around in his underwear all day, eating pickles. My Aunt Helga was stuck working until she was seventy to pay their bills." He thumbed his moustache philosophically. "They say depression runs in the family."

"It can." I thought about what Norb had said. "Pickles, eh? I prefer ice cream. Best depression medication ever."

Across the street, I noticed a blonde woman entering the Blue Ball, and I instantly thought of Sheena. My heart leapt. My stomach fluttered. I hadn't felt that way since Sophia. *No, forget it, I'm never falling in love again! Can't happen! Won't happen!*

"I'm really sorry about your divorce, John," Norb said. "I always wanted to tell you that but I was afraid you'd bite my head off." He gnawed his lower lip, obviously afraid I *was* in fact going to bite his head off.

The familiar Sophia pang knifed my gut. "Thanks, Norb, I appreciate that. But do you mind if we don't talk about it anymore?"

"Sure thing, buddy. No problemmo." Norb polished off another wing in record time.

"Hey, John!" he cried, staring at his fries as if he'd discovered they were made of gold. He leaned forward, excitedly. "Have you ever considered becoming a psychonaut?"

"A psychonaut? What the hell is that?"

"He's like an astronaut, except, instead of travelling into space, he travels inside his mind while he's high on psilocybin. You know, magic mushrooms?"

"Magic mushrooms? You're kidding, right?"

I realized I'd raised my voice. Omar, the owner, gave me a dirty look.

"Sorry," I mouthed.

"I'm not kidding! It's the only drug I've ever tried, outside of coffee and cough syrup—and cheesies, which aren't technically a drug but should be, they're so fuzzin' addictive." For a brief moment, he went into a snack food fantasy.

Then he roused himself. "Don't worry, buddy. Mushrooms are natural." He gave me a pleading look. "They helped me. After Mutti died. They're...therapeutic."

I was stunned. In a million years, I would never have imagined Norb getting high on mushrooms. Or anything illegal, for that matter.

"I've smoked a little weed," I offered weakly, trying not to sound too pathetic in the wake of Norb's epic revelation. But that had been in my teens. I'd hated how paranoid it made me feel, so I stopped. I hadn't smoked up since.

Norb was licking his lips. I wondered if he'd heard a word I'd said. "Once, after I drank the tea, I saw all these beautiful kaleidoscoping colours, and then I died, and, at first, I was terrified, but then I found myself in a beautiful forest, and Mutti was walking towards me, and she suddenly stopped and plucked a leaf off a tree and that leaf was actually fuzzin' *me!* It was so profound! When the trip ended, I felt super spiritual, and I felt lighter, like a heavy weight had been lifted off me. And I knew then that Mutti was going to be okay, wherever she was." He spread his hands out, palms up, like a BBQ sauce-stained Buddah. "Afterwards, I was so happy and relieved, I wept with joy."

"Oh my God, Norb. It's so risky! What if the mushrooms had made you crazy? Weren't you scared?"

"Sure, of course I was, that's to be expected. But I figured whatever happened couldn't be any scarier than what happened to my mother. And getting high was way less scary than jumping off the Irondale Lanes rooftop. *Way* less. What made things less scary was having a trained therapist guide me. I hired a guy named Dr. Michael Ferguson. He was a very nice man and he put me totally at ease."

"Wow, Norb, I can't believe you tripped."

"Before Mutti passed, I had zero interest. But grief was killing me, and one day, while I was online researching anti-depressant medication, I stumbled across an article on the therapeutic value of psilocybin. Then I found forums full of people who'd had great success with it, and, of course, some who'd had a bad experience, but I was so busted up I had to try."

"I'm glad for you, Norb. But *I'm* not ingesting mushrooms, or smoking them, or whatever you're supposed to do with them. A hallucinogenic trip sounds absolutely terrifying. Especially with the state of my psyche these days."

"But it might help you deal with—" He stopped himself from saying Sophia's name. I checked my watch. It was already eight p.m.! *Shit.* I wasn't sure how much longer I could keep up my nice guy ruse. My nerves were frayed, and I realized I'd eaten way too many wings.

"I just want you to be happy," Norb said shyly.

And that's when it hit me like a ton of bricks. Norb's heart was so much bigger than mine. Mine was tiny, and malnourished. I was practically The Grinch.

I was desperate to have a heart as big and generous as Norb's. I wanted to be a better man. I wanted to love again. But I'd long since given up on that possibility. I was "beyond the pale", to use one of Archie Love's expressions. The cost of my bitterness and anger overwhelmed me.

Embarrassed, I hid my face behind a menu, grabbing up napkins and daubing up tears. I was just about to leave when, like a bat out of hell, Donny flew up to the table. "Hey gents! Hidey-ho!"

Donny had this uncanny ability to locate his friends, especially when they didn't want to be found.

I composed myself as best I could. "Freakin' allergies," I lied. Donny looked skeptical and plunked himself down beside Norb.

He seemed reasonably calm, like he'd been when he'd first landed back in Hamilton, pre-Dumpty, pre-Vigilante, pre-*Making Steven Famous*. I wondered often—we all wondered—if Donny was now taking meds to even himself out. No one had the heart to ask him. When Donny wasn't out of his mind, he really was a fun, easy friend.

He gave me an odd look. "You okay, John?"

I shrugged. "I'm fine. Don't worry about it."

"We're getting our wings on," Norb enthused, rubbing his tummy and winking at me.

"So, I want you to meet a guy, John," Donny said, "A *good* guy."

I barked out a laugh. "A good guy? Yeah right, since when do you know a *good* guy?"

"C'mon, finish up. He's outside waiting. You'll love him, I promise."

"No way. Forget it." I would accept help from Norb, especially of the wings and beer variety, but there was no way in hell I was putting myself in the hands of one of Donny's sketchy acquaintances.

"Your life's about to change brother. You have no idea. Trust me."

Cultivate your gentleness, I told myself. I sighed. "Donny, I know you're trying to help me, in your own unique way that is uniquely you, just like Norb here, but I'm going to pass on whatever it is you have in mind. Thank you, though." I stood up to go. "Norb, thanks for the beer and wings. And thanks for trying to fix me, even though we all know I am deeply unfixable."

Norb gave me a BBQ sauce smile. Despite his distasteful table manners, I loved that big lug. But my benevolent mood crashed when I turned.

At the door was Donny's *good* guy, waving to me, a big grin on his face. *Please tell me this isn't happening. What could this guy possibly want with me?*

Donny held the door open. "Rock 'n' roll Barry!" he cried. "And he's about to rock your world, Johnny Boy!"

"I didn't ask to be rocked, okay!" I'd shouted so loud everyone in the place had stopped eating. You could hear a pin drop.

Humiliated and furious, I marched out the door into the night and stood in front of Barry, growling, daring him to speak to me. But he wasn't intimidated. His smile grew even brighter.

I spun around and faced Donny.

"My life is none of your frickin' business! Or anyone else's for that matter! And the same goes for you Norb, goddammit!"

So much for cultivating my gentleness. *Fuck!*

Chapter 6

TOO LATE, I NOTICED a little girl clutching Barry's leg. Terror was on her sweet face, as if she'd just met the big bad wolf. Me. I felt crummy for yelling and scaring her.

Norb was shrugging on his jacket as he and Donny went to leave.

"No, you don't!" I blocked their path.

Donny threw up his hands.

I turned back to the man. "So, you're Donny's guy, huh? Excuse the language, but what the eff do you want with me?"

"I'm Barry Supinder," he said, pleasantly, his accent thick.

He looked to be in his early sixties. His hair was short and grey, parted at the side, and he wore a baggy red Adidas track suit that clung to his wiry frame when the wind blew. His brown eyes were warm.

He extended a hand and I grudgingly shook.

"This is Devisha, my granddaughter," he said. She shyly tightened her grip on her grandpa's leg.

"Hi, Devisha," I said, smiling as best I could under the circumstances. "Sorry, Barry. Whatever you're offering, the answer is a big no."

"I own this strip mall," he said. "I have a small unit for rent upstairs. Donny says you want to open a dance school. He says you're super-talented." He smiled encouragingly at me.

Move forward, leave the past behind.

"He did, huh?" I threw Donny a death stare. Same crap since Grade Three.

"Come see it," Barry said "You'll love it!"

"Fine, let's get this over with."

I pushed away from the door and Donny and Norb spilled out like excited kids at the end-of-year school bell.

Develop greater self-awareness. Like maybe how my anger was affecting Barry's little granddaughter?

"Devisha, what do you want to be when you grow up?" I asked.

"A veterinarian!"

"Wow, that's great. I bet you'll make a fine veterinarian."

"Thanks, Johnny!" She giggled.

I laughed. The kid had chutzpah! We were now on a first-name basis. And I was no longer the big bad wolf. Progress!

At the end of the strip mall, beside Wing Man, was a door. We went through it and up a flight of stairs to the second floor, then down the hallway past street-facing offices. On the walls were placards—All State Insurance, J.M. Barrie Law Office, and Steel Town Driving School. The hall smelled like beef soup and old carpet.

At sixteen, we four buds had come here to sign up for driving lessons. Norb failed his test five times before he passed. Our instructor, Fred, must've heaved a sigh of relief.

Remembering my past life at this puny-ass driving school made me feel queasy. Is this how that poor bastard Donny felt, always romanticizing the past? Sick to his stomach? I didn't think so. Donny seemed to get high on this kind of stuff.

The thing is, unlike Donny, I didn't romanticize my past. I *un*-romanticized it, ruining all that had been good and wonderful and beautiful. Everything ended up tainted by cynicism and bitterness.

Donny had kept his distance behind me, probably afraid the slightest thing would set me off. He was right to do that. At one time or another, my mood had made all my friends nervous around me, even Tony. *A shit friend, that's what you are.*

Barry unlocked the fourth door and in we went. The office was maybe eight hundred square feet, with wood parquet flooring. Two large windows fronted Flux Road. I was pretty sure we were directly above Mike's Submarine Shop, Norb's favourite snack shop. An alarming image of Norb showing up for a dance class, wearing a tutu and a toting a meatball sub, spiked my brain.

I told myself to politely say no to Barry then fuck off. "Sorry, Barry, too small. Thanks, but no thanks." I tried to leave but Donny blocked me.

"Baloney. You're telling yourself that so you won't have to move forward in your life. Grow a pair, buddy."

I snorted in anger. "That's pretty rich coming from you, Peter Pan."

"True dat, Johnny."

"True dat? How old are you, Love?"

"Old enough to know better," he said, avoiding my hard gaze. "You know I'm right."

I gave the room another once over. "I'd be lucky to cram fifteen students here."

"You could offer more classes," Norb said, "Make people sign up for a month. And if business goes crazy, you rent a bigger space. Easy-peasy."

"Not interested," I said. "Teaching part-time at Lyle's is enough. The last thing I need is the hassle of running my own business." I pushed past them out into the hall.

"Two hundred a month!" Barry cried.

Slowly, I turned back to face him.

He was grinning like the Cheshire Cat.

"Two hundred bucks?" I said, incredulous. "That can't be right. What's the catch? A place like this must usually go for at least eight hundred."

"Barry owes me a favour," Donny said, squeezing in beside him. "Well, not a favour exactly, but he wants to pay something forward."

"Pay what forward? And what kind of *favour* are we talking about, Donny? No, actually I don't want to know." What bullshit scheme was he pulling on poor Barry? Or me, for that matter?

Donny looked really proud of himself. "I got Barry's son a six-month internship at *The Gazette*."

Barry beamed at him. "Donny, you are such a good man. Farida and I are so grateful for everything you've done for our Darsh. This Sunday, we want you to bring your family to our place for dinner."

"I'd be honoured to," Donny said, placing his hand over his heart. "I'll check with Allison and get right back to you."

Barry's kind words riled me. Clearly, he had no idea who he was dealing with. *Donny's the Devil!* I sighed. Okay, Donny wasn't *always* the Devil. Mostly, he was a loving husband and father, and currently he was holding down a good job.

You're a better man than I am, I thought. *You've found a new friend and you're generously helping his son.* And what was I doing? Moping over my ex-wife like some self-absorbed narcissist.

Still, I couldn't quite quell my sarcasm. "What's next, Love?" I grumbled. "The Nobel Peace Prize?"

Donny just grinned and shrugged.

"Donny tells me you dance just like Gene Kelly," Barry said. His eyes practically pinwheeled. "I *love* Gene Kelly! *Singin' in the Rain! An American In Paris!*"

I threw Donny a dirty look. "Barry, I'm no Gene Kelly, trust me."

Donny's grin got wider.

What the frig was he up to?

"Barry," I said, trying to change the subject, "I've seen you outside The Naan. Do you work there?"

The Naan was an Indian restaurant two stores east of the Village Variety, beside the laundromat. It was the latest entry in the four strip malls that populated the Village corners.

"Oh yes. I help my oldest son Viresh run his restaurant. You should come by. We'll treat you like royalty, Gene Kelly!"

I was getting sick of cold pizza. "You never know, Barry. I just might."

"Did Donny tell you about Dirk?"

"Dirk?"

"My other son. He lives in Brampton, and he's a budding Bollywood film maker. He's looking for excellent dancers for his movie. He'd love you Gene Kelly!"

This Gene Kelly bit was beginning to grate on my nerves. *Be kind, John.* "I heard the movie business is a really hard nut to crack. I wish Dirk the best of luck."

"Thank you so much, Gene Kelly," Barry said. "I will tell Dirk you said that."

"Barry, please stop calling me Gene Kelly."

My words had no effect on his cheery grin.

"What do ya say, John?" Donny chirped. "The rent's dirt cheap. It's clean. Bright. Very affordable. If it doesn't work out, so be it. At least you can sleep at night, knowing you finally took a risk."

Find your courage, like Norb and Donny did.

If I was being honest with myself, it wasn't opening a business that was the problem, it was the fear of failure and what that would do to my reputation. I liked being thought of as the good son who'd foregone his own dreams to help his parents run the family business, while fools like Donny selfishly pursued their own dreams. But maybe I wanted to be selfish, just once.

"Do I have to sign a lease?" The words had just popped out of my mouth.

Barry looked at Donny, then me, "For you Gene Kelly, six months. Best deal in town!"

It definitely was.

But I couldn't answer him. My tongue had gone numb, and everything around me pulsed small and distant. Fear coiled inside me.

Don't do it! You want to be a self-serving loser like Donny? But another voice piped up in my head: *Donny tried a bunch of stuff, somehow landed back on his feet, returned to Hamilton, scored a job at the newspaper, dutifully pays his mortgage, and raises his son with an awesome woman who loves him to bits despite his bullshit. He's living proof you won't end up a homeless loser! So do it!*

I wanted to shout, "Forget it, I'm out!" and bolt down the hall.

Move forward, leave the past behind! I swear that God himself was ordering me. I clung to the door jamb, trembling. Inside me, something cataclysmic was taking place.

Donny patted my back. "C'mon buddy, I know this is really hard for you, but running a dance school might just save you. You need change, brother. I'll help you. I promise."

The words stapled out of my mouth, each ejection a hard-fought syllable through a tight jaw and clenched teeth. "Okay, Barry, I'll give it a shot. But only for six months."

"Awesome!" Norb cried.

Barry looked elated.

Devisha was bouncing on her toes.

Donny grabbed Barry by the hand and swung him into a merry celebration dance, and Norb and Devisha joined in. The four of them were shockingly happy for me. It was actually very touching, so when Barry reached out his hand I felt a tight band inside me finally relax and I joined them.

My smile probably looked more like a Halloween grimace, as I found myself thinking of creative ways to dispose of Donny's body. John Pappas, a middle-aged sad sack, was opening a friggin' dance school, of all things.

Chapter 7

IT WAS TWENTY-FOUR hours later, and all my good intentions had ebbed away. The gloom was back, baby.

The only thing I was determined to do today, other than sit around in my underwear, moping and drinking heavily, was to finally burn my wedding photos.

My phone rang twice that morning. One call was an anxiety-inducing shocker, and the other was, to quote The Cars' song, "Just What I Needed", although I didn't know it at the time.

I was pacing in the kitchen, desperately trying to process my insane decision. *Who opens a dance studio at my age? No one. Ever!* When I'd signed the rental agreement, my hand hadn't even felt like it was mine. Had Donny signed for me? I was seriously losing it!

I swigged from a vodka bottle.

I'd acted impulsively. Twice now. First by jumping ship from the Olympia, and now this! I imagined the *Weekly World News* headlines: "Lovesick Loser Quits Family Business to Read Self-help Books Eight Hours a Day!" Underneath, a picture of me strung out on my bed, surrounded by dirty dishes and whisky bottles.

I tried to get a hold of myself. I could run a dance studio. After all, I'd been teaching dance for years. And it would probably be easier than running the Olympia.

I took another swig. But what if the studio failed? And what if the restaurant failed because I wasn't there to help my folks? I couldn't live with myself if that happened.

And then came the familiar searing guilt—I'd left my parents in the lurch, with poor, doddering Uncle George waiting tables. What a horrible son I was!

A frightening thought occurred to me: what if the dance studio actually *succeeded*? I'd have to permanently quit the Olympia. My parents would be devastated. The understanding had always been that one day they'd pass the business down to me. If I didn't take over, the Olympia would just cease to be.

I swigged hard.

Predictably, I then obsessed over Sophia.

Even when life was a bowl of cherries, I made myself think of her, but of course it only made things worse. My sick, unbreakable pattern! I'd have paid a million dollars for a surgeon to drill my skull and excise her permanently from my brain.

I plopped down at the kitchen table, already buzzed, at ten in the morning for frick's sake!

Ma had left a voice message earlier but I'd been too funked out to talk.

"I hope you can forgive me, Johnny, but I've arranged for you to meet with Sophia at the Andonises' house on February 22 at eleven. Sophia's very nervous, but she also wants to make things right..."

My stomach dropped and my heart began to thump.

"...You deserve closure, honey. You didn't deserve what she did to you." Ma had lowered her voice to a whisper. "I love you so much."

The message ended with a beep.

Mom's words slowly sunk in. Knowing I'd be seeing Sophia felt different than I'd thought it would. I wasn't jumping for joy. Seeing her would somehow be *wrong*. But that wouldn't stop me. She had to hear my shit. She owed me that much.

Would she break down and tell me she'd made the biggest mistake of her life? That she wanted to reconcile? At one time, I'd longed for her to say that. But now? Who knew?

How long does it take for a broken-hearted man to get over his first and only love? A week? A year? Ten years? A lifetime?

One of Tony's favourite sayings wrenched inside my head, "Shit's getting real, buddy! Deal with it!"

"Fuck off, Tony," I muttered. "I *am* dealing with it."

But my mother was right. I deserved closure. I would go to the Andonises'. And if it went horribly wrong, at least I'd know I'd mustered the courage to face Sophia and tell her exactly how she'd single-handedly ruined my heart and my trust in women.

I stared at the list on the fridge. Determined to leave my past behind, I punched Donny's number into my phone.

Typically, after one ring, he answered. He could retrieve his phone with just a flick of the wrist.

"Is Sheena single, Love? Tell me fucking straight!"

"Woah, easy, John. Yeah, yeah, sure, she's single. Are you—?"

"Give me her number."

"Okay," he said hesitantly, "but I think her phone is on the fritz."

"So how do I get a hold of her?"

"Try her apartment."

"Where's that?"

"You'll never guess."

"*Where* is her apartment?" Okay, I sounded very intense. Even I could hear that.

He chuckled. "Right beside Norb's old place, right above the barber shop."

"You put her up there? Couldn't you have found something nicer?"

"Woah! Listen, Mr. Judgemental, those apartments might not be so hot on the outside, but inside they're clean, and bed bug free, and I can be there in a jiff if Sheena and Agnes need me. I even paid the first month's rent for them."

"Okay, sorry," I grumbled, "yeah, I'm sure it's alright."

"And don't forget, Morag and Norb were once very happy there."

I willed myself to breathe deeply. "Listen, Donny, sorry for being such a dick. I'm having a bad day. Again. Still."

"Sure, sure, I totally understand."

"Donny, I owe you an apology. The other night I was drunk and acted like a total idiot in front of Sheena and Agnes."

"Are you kidding, man? You were the life of the party. Sheena really dug you."

"She did? You sure about that?"

"Sure I'm sure."

A glimmer of hope grew inside me. I'd carried a lot of shame about that night. "She must have been pretty hammered if she liked me when I was like that."

"No, she wasn't hammered, just tipsy. Some Scots have a high tolerance for alcohol."

"I thought I'd stop by and see if she needs help unpacking," I said.

"Sure, why not? Anyway, gotta go, on a deadline for the column." He cleared his throat. "John, Sheena's really sweet, so be good to her. Okay?"

"Of course I'll be good to her, Donny. I'm not a fucking monster! But just so you know she's not my type, so my visit is strictly an act of Canadian hospitality."

"You know she's my cousin, right?"

"Yeah, you told me that before I got drunk."

Anyone seeing her hair and watching her dance would know she was a Love—she had the crazy gene.

"Later," I said, and hung up.

I dumped out my box of photos of my life with Sophia onto the kitchen table. There was one that wasn't a wedding photo—seventeen-year-old Sophia and I snuggled up on my parents' couch, our eyes shiny with love. Seeing it always screwed me up.

Determined not to let it get to me, I shoved it under the pile.

On top was a shot of us signing the wedding register at the St. Demetrius Greek Orthodox Church altar, the same church I'd attended as a kid. I hadn't stepped foot in there, or any other church, since the divorce.

Leave the past behind! And, this time, don't chicken out!

I grabbed the pile of photos and threw them into the sink. I flicked the lighter and edged the flame towards the photos. My hand was trembling. *Goodbye, Sophia.*

The landline phone rang and startled me.

Call display said it was Tony. "Shit!"

Tony was the boss you didn't want to piss off first thing in the morning or the rest of your day would be hell. If Norb or Donny had called, I wouldn't have answered. But I couldn't ignore Tony. None of us could.

"Hey, Tone."

"What are you doing Sunday afternoon?" he grunted through a mouthful of food. I figured he was on a coffee break.

"Nothing. I'm a shut-in. I don't go out—"

"After road hockey, dinner at my place. End of story."

"Forget it, I'm—"

"Disappoint Angelina, and I'll take a hammer to your friggin' balls." Tony's daughter Angelina actually liked me, for reasons none of us could ever figure out.

He hung up before I could say no.

I slammed the phone into the receiver.

Then I reminded myself that Tony wasn't manipulative. He was simply trying to help me.

I wondered how was it that a man once so confident and sure of himself in his youth had become a depressive, middle-aged recluse? So much so that his friends felt a desperate need to help him?

As I turned back to the sink, I was shocked to find that the pile of photos was now a raging, smoking inferno! The flames licked at the bottom of the kitchen curtains.

Fear paralyzed me, just for a moment, but then I snapped out of it and jerked the fire extinguisher off the wall. But when I spun around, I tripped over my own feet, crashing to the floor and landing on my elbow.

Zapping pain ran up my arm.

I scrambled to my feet and blasted the fire. I'd had practice at the restaurant, over the years. Kitchen fires were my forte. The acrid reek of the smoke made me hack my lungs out.

Once I was sure the fire was out, I slid down the wall beneath the cuckoo clock. The room was a haze of black smoke and white powder.

I should have opened the window to air the place out, but I didn't. Maybe I was hoping it would suffocate me. Then, like a bolt from the blue, deep wracking sobs rag-dolled me. Leaving the past behind hurt like hell.

Chapter 8

As I walked south on Steel Street towards Sheena's, I fully intended to apologize for my drunken behaviour then offer to help her settle in. If things went well, I'd gather up my courage and ask her out on a date.

Earlier, I'd cleaned up the mess from the fire and aired out the house. I'd showered twice to get rid of the burn smell on my skin, and hit the cologne harder than I should have. Hopefully it didn't make her sick.

I argued with myself about the wisdom of getting involved with *anyone* again, much less the exciting crazy-train girls I'd only just met four days ago.

I was about to knock on Sheena's door at the back of the bowling alley, when I heard a woman shrieking bloody murder.

Heart racing, I booted towards the racket. In front of the strip mall, tearing a strip off of Jimmy the Barber was a chic middle-aged woman wearing an expensive wool coat, a smoke dangling from her red lips.

Old Jimmy's arms were crossed against his pale blue smock. He was slowly shaking his head. Smoke from his cigarette steamed the air like mist.

She shot him the bird, then stomped over to her black Mercedes parked on the narrow tarmac strip next to the sidewalk. She whipped open the car door and spun around dramatically. "You two-timing piece of shit!" She reached inside, grabbed a coffee cup, and chucked it at him. The cup arced through the air. Jimmy scuffled out of the way, but not quite fast enough. The cup struck the tarmac and splashed coffee against his brown polyester slacks.

"Ach, I just washed they." He shook his head ruefully. "Aye, I guess I had that comin', Catherine."

"How could you cheat on me?" she cried.

"I said I'm sorry, dear. I apologize."

"This isn't the first time!"

"Keep your voice down, hen," he said casting his gaze about. "The entire Village doesn't need to know our business."

"I'm not your goddamned hen. Not anymore!"

"Okay, aye, no problem."

The rage on her face loosened. "I love you, Jimmy. How could you do that to me?"

I stood frozen on the spot, embarrassed to be witnessing this scene. Luckily, it seemed that neither of them had noticed me, yet.

He pleaded with his hands. "Catherine, I was honest with you from the start. I'm no' a one-woman man."

The rage returned. "Fuck you, you Scottish bald-headed loser!"

"Ach, Catherine, you're over-reacting!"

She piled into her car and screeched off the curb, westward along Flux.

Jimmy turned his head and squinted at me. "Is that you, Johnny?"

"You know it is, Jimmy," I said, awkwardly. "Uh, everything okay?"

He sized me up. "I didn't recognize you without your stylish clothing. You look like a bloody bum. Are you sick?"

"No, I'm not sick."

"Shouldn't you be at work, then?" He picked up the coffee cup.

I shrugged.

"You're no' yourself, son, I can tell. Come inside. I've got something for you."

What could he could possibly have for me, other than another bad haircut?

"I can't stay long," I warned, following in behind him. In a way, I was glad for the diversion. My resolve to see Sheena was weakening.

The barber shop hadn't changed, at all. The guys and I had started coming here for haircuts since elementary school. But not too long after my divorce, Jimmy had cut my curls too short and I'd freaked out on him. He'd apologized, but I was so upset I'd stormed out and refused to pay. Later that day, I'd wordlessly tossed a crumpled up ten-dollar bill inside the door of his shop and hit the road.

Suffice to say, I hadn't returned. But Jimmy had been pretty magnanimous about it, and he'd wave through his window whenever he saw me walking by. Sheepish, I'd wave back, knowing I'd abandoned him. So many times, I'd almost gone back, but my pride and vanity wouldn't let me.

I'd opted to go downtown to hoity-toity Robertson's Boutique Hair Salon on King Street, paying five times Jimmy's rate. My buddies teased me for being a phony and a sell-out, and they were right. But at least the stylists never messed up my hair.

While cutting hair, Jimmy smoked hand-rolled cigs. For some reason, the city bylaw officers hadn't caught on to him, or maybe they turned a blind eye because they took their own kids there for haircuts.

Looking around the old shop, I realized that like Archie, Jimmy was a dinosaur facing extinction. Nothing would be the same in The Village after their generation blasted off in their Tartan spaceship.

When we were kids, he'd give us an old penny to insert into his ancient gumball machine, and a couple of turns always delivered a shiny, rock-hard behind the candy door. I'd always suspected that it had been his way of apologizing for dropping cigarette ash in our hair.

The adults kept coming back, too, although I was sure that had a lot do with the Playboy magazines fanned out on the table in the waiting area.

His barbershop was pure time warp: four red barber chairs, mirrors, six brown vinyl waiting area chairs, and on the wall a bulletin board loaded with local business cards. On a small divider were framed headshot pictures of male models, and just inside the door, on the counter, was a small cash register. The floor was tiled beige, scored and pocked and deeply faded. Jimmy had been cutting hair here for fifty years. I admired his work ethic. Fifty years was a long time to be on your feet all day.

On his counter, next to razors, combs, and shavers, a battered transistor radio played CKOC. Seventies' superstar Tom Jones was singing, "The Green Green Grass of Home". You could always take a trip back in time with AM radio.

Hank was in the waiting area. He didn't work at the shop but for some reason was always there. He was immersed in Playboy heaven.

"Good thing Hank's as deef as a bloody doorknob," Jimmy said. "And it doesn't hurt that he loves the girly magazines. So, he won't mind if we have a wee chat."

A wee chat? Since when?

"Have a seat, Johnny," Jimmy said, pointing at his barber chair.

"I'm not here for a haircut."

"Aye, I know that."

Reluctantly, I sat.

"Johnny, you haven't stepped foot in here since you were twenty-three. I've been told you broke rank and went to Robertson's."

"Did you invite me in here to scold me?"

"I've cut all you lads' hair since you were wee, and your fathers' hair, too." He *humph*-ed.

I hoped he would get to the point. I could feel my temper rising, as it constantly did these days.

"All of youse wore your hearts on your sleeves, but you more than anyone else, until your divorce—", he turned down the radio volume, "—and that's when you stopped coming. And I don't think it has anything to do with the time I nicked your curls."

"Gee, Jimmy," I said sarcastically, "why don't you tell me why then, since you're clearly a barber *and* a psychologist." So much for Step Number 3, but at least I'd nailed Step Number 1 and was *aware* I'd been sarcastic. *Progress.*

The mirror reflected back a hungover misanthrope. What a cruel bastard he was, making me look at myself. There were dark circles under my eyes. I looked and felt like shit. Now I felt even angrier.

"Who the hell told you about the divorce? Let me guess, Donny, right?"

"Aye, and everyone else. It was public knowledge."

I jumped up to leave but what Jimmy said next stopped me cold.

"I'm sorry about your divorce, Johnny. I've had four of the nasty buggers myself."

"Four?" I sank back into the chair. I'd always thought of him as a bachelor. But married *and* divorced? Four times?

"So, basically, you're telling me you're the last person in the world who should be giving relationship advice?"

"Bingo."

He spun me around to face him and sat in the chair across from me. Behind him, tucked into the edges of a mirror, were at least thirty photos of him posing with women he'd dated throughout the years. Old Jimmy the Barber was a total womanizer! It was mind-boggling!

"Look, everyone in The Village knows what I am, Johnny. A failed father *and* a failed husband, and a skirt-chaser. Most of my adult kids have estranged me. Some judge me for what I've done, but I don't judge myself. Not anymore. After all the years of beating myself up with booze and self-hatred, I said, fuck it, I did my best, the past is *deed*. So, I quit feeling bad about myself, and I gave up the booze. And when I'm not too knackered from a day's work, I enjoy the ladies and they enjoy me, unless they fall in love with me, like poor Catherine did. Then it's always an unhappy ending. But, fortunately that doesn't happen very often." He puffed on his smoke. "I've been living this way for near thirty years now. And it suits me very well."

"Okay," I said, tentatively. How was it a man I barely knew had kept me in his thoughts and felt comfortable telling me his life story?

"I really do feel bad for Catherine," he said. "She is a lovely lady and I wish her well."

"Okay, but let's get back to why you think I stopped coming here." I crossed my arms defensively.

He eyed me like a drill sergeant. "After your divorce, you compensated for your pain. Not a delicate curl or stitch of clothing out of place, always ponced up, always wearing dress shoes, even with two feet of snow on the bloody ground. Either you were trying to build yourself up to meet the future Mrs. Pappas, or you were coming out the of the closet, which you're obviously not."

He dragged on his cig. "Afraid to be hurt again, you hid behind fashion. And, worse, you stopped dancing and following your dream. Oh aye, I remember what a natural-born dancer you were, Johnny." He lowered his voice. "After my second divorce, I buried my emotions so deep they blew me a new arsehole."

Then he jabbed his blue-veined middle finger at me. "You're me, Johnny Pappas, and I'm *you.*"

I was too stunned to be angry.

"Just go see a shrink, lad. I could have saved myself and my family a lot of grief if I had. Find your happiness now, don't wait until you're old and your prick falls into your sock. Meet a lass and have the time of your life. Tomorrow's no' promised to anyone." He gave me a soldierly nod.

While I sat there in stunned silence, the door suddenly swung open, ringing the bell at the top, and in walked a father and his two sons.

Hank hadn't once looked up from his Playboy. He was obviously in the grips of a powerful article, one that could only be read by turning the magazine sideways.

Jimmy pointed. "Right, John, this way." He led me over to the gumball machine and slid in the same grimy penny he had when I was a kid. He opened the candy door. A pink orb dropped into his hand.

I dumbly accepted it.

"Thanks, Jimmy." I swallowed my pride. "For everything."

"Gumball wisdom," he said, patting my back.

"Gumball wisdom." I popped the ball into my mouth and went out the door. Suddenly, I felt really positive about seeing Sheena—Jimmy's life philosophy had set me straight again.

Chapter 9

JIMMY'S WORDS STILL rang in my ears as I knocked on the door at the back of the strip mall bowling alley. There was a loud thumping sound of bass and drums. I figured it was the music from the Blue Ball, reverberating through the walls. I banged harder.

I noticed the old gouge marks on the cedar tree where Norb and Morag used to chain up their scooters. Seemed like they'd lived here only yesterday. I remembered the terrible times they'd faced when The Screw had come after Norb. I was so glad that nightmare had ended.

Nearby, cars inched slowly through the Tim Hortons drive-thru. The main parking lot was badly potted and slicked with dirty slush. Snow drifted dopily from a hazy grey sky.

Apologize to Sheena and Agnes, I reminded myself. *Then offer to help.*

I pounded again, and the metal door creaked open. It hadn't been latched properly.

Peering up the stairs, I realized the music was coming from Sheena's apartment. She and Agnes were on the landing at the top of the stairs, dancing to "Tainted Love". I sighed. Another 80's break-up song that had foretold my future!

The girls suddenly noticed me and screamed.

"I'm sorry!" I cried. "It's me! John Pappas! I'm not a peeping Tom, I promise!"

"John?" Sheena said, peering down, her arms crossed against her chest, as if she'd been caught naked. Then she laughed as Agnes ran into the apartment, turned off the music and came back.

I barely recognized her—her poofy hairdo was gone. Instead, her auburn hair was full and natural on her shoulders. She was beautiful. Sheena's hair, on the other hand, was still full-on electrostatic.

"I came to apologize," I said to Sheena.

"Apologize? For what?"

"I was drunk the other night, and I'm pretty sure I said and did some stupid things."

They both laughed.

"Achh, no," Sheena said. "You were fine! Where we come from, you'd be considered an absolute saint!"

"Aye, it was a great Canadian welcome," Agnes said. "Not to worry."

I sighed with relief.

"I was wondering if you two need help settling in?" I gazed up at them hopefully.

They exchanged a glance.

"We've done all the hard stuff, John," Sheena said, "but thanks anyway." Her eyes lit up. "Em, how about we all go to Tim's for tea? Donny tells me they have fancy Canadian donuts."

Fancy donuts? At Tim's? *Yeah, right, Donny.*

"Sure," I said. "Fancy donuts it is. My treat."

"You go ahead," Agnes said to Sheena. "I've got a bathtub to scrub."

Sheena looked surprised. "Oh, aye, okay." She smiled down at me. "Be there shortly, John."

A moment later, Sheena Stirling practically danced down the stairs and smiled up at me like an expectant kid. I'd forgotten how short she was—barely five feet.

Under her unzipped blue parka, one Donny had no doubt purchased used for her from the thrift store, she wore a tattered Simple Minds t-shirt and grey baggy sweatpants with holes in the knees. I could easily imagine her with a baby on her hip and a fag in her mouth, like some Dickensian washer woman.

Her blue eyes reminded me of what a clear Scottish lake would look like, not that I'd actually ever seen one.

And her face! Talk about warm and welcoming! She smiled up at me as we strolled across the parking lot.

"What kind of donut do you suggest, John? I hear the chocolate dips are crackin'."

"Yes, they're good, but I'm partial to sour cream glazed. How about we order a variety and you can bring some back to Agnes?"

"That would be fab."

"Fab? Are you a Beatles fan?"

"Oh aye, isn't everyone?"

Then she must have seen something in my expression, something fleeting but mean-spirited. "Are you okay, John? Is there something bothering you?"

Shoot! Why did my brain always go to mean shit like this? I'd just automatically thought about how easily she'd fit in with the coffee shop riff raff. And I realized I'd been ready to pull the plug on our little date, without even giving it a proper chance. Damn it. I was a messed-up bastard.

"No, I'm fine," I lied.

She smiled, but I could tell she didn't believe me.

At the coffee shop, we sat by the front window with our order. I picked away at my donut while Sheena inhaled hers.

"This is delicious!" she enthused. "Mmmm." Thankfully, she ate with her mouth closed, and didn't play show-and-tell the way Norb did.

"Don't they have donuts in Scotland?" I asked.

"Not in my town," she said between chews. "When I get back home for a visit, I'll be sure and give a full recommendation to Charlie MacDonald. He's the baker up the road at McVee's."

I enjoyed watching her simple pleasure. She swung her legs under her seat like a kid, her face lit up as she took in her new surroundings. She didn't know it, but she was nailing Step Number 5: *Find Joy in Life.* I envied her. It seemed to come naturally to Sheena.

I guessed her to be in her mid-thirties. If Donny hadn't married Allison, and Sheena wasn't his cousin, they would have made a great couple. Crazy hair and crazy brains! Perfect match!

She'd caught me staring at her. I quickly looked away, heart thumping.

I drank some coffee and tried to act nonchalant. *I'm not falling for UK Madonna!*

"Did Donny tell you Agnes and I were coming the other night?"

"No, your arrival at the Blue Ball was a total surprise."

"Oh, The Blue Ball! I loved it there! Great place to fly your freak flag, right?"

"Mm-hm," I murmured, trying my damnedest not to sound sarcastic.

She leaned forward, icing rimming her upper lip. "Isn't Donny the best? Not only is he my cousin, he's been my constant pen pal since we were kids. When I wrote him and told him I needed a change, he suggested moving to Canada. He said he knew a guy who could get Agnes and me a job. Right here in this beautiful neighbourhood." Her eyes brightened.

Beautiful? If the Village was beautiful, I shuddered to think what *her* town was like!

"So what kind of job did Donny's guy get you?" I asked. *Humpty Dumpty, Village Vigilante YouTube video editor? Bogus column writer? Self-published author? Perpetual dreamer-schemer? Comeback concert impresario?*

"Discount Vacations."

"The one between Budget Cremation and Burial and Mike's Submarine Shop?"

"Aye, that's it." A fresh smile sweetened her up.

"Hey, that's right below my dance studio." Coincidence? I thought not.

"You run a dance studio?" She looked as though I'd just told her I'd won the UK National Lottery. "Oh, me and Agnes just love to dance! Sign us up!"

Well, this was an interesting development. I wasn't too sure how I felt about it. "Sure, yeah. Monday night at 7 p.m. First class is free. Wear something comfortable." Automatically, my eyes flicked to her dowdy sweat pants. What an asshole I was. But Sheena just gave me a kind, sweet smile, one that I absolutely did *not* deserve.

And that's when I did what I'd promised myself I'd never do: crack open the Sophia vault.

And boy did I ever. All the gruesome details of my divorce, the pain my ex-wife had caused me, and how she was the reason I'd suffered a breakdown and had to take time away from the Olympia.

By the time I'd finished, Sheena looked like she'd been hit by a transport truck. She'd polished off six donuts. Her skin was pale, and there was a dollop of icing between her nose and lip.

My bitterness had drained Sheena's joy. She cast her eyes down, deep in thought as she chewed on her fingernails.

"I'm so sorry," I said, suddenly ashamed of my tirade. "I didn't mean to go on about myself. That was never my intention. I don't know what came over me."

An old guy, two tables away, took time away from scratching his lottery ticket and grumbled, "No one wants to hear about your ex on a first date, dummy."

I felt the rush of blood to my face.

"I'm sorry, John," Sheena whispered. "That must have been very hard for you." She went back to gnawing on her fingernails.

A nail biter. *Classy. Now I definitely know you're not my type. Thanks for the warning.*

She picked up on me silently judging her again. This time her expression cooled. "I better be going."

Why was I such a damn jerk? "No, no stay, please. I'm sorry, okay?"

"I need to help Agnes." She brightened. "I can't wait to see the look on her face when she tries her first Canadian donut."

"Ah, come on, Sheena, give me a second chance? Please?"

Right away, I realized my mistake. I'd begged her for a second chance as if she was my ex-wife. I was sure I looked as confused and messed up as I felt. Now I knew for sure I wasn't ready to date. There was just way too much for me to sort out. I sank.

But Sheena looked thoughtful. "Second chance, John? Aye, sure. Give Agnes and me the best free dance lesson ever and you're off the hook."

She drum-rolled the table and collected up the donut box.

"Good night, John Pappas," she said with her sing-song voice. "And thanks so much for your Canadian hospitality." She raised the box in appreciation.

"I'll walk you home."

"Very chivalrous of you, John, but I'm a big girl, so no thanks."

"Of course."

And she was out the door and gone.

"You buggered it asshole," the old guy grumbled, "you made the entire conversation about yourself. Women hate that."

"Shut up, old man," I muttered.

He shrugged me off and went back to his ticket.

I bustled out the far exit, equal parts humiliation and anger.

The old guy was right—I'd fucked up with Sheena.

Instead of dishing out my story in bite-sized segments, I'd vomited up my entire Sophia story. *Stupid, stupid, stupid!* And I'd been judgemental and snotty, which she absolutely hadn't deserved.

For some reason, Sheena had been the first person I'd trusted with *all* the painful details of my divorce. But why her? I hardly knew her.

A bitter wind stung my face as I stumped home along Steel Street. Traffic heaved and rumbled along the icy road.

I couldn't help wondering if I'd subconsciously used the gruesome details of my divorce to destroy any and all chances with Sheena. To make her hate me the way Sophia did. Maybe I should start wearing a t-shirt that read: Self-sabotaging Nutcase! Don't Waste Your Fucking Time!

What a piece of shit I was for ruining her evening. I should have made it fun and memorable. *Piece-of-shit*!

I re-traced my steps and footed west to the liquor store in the Dominion Mall. I bought a forty ouncer of cheap, cruel, punishing whiskey, and guzzled it on the way home, groaning after each throat-burning chug, determined to get so drunk I'd pass out and freeze to death on a snowbank.

Chapter 10

Sadly, I'd made it home *alive*.

I'd awakened with a terrible start.

Waves of guilt and shame and nausea pounded me, each one bigger than the last. And the belly sickness was the worst ever.

Still wearing my boots and coat, I crawled out of the bed and somehow made it to the washroom in time to retch my guts out.

I popped two extra-strength Tylenol to ease the ice pick stabbing my right eye, swallowed two ginger anti-nausea tablets and slunk back into bed. I'd forgotten just how unforgiving a whiskey hangover was.

I re-played my disaster with Sheena. Then, apparently needing to feel worse, I slid open the bottom dresser drawer and pulled out a crinkled paper bag stuffed with old love letters from my early days with Sophia and sat on my bed. After our divorce, I'd literally *studied* them, trying to divine a reason for her sucker-punch decision. Twice, I'd almost burned them. After a year of torturing myself, I'd finally stuffed them back in the drawer. Until today.

I was pretty sure Sophia had long since burned my love letters.

That would have been the smart thing to do. She'd once cryptically said she'd heard that the best way to get over a break-up was to hate your ex. At the time, I hadn't given that much thought. Obviously, she'd been preparing me. I wondered if that's how she got over her break-up with me, by hating me.

But I couldn't hate her. Yeah, I was angry with her, but I wanted to remember her as the sweet, wonderful woman I'd married. I wanted to remember that *she* had loved *me*, for a while.

I knew reading the letters would fuck me up all over again, but I was desperate to feel something other than my blistering hangover.

I opened the crypt and dug out three letters and two birthday cards.

Saturday, March 1, 1981

Dear John,

I really enjoyed meeting your family at Christmas. Your mom is very nice, as is your dad. Your sister Amara is very funny and smart, and I bet she will do very well in life.

Also, I love your Greek family. Greek like mine! Haha!

Things are going very well in Paris. I imagine this will be our last family vacation together, as after all I am 19 and not a kid anymore. I'm doing my best to appreciate my parents before I get too busy being married (and raising kids? Wink!).

The food here is spectacular. My parents and I went up the Eiffel Tower, and we enjoyed a cruise along the Seine. The Louvre Museum was fascinating. I highly recommend it.

Back in a couple of weeks.

Sophia :)

A smiley symbol? Not "Love"? How had I not noticed that before? I felt like I was seeing her words for the first time. She'd shown very little real emotion, except for the part about our families being Greek, and her feelings about the touristy stuff. The letter was guarded, even though we'd been dating hot and heavy for seven months. No powerful longing or love for her future husband. In my letters, I'd poured my heart out to her—they'd easily run four pages.

Had I been too young and love-struck to see the obvious? Had I been afraid to face the truth that she didn't really love me? Or had she been so scared of her love for me that she couldn't show it? Or had she just settled for me? Greek man to placate her Greek parents?

I swallowed a hot lump in my throat. On top of the pile was the only birthday card she'd given me when we'd been married. I steeled my heart and picked it up. It was colourful, but non-descript, with birthday balloons and a cake. Inside, she'd written: "1983 will be a great year! Hope it's your best yet." She'd signed it: "Your partner in crime, Sophia".

No hearts. No "love" or "honey". It was a card you'd give a friendly acquaintance!

I'd balled my hands into fists. How could I have been so blind? *And* so stupid? The card trembled in my hands. Had I imagined our entire relationship?

My self-constructed trauma wheel was spinning full-tilt. I bagged the letter and card and jammed everything back into the drawer.

Had our whole marriage been a romanticized fantasy? Why did I still hold onto her, all these years later?

Had I even really known Sophia? Why was I still addicted to the idea of her?

I wished I were more like Norb. When it came to loving and living in the moment, he was a natural. But if Morag ever left him, he'd probably die of a broken heart, he was that sensitive.

Breathe. I tried to slow my ragged pulse.

How had John Pappas—businessman, dancer, faithful friend and son, Village home-boy, Tim Hortons psychologist—become such a deranged, self-deluded, broken-hearted loser?

And why couldn't he escape his dumb fucking past?

Familiar revenge-plot fantasies trudged through my head—me throwing a cream pie in Sophia's face, cutting the brake cables on her car, getting Donny to shame her on YouTube.

I called my friends and arranged an emergency meeting at Tim's. For once, it was *my* emergency, not Donny's or Norb's.

Chapter 11

Coming to the coffee shop *before* our weekly hockey game was a rarity, but the urgency in my voice had convinced them.

Tony narrowed his eyes like a gunslinger. "...So, you're asking me, do I have revenge ideas to pay back Sophia for what she did to you?" He leaned forward in his chair. "No, John, I sure as hell don't, and you better not either."

I just stared at him.

"Johnny," he growled. "You better check yourself. You look like friggin' Norman Bates."

Donny grinned darkly as he sang the Talking Heads' song, "Psycho Killer".

Perfect! If anyone could get behind my revenge plan, it was psycho Donny!

But Norb nodded in solemn agreement with Tony's assessment of me and the wind went out of my sails.

"I'm not a psycho," I said, hoping that I wasn't. My anger sputtered out of me and I clamped my jaw shut.

"Say it, brother," Donny said, "You're amongst friends. No judgement. Right, guys?"

The usual lottery-card-scratching patrons were staring at me in anticipation of drama.

I glared coldly at them all. "Do you mind?"

One by one, they went back to their cards and coffee.

I stared down at my mug and lowered my voice. "I loved Sophia with all my heart and soul, then she walked out on me, and I have no real idea why, and I know it's wrong, but I want her to feel my pain."

Tony was shaking his head. "Just what kind of pain?"

I squeezed and un-squeezed my fists. I could barely choke the words out. "Anger. Jealousy. Hurt. Loss. Betrayal. Maybe it's time *she* felt what I've felt every day for seventeen years. See how *she* frickin' likes it."

"I get it, John. Remember when Bootsy died?" Norb mused. "That must have been thirty years ago, but I still think about her every day."

"Yeah, we know her death was hard on you, pal," Tony said. "Boots *was* a lovely dog."

"Lovely for sure," Donny echoed, "really, really lovely."

This was exasperating. "You guys are actually putting the death of Boots on the same level as my *divorce?*"

"Easy, Johnny," Tony said. "You don't have a monopoly on heartache."

Norb was rubbing his cheek. His face was flushed. "Sorry, John. I was just trying to help."

"I know you were, Norb." I tried to summon a bit of kindness. "Boots was a great dog, my bad."

"John," Donny said, "this is the first time you've opened up about your divorce. I'm really proud of you, man." He sounded cheerful that I was such a vulnerable wreck.

"Are you?" I said, sarcastically. I slugged my coffee, pissed off and grateful at the same time.

"I know!" Norb piped. "Let's order fourteen pizzas and send them to Sophia's house! Imagine the look on her face when they arrive and she has to pay for them!" When he saw the looks on our faces, he slumped a bit. "What? Mike Zerbinsky and his pals did that to me in Grade 9. It's a legit prank, OK? Very effective."

He slurped his 3X3 coffee—three creams, three sugars—he'd cut back from 4X4's so he could be a healthier future father for his baby, due to arrive in February.

"Hey, how about the old pie-in-the-face routine?" Donny said. "Message sent, no one gets hurt. Classic."

"Guys, I don't want to prank her, OK? She deserves worse, much worse," I said.

"You probably don't want to hear this, John," Tony said, "and don't go running off in a huff when I say this, but I'd always found Sophia to be very nice. In fact, we all did. Right, boys?"

Norb and Donny nodded in agreement.

He continued: "Of course, what she did to you was friggin' awful, but other than that, I don't have anything bad to say about her."

"You found her *very nice*?" I said, my anger rising.

"Well, mostly," Donny said. "Obviously, if you didn't know her, you would have said she was uppity. But we knew her, and we knew she was nice. And also, if you don't mind me saying, drop dead-gorgeous."

I glared at him, but he wasn't fazed. "Just stating a fact, man. Don't take it the wrong way."

"She *was* drop-dead gorgeous," Tony said philosophically.

"None of this is what I need to hear," I groused. A pulse throbbed in my temple. "I need everyone to tell me right now that she's a piece of shit and how completely right I am about that."

"Maybe she is a piece of doodoo," Norb said, "I mean, think about it, she walked out on you without an explanation. Nice people don't do that. June Cleaver never would have walked out on Ward Cleaver, not a chance. You didn't deserve that, John, you're a good guy. Her loss, for sure."

"Thanks, Norb, but I'm not a good guy."

"You *are* a good guy, Johnny," he retorted.

"If you say so," I grimaced.

"So how does this end?" Donny asked. "Do you spend the rest of your life messed up, or do you finally find a way to move forward?"

Donny had just hit on Step Number Four. Had Norb shared my damn list? Now, for some reason, knowing that might be true didn't bother me. I had way bigger fish to fry.

"Really, Donny?" I said, defensively, "You're suggesting *I* move forward? This from the guy who practically raised Steven from the dead?"

He threw up his hands. "I know, I know, Donny Love can't let go of the past, he's sick with it, blah, blah, blah, but *just* so you know, I'm back on my meds, so I'm definitely moving forward with my life. And Allison's top-notch proud of me for trying. So, there you have it, boys, everyone's new favourite TV show, *The Donny Love Confession Hour*, starring the one and only!"

He bowed.

"Medication?" Norb said.

"Just said that, Norbster," Donny said sitting down.

We were dead silent for a few moments, trying to take in this new information.

"We're all proud of you," Tony said, "right, boys?"

"Super proud," Norb chimed in.

"Wow," I said. "Yeah, great. Hope it helps you be, uh—" I couldn't find the words. *Less Donny?* "More consistent."

"Why, thank you, my good man." He did a wee jig. He must be on a low dose, I thought, or maybe the meds hadn't completely kicked in.

Another lightbulb went off over Norb's head. I had no idea he had so many. He pointed finger-guns at me. "I know, Johnny, you're like Ophelia. You know, from Hamlet? Remember how she was so distraught she drowned herself in a stream? Just don't go doing *that*, man!"

I just gaped at him.

"Cool it, Shakespeare," Tony said.

"Stick with comics, Norb," Donny added.

But Norb was on a roll. "And you're so normal now, Donny. So relaxed."

"I am? Okay. Cool." He looked pleased. "I'm on the meds for Allison and Stewart's sake. The day I suggested that it wouldn't cost much to make Jerry the banjo-playing janitor famous, she totally freaked out and threatened to leave me, again. I had to deal with my problems or lose everything, you know?"

Tony was shaking his head.

"I'm glad you're on meds," I said. "Good for you, buddy."

"Thanks."

We sat silent for a while. I liked that about us—we didn't always feel the need to fill in the gaps, even after hearing something crazy come out of Donny's mouth. Also, I think we were happy just quietly chewing on the idea that Donny was getting better.

"Shit!" Tony said, checking his watch. "We're late! So much for warming up."

Tony was always worried about blowing out his knees. Our road hockey games had led to more than a few injuries.

The three of us rose to go.

I didn't move. "I'm not up to it today."

Tony turned around. "Yes, you're up to," he scolded. "Atkinson and Monaco called in sick. You don't show, we get disqualified. We need the points to make the play-offs. End of story."

"I'm *not* going, Tony. End of story."

"Listen," he said, "just show up and be a statue, okay? That way we won't get disqualified."

Next thing I knew, he'd grabbed me under the arm and was dragging me outside to his pick-up truck. Tony was brutishly strong. I didn't know whether to hate him for taking me against my will, or hug him for rescuing me from my deep dive into the ex-wife rabbit hole.

Either way, my revenge plan hadn't sold. And I knew that was a very good thing. Mostly.

At the hockey game, my troubles vanished. I flew into action, like John Travolta on skates. I scored three goals, giving us a much-needed win against the scrappy Hamilton Headbangers, in an amazing game that should have stuck in my mind for years, if I hadn't discovered that our new ref was Sophia's fucking husband, Ben Wiley.

At first, I'd no idea who he was. After the game ended, and I'd been safely tucked away in Tony's truck, he'd come clean. My state of shock quickly gave way to powerful feelings of hostility and jealousy. "So, she's Sophia Wiley now?" I'd cried. "Like Wile E. Fucking Coyote? Nice fucking last name!" I'd hammer-fisted the dashboard. "Fuck, he's not even Greek!"

Even worse, I remembered liking the way Wiley reffed, the way he conducted myself, thinking he'd be a cool guy to get to know. But now, just *knowing* he was a good guy, a *nice* guy, royally fucked me up, and I burned with jealousy. He was better than me, and that's why Sophia had chosen him. I felt like slitting my wrists.

Ben Wiley was a high school history teacher and football coach at Jay Prentis Secondary School. Tony's cousin, Loretta, was a custodian there and had given Tony the scoop on Ben. Apparently, everyone *loved* him. Guess they didn't know he was a fucking wife-stealer! If they did, then maybe they wouldn't think he was such a swell guy!

"Turn the fucking truck around!" I cried. "Take me home so I can process this shit." Sure, I'd known that Sophia had remarried, but always nurtured the idea that Sophia's husband was a rich sleazeball, or a tall and skinny version of The Screw. In either scenario, it was easy to hate him, but now I couldn't.

"Not yet, John," Tony said, turning down his street. "I need to show you something."

"Show me what?"

"You'll see. Afterwards I promise to take you home." Tony didn't make promises lightly.

"Make it quick," I groaned. "I don't know how long I can hold off raging in front of your family."

He soft-punched my shoulder. Instead of wondering what that was about, I went back to obsessing on Wiley.

I'd always accepted that a jilted husband should never meet his ex-wife's new husband. It would be too painful, knowing he'd won, that your ex saw him as a better man, that you just weren't good enough and never had been.

Still, I'd rehearsed hundreds of ridiculous meet-your-ex scenarios. One had me randomly bumping into Sophia and Ben at the mall and destroying them with my brilliant digs. But no matter how hard I tried, even in my fantasies, I couldn't find the perfect zinger that would shame them or heal me.

I knew I could never play road hockey again with Wiley refereeing. I couldn't handle the pain, couldn't trust what I'd say or do. I *made* myself imagine Sophia making love to Ben—how sick was that?—until it knotted up my stomach so bad I had no choice but to stop.

After the divorce, I'd torn a strip off of anyone if they so much as *whispered* her name, but today, at the coffee shop, I'd broken my own effing rule.

After I was done with Sophia, she'd know in exact, technicolour detail just how much her cowardly act had ruined me. I'd make it very clear to Ma to make sure Sophia didn't bring her goody-two-shoes-apple-cheeked-doogooder-referee-husband along!

Deep breath in. Slow breath out.

I prayed Tony's surprise didn't involve Ben and Sophia jumping out of a wedding cake and having rip-roaring sex. I cringed. Why did I always imagine them having sex? *Why do I keep hurting myself like this? What the fuck is wrong with me?*

Chapter 12

"GET IT INTO YOU, BUDDY," Tony said.

We'd just stepped off the basement stairs into Tony's basement.

He lived on Shunt Street, two streets east of Irondale Middle School, a stone's throw from Steel Street. Like the rest of us, he'd found great comfort growing up and living in a brick bungalow, in the Village. It was home.

Three swivel chairs flanked a battered wooden bar. Behind it, sunk into mirrored tiles, were liquor bottles on glass shelves. A huge Italian flag was draped overhead.

Nascar posters plastered the wood-panelled walls, along with framed photographs of Tony's kids smiling with their baseball, hockey, and football teams. Angelina was inside a GoKart, grinning-ear-to-ear and waving.

Twenty-year-old Tony was giving a thumbs up from inside a sprint car at Hermonville Raceway. Leaning against the car were his pals, Larry "Hoffy" Hoffman and Luke Ranger. Luke was their mechanic, an old auto buddy of Tony's from Irondale, and Larry was the money man. Together, they'd made a helluva team. Tony had won seven consecutive racing titles, an unbroken track record that still stood.

His racing future had been so bright, yet he'd quit. The handful of times we'd asked him why, he'd brushed us off, saying he'd made his decision and to drop it. "The past is *dead*," he'd always say.

He *had* told us that he'd quit to focus all his attention on raising a family, that he'd outgrown racing, but we'd always suspected his decision had everything to do with his dad, and the last time we'd pried, about ten years ago, he'd gone stone quiet.

Donny was right when he said that Tony was lying to himself, and I believed Donny, who knew a thing or two about lying. Donny Love didn't always lie, but when he did it was such a doozy that you started to wonder if anything he'd ever told you had been one hundred percent true.

Tony reminded me of myself. I could also be stubborn and private with my feelings. I suspected that none of us had ever seen the *real* Tony, that deep part of himself he kept buried.

Donny, on the other hand, spouted his real self on a daily basis, and Tony would often respond with "too much information, Love!", but that never swayed Donny. He just kept on, like a flasher—showing you stuff you *really* didn't want to see.

Norb was a close second to Donny, but, unlike Donny, Norb *almost* knew went to shut up. Sometimes, he'd realize he was embarrassing himself and shake himself into silence. Or, he'd stop cold turkey when Tony gave him the stink eye.

Norb used to remind me of a baby bird squawking in his nest for his mama to feed him. But after his mom passed, he'd matured a bit.

Here we all were now, middle-aged, with half or more of our lives behind us.

Tony turned me to look at the goal of our visit. On a large rectangular plywood table were six brand new boxes of Carrera slot car tracks and cars. I'd loved racing them as a kid.

"You're still a kid at heart, Johnny" he grunted, "and so am I. And we're gonna build the most kick-ass slot car track in Steeltown."

I felt my anger rising. I refused to be placated by playing what was basically a kid's game.

"Valentini, take me home, *now!*"

He threw out his hands out in supplication. He wouldn't look me in the eye—a first!—and said, "Maybe *I* need you to hang out with me, okay? There, I said it."

I was stunned!

His plea had unscrewed something deep inside me. Tony never *needed* his friends. He liked them. He helped them. But he didn't actually need them. Or so I'd thought.

"Okay, when you put it that way, I'll definitely stick around."

"Thanks, buddy."

We stared at the race set.

"Carrera, huh?" I remembered lusting after an expensive racing set from Booth's Hobby Shop on Concession Street when I was eight. Although I'd bugged my parents to buy me one, they wouldn't or couldn't fork out the money. Instead, for my birthday, they'd bought me a Hot Wheels track, which I'd loved. "How much did this run you?"

"Too much."

He cut open a box. "But staying busy is a good way to fight depression."

Depression? Tony? What the hell? "Are you talking from personal experience?"

He lowered his voice. "Naw, not me, Angela."

My heart sank. Angela had always been one of those people who seemed unshakeable.

"I know, right?" He cut a tape seal. "You wouldn't think she's depressed. But if she doesn't take her meds, you wouldn't recognize her. It's painful, trust me."

"I'm really sorry, Tony. I had no idea." Stuck in my misery, I'd forgotten that other people might suffer, too. What a selfish idiot I was.

"I haven't decided if I want everyone to know, so I'd appreciate it if you kept it to yourself." He cracked open a lid.

"Of course."

He slid the box in front of me. "Depression's a bitch."

"Yes-sir." Straight from the horse's mouth.

I wondered if I needed medication. I wasn't *that* far gone. Was I?

As we unpacked the cars and tracks, a weight had been lifted off my shoulders. I suddenly felt like a kid again, hanging out with Tony in his parents' basement, immersed in the magical world of slot car racing. *Find the joy in life.* Well, thanks to Tony, I had!

"Thanks for trying to cheer me up, Tony," I said. "I appreciate it."

"Stay cheerful while you can," he said. "Because when I'm done kicking your Greek ass on this track, you'll be begging for Angela's meds."

"You wish, Valentini!" We shared a grin.

"Hey, maybe next week Donny and Norb could come, too. We can make it a weekly thing."

Tony frowned. "Enough of the weekly things. Any more time spent with you knuckleheads and Angela will divorce me. Or I'll kill youse. Take your pick."

An hour later, the massive track partially laid, we took a beer break at the bar.

Tony swallowed a mouthful of cold Labatt's Blue, and passed me a Molson Export. We sighed with pleasure. Back at Irondale, Blue was considered rocker beer and Export was disco beer, according to the tough guys who hung out in the smoking area.

"Speaking of hobbies," I offered. "I'm still busting out the moves in my basement studio."

"Why not?" Tony said. "Dance therapy. And it keeps you in good shape. And you've always been in good shape, Johnny. You and Donny both." He patted his belly. "Me and Norb, not so much."

"Maybe, but I envy you, Tony."

He eyed me skeptically. "Right."

"You have a good life."

He tilted his head. "It ain't perfect. Sometimes Angela and I fight like cats and dogs. And, to be honest, a few times she's had the suitcases at the front door."

I was shocked. These two always seemed rock-solid to me. "Really? Why didn't she leave?"

"She couldn't. She loves me. And I love her. End of story."

"Tony!" Angela shouted down the stairs, raising my arm hairs. I almost dropped my beer. "You didn't pick up the Ragu! I can't make lasagne without Ragu!"

"Aw shit, I forgot. Okay, I'll go get some."

"Forget it," she said in exasperation. "You have company. I'll go."

Tony winced. "Thanks, honey, I owe you."

"Don't you always? By the way, hi, John."

"Hi, Angela," I called up. "Thanks for having me over. Very kind of you. Sorry I didn't say hi when I came in. I'm, uh, not at my best these days."

"No problem, Johnny, I get it." She closed the basement door.

Angela Valentini had just said what I needed to hear. She could be prickly, but I felt a wave of affection for her.

The basement door swung back open and Angelina thundered down the stairs and gave her dad a big hug. "Thanks again for the slot car track, Daddy!" She was the spitting image of her mother, lean and tomboyish, with short brown hair and brown eyes. She was wearing blue Adidas track pants and a Toronto Maple Leafs hockey jersey.

Tony winked at me. "Okay if Uncle Johnny gets in on the action?"

"Sure!"

"Uncle?" I felt a powerful pang.

"Of course, *Uncle*," Tony said. "We always call you Uncle, right Angel?"

"Always," she chirped. She gave me a high-five. I was choking up with emotion.

Like a wild animal, she quickly pieced together the remaining track. Her hands were lean and intelligent, her energy infectious.

Thirty minutes later, we'd assembled a huge oval track complete with power transformers, bleachers, and two red and white pit stops. I'd settled on a black car, Tony on the red one, and Angelina on yellow. Tony returned from the bar with three cans of Orange Crush. Then Angelina waved the green starting flag. Game on!

After zipping our cars around the track for a good hour, it was dinner time.

Don't overstay your welcome, I reminded myself. The past few hours had been so good. I really didn't want to sour it.

At one end of the kitchen table was Angela, on the other Tony. Angelina plunked down across from me.

"Thanks again for the slot car track, Dad!" she cried. "It's so awesome!"

"No problem," Tony said. "And you're okay if Uncle Johnny comes over and plays with us again?"

She nodded enthusiastically and dug into her lasagna.

"Angel's a Junior Kart racer at Rockford Speedway." Tony sounded very proud. "She's ranked second in the province."

I wondered if Angelina knew what a phenom her dad had been.

"That's great, Angelina," I said, "Are you going to drive Nascar one day?"

"Nope. Sprint cars only."

"Really? That's awesome."

"Girls are getting into the sport now," Tony said.

Angela scoffed. "It's time those sexist pigs at Rockford realize women can race just as well as men."

"Absolutely," I said.

"Personally, John," Tony said, "I prefer my woman barefoot and pregnant in the kitchen."

"Dad!" Angelina growled.

Tony raised his palms. "What? What did I say?"

"I prefer my husband wearing cement boots at the bottom of the bay," Angela retorted. Angela wasn't anything like my precious Sophia. She was down-to-earth blue collar. She traded a grin with her daughter and they high-fived.

"Good one, Mom!"

"Sorry, John," Tony said, laughing, "this is us at our civil best. Hope we don't scare you off." He snatched a piece of garlic bread out of a basket. I saw for the first time just how cracked and calloused his hands were. They looked permanently fissured with grease.

"Not scared at all," I said. "I grew up in a Greek family, remember? I don't scare easily."

"You should have come by when the whole family was living here," Tony said. "It was like the battle at the Tartan Club times ten. Surprised we didn't kill each other." He forked a hunk of lasagna into his mouth.

"You okay, Johnny?" Angela asked, her fork frozen in mid-air.

"Oh, sorry, I drifted off."

All this nice family time had triggered a longing in me. I'd been wondering what our kids would have looked like if Sophia and I'd had them.

A familiar heaviness crushed my chest. I did my pathetic best to ignore it and forced a smile. *Fake it till you make it.*

As I raised a forkful of carrots to my mouth, I realized an uncomfortable silence had fallen at the table. All three were watching me carefully. Did I look wounded?

Despite being surrounded by good people who clearly loved me, my good feelings had dissipated, but that's how post-Sophia life went: an unpredictable lightning bolt through my head and heart, usually when things were going well, triggered by virtually anything.

Tumbling down the familiar rabbit hole, determined not to infect this imperfect but perfectly loving family, I wolfed down my dinner and excused myself from the table. "Darn, I completely forgot," I lied. "I have to run errands for Pops."

"Can't you stay for dessert, Uncle Johnny?" Angelina said. "We're having chocolate cake!"

Before I could say no thanks, she piped, "Take some home with you, Uncle Johnny. Please! It's so good!"

"Sure, sure," I said, forcing a smile.

Tony eyed me with compassion and skepticism. I was thinking he knew why I'd lied, and perhaps was as relieved as I was that I hadn't had a meltdown in front of his family.

At the door, Angela handed me two Tupperware containers, one stuffed with lasagna, the other with chocolate cake. Her generosity made me feel fragile. I began to tear up.

I bustled outside, before I embarrassed myself even more. "Thanks for everything, Angela," I croaked.

"Let me give you a lift," Tony offered, following me out the door.

I waved him off. "Naw, a walk will do me good."

"Come back, soon, Uncle Johnny!" Angelina cried. "Next time I'll let you beat me!"

"Haha, you bet," I managed. I waved from the end of the driveway.

On the sidewalk, I bowed my head against an icy wind, glad for its punishing bite. What was so bad about me that Sophia hadn't wanted me as the father of her kids? Especially with my smarts and good looks?

Like a fool, I spiked my pain by re-imagining Sophia having sex with Ben Wiley. Then I thought about how I'd abandoned my parents, just as Sophia had abandoned me. "You're a hypocrite, Pappas!" I shouted.

Backyard dogs started barking.

"Shut your fucking yaps!"

A rotten desperation seized me. I ran south along Rendell Boulevard towards the 7-Eleven at Steel and Flux. My face was completely numb. Anyone seeing me would have been right if they thought I was an angry, washout junkie desperate for an emotional fix. *Sorry, Angela, but cake is not enough.*

Chapter 13

I wakened with a nasty sugar hangover and a crick in my neck from sleeping on the couch. My stomach was burning with acid. I'd consumed two buckets of Neapolitan ice cream, a family-size bag of salt and vinegar potato chips, three Twinkies, a litre of chocolate milk, and all of Angela's cake. Hurting myself with sugar was almost better than killing myself.

I'd tossed and turned all night, trying to decide if I should just return to the Olympia. Should I cancel my dance studio? Cancel my meeting with Sophia? Burn down my house? Just leave the frickin' country? The urge to run away tugged at me.

I listened to my voicemails. One was Norb and Donny wanting to hang out. Goliath Communications was offering me an internet deal, The Weed Guy was promising me a pre-season discount if I called back and signed up within the hour, and Ma was checking in on me to see if I was okay. I didn't respond to any of those messages.

Instead, I pulled out the list and stared at it. Maybe if I resolved my issues with my ex-wife I could fall in love again. My thoughts strayed to Sheena.

I dragged on yesterday's clothing. Predictably, the guy in the mirror looked like he'd been on a two-week bender, but then I thought, *fuck it.* I decided to embrace my downward spiral.

I shrugged on my boots and coat and headed to the library.

A sliver of sun cut through bruised clouds, temporarily blinding me.

Hopefully, I'd discover a new self-help book. Every six months or so a new one arrived.

One of my favourite techniques was witnessing from a book by Wayne Dyer. It's called *Your Sacred Self,* and it showed me how to tap into the power of my higher self and live with a greater sense of peace. I tried to live in the moment as Eckhart Tolle urged. His book *The Power of Now* is about transcending the ego and finding inner peace. I'd also begun re-reading the Bible, although there was a lot to sort through before you could find the self-help bits.

All the books worked until they didn't, and then, like returning to back exercises after throwing out your back yet again, I'd re-read them and that would help for awhile.

Sometimes old-fashioned distraction was the solution, like watching TV, reading, socializing, or working. But, sooner or later, she'd haunt me again.

At the library, I was on the stairs, heading up to the psychology shelves, when Morag whispered loudly. "John!"

She waved me over to the check-out desk and handed me an audio book called *Secrets of Your Own Healing Power*.

She knew why I was here—everyone in the Village did, thanks to Motormouth Donny—and the books that interested me. She'd always had my back that way.

"Dyer," I said, sheepishly. "Good old Wayne. Thanks, Morag."

Determined to show my gratitude, I drummed up a smile. "I've seen this one here before, but for some reason I resisted."

"I know you did, John." She smiled knowingly at me.

"You did?"

She kept her voice low. "Good luck, John. Don't forget your friends love you."

I choked up.

It didn't bother me that she knew I was a tortured soul. At the library, Morag was like a doting big sister. Norb really had lucked out.

"I already checked it out for you so you're good to go. Let me know what you think, okay?"

And then she turned her smile to a customer searching for a book on conspiracy theories.

I waved goodbye and headed for the door, my eyes blurred with moisture. Why was I always tearing up and leaving? Was that John Pappas' new signature exit? I sure as hell didn't want it to be.

It dawned on me that there are self-help books, and then there are people who care enough about you to actually give you self-help books. Maybe it was time I became a giver like Morag, not a pity-taker.

Again, I reflected how lucky Norb was to have Morag in his life. Despite his peculiarities and perma-poverty, she'd fallen in love with him and married him. I doubted there were many women as big-hearted and beautiful.

Visually, they were a total mismatch, Morag being a sexy, red-headed cosplay-type, and Norb being an overweight, blonde comic book nut, and people often were shocked to discover they were married. I teared up again. Self-pity yanked on my heart strings. I wanted to have what they had! *Where's my Morag? God, please send me my Morag!*

After I'd crossed the road, I looked past the intersection at the windows of the dance studio. *Dance Studio? What had I been thinking? This was all Donny's fault!*

As I trudged through heavy slush on Steel Street, fear repeatedly knifed me in the back. I created a *new* list: Reasons Why A Dance Studio Is A Terrible Idea:

1. I am forty-one
2. Dancing is exhausting
3. Teaching dance is exhausting
4. Dancing and teaching are exhausting when you're forty-one
5. I am a forty-one-year-old coward!

I whacked a telephone pole. Bad idea! My palm burned.

I decided that if reading Dyer didn't fix me by seven p.m., I would run over to Barry Supinder's house, pay off the entire lease and hand him back the keys. Then I'd go back to the Olympia, tail tucked between my legs. *End of your stupid dream, Donny!*

But if I was being honest, it was really *my* dream. It had been for more years than I cared to admit.

Morag's words danced in my head like twinkly Christmas lights. *Good luck, John. Don't forget your friends love you.*

Across the street, a guy wearing a Hamilton Tiger-Cats cap was staring me down as his dog took a leak against a fire hydrant. I realized I'd been boxing the air, like a lunatic, trying to punch some courage into my chicken shit self.

"Yeah, I'm crazy!" I yelled at him. "So what? So's everyone else in this shithole town!"

He scowled and gave me the finger.

I *skipped* across the street, just to really own my insanity. I got weird looks from the bus shelter people but I didn't give a shit. My breakdown had to go somewhere, and I was glad as hell it had me skipping home, rather than leaping off a bridge.

Chapter 14

NIGHT HAD FALLEN. SNOW whipped through the streetlights. In half an hour, I was supposed to teach my first dance class in the studio.

I slogged past Crazy Bob's Head Shop, puzzled by how I could have spent the entire afternoon listening to Wayne Dyer's audio book but now couldn't remember a damn thing. I swear the portrait of Bob laughed at me from the sign above his store, stoned yet superior. *Fuck you, Bob!*

I guessed some of Dyer's wisdom must have hit home, otherwise I wouldn't have found the strength and conviction to leave the house tonight.

Then I realized that real-life Bob was waving at me from his shop window. Why? I barely knew him. To be honest, I didn't care much for him. He was like a combo of mad scientist, praying mantis, and Lemme from *Motorhead,* and also a total dopehead. Last spring, at Home Hardware, Donny and I had been in the plumbing section picking up copper pipe so we could install a bathroom in his basement when we'd bumped into Bob.

Donny had introduced us. He'd seemed nice enough. But what really struck me about him were his eyes—they were so heavily-lidded and glazed. How could a guy be that high and still function?

Half-heartedly, I waved at Bob. He made me uncomfortable, like most of Donny's "guys" did. I found them shady and weaselly. Did that make me a snob? I knew what Donny would say about that.

A bizarre mirage on the other side of Flux Road froze me to the sidewalk.

Barely visible through a sheet of snow were the Steeltown Avenger, his icy breath steaming out of his mouth, and John Travolta, busting out dance moves while juggling miniature disco balls. They were both wearing sandwich boards and gesturing excitedly at passing cars.

Donny and Norb!

My heart panged when I realized they were freezing their asses off in an effort to drum up business for me. I didn't know whether to get down on my knees and thank them for helping, or tear a strip off them for not asking permission.

Their love for me was hard to take. In a million years I couldn't give back half of what they were giving. A powerful cocktail of humiliation, anger, and gratitude ran my veins.

Norb had removed his mask and was chomping on a 7-Eleven chili dog, his smiling face totally unperturbed by the driving snow.

On the boards, in scratchy red handwriting, they'd painted, "Free Salsa!" Red arrows pointed towards my studio.

What? "Norb, you idiot! It's a free salsa lesson, not *free salsa!*" But he couldn't hear me through the whizzing traffic.

What if people showed up looking for free salsa? Shit!

Bob was nodding, as if he'd astral-projected this Norb-and-Donny-hallucination into my brain. I threw him a dirty look then hustled across the intersection towards them.

Traffic was heavy. Not surprisingly, no one paid any real attention to my marketing genius friends. Maybe it was because it was too cold to stop for salsa, or people were afraid to approach two weirdos out parading in a blizzard.

A pick-up truck flew past Norb and sprayed slush all over his tights. His last bit of chili dog spilled out of his cold, red hand and hit the dirty slush.

He stared down at his dog, blinking against the stabbing snow. The last time I'd seen him that sad had been when MegaFreak had cancelled their Buffalo concert.

When he saw me approaching, his eyes lit up. He waved me over.

"John!" he wheeze-cried, "Me and Donny are promoting your studio!"

"Go home and be with Morag, Norb. This is totally unnecessary. You too, Love." I wasn't sure Donny had heard me, he was so caught up in his juggling. "Why aren't you guys wearing gloves?" I said. "Your faces and hands are just about frozen!"

"It's not that cold," Norb said.

"Are you crazy?" I had to turn my head away from a powerful gust.

"Gloves and juggling don't mix," Donny said, shrugging. "Hey, check out our marketing strategy!" He pointed at the telephone pole beside him.

There was a poster exclaiming, "Want to meet sexy singles? Try a free Salsa lesson!" At the bottom was Donny's phone number. No mention of my studio! A second poster below it shouted, "Where the fuck are you, Steven? Call me!"

The absurd had become real.

Winter thunder shook the neighbourhood.

"Cool!" Norb said, dreamily, through chittering teeth.

"I didn't ask for this!" I groaned.

"This is what old friends do for each other," Donny cried above the traffic. "So far, we've handed out a hundred business cards. Norb did an awesome job designing them, don't you think?" He handed me one. At the top it said *Pappas' School of Dance*. Beneath it, was the silhouette of a dancer, presumably me. I could tell Norb had put a lot of effort into it. At the bottom, he'd added my number. But instead of being happy they'd done this for me, I felt fucking guilty.

"Look, I can do this on my own!" As soon as I said it, I realized it wasn't entirely true.

"But what fun would that be?" Donny said, rubbing his hands together for warmth.

Suddenly, like a bolt of lightning, I realized I wasn't and could no longer be the same guy hanging with his friends at Tim's, waiting for an opportunity to cut them up and get a laugh at their expense. I was now a new John Pappas, one that needed these Village Idiots as much as they appeared to need me.

"We knew you could do this on your own," Donny offered. "But you haven't been doing so good lately, so we thought we'd lend a hand."

Norb heartily agreed.

Changed or not, I could only handle so much bleeding-heart stuff, so I pointed at Norb's sign. "Free *Salsa*? Who am I? Mr. Tostitos?"

When he looked down, his jaw dropped. "Aw fuzz, me, man!" He stared daggers at Donny. "No wonder your sign guy was so cheap. He forgot to add *Lesson!*"

"Hey, woah," Donny said, making his trademark innocent face. "I was trying to save us a buck. You get what you pay for, right?"

Cultivate your gentleness. I could do that. I would try, anyway.

I checked my watch. I was almost late. "Gents, apparently I have a class to teach." I turned around and jogged down the sidewalk towards my studio.

"Break a leg, Johnny," Norb cried. "No pun intended." He threw on his mask and went back to work, waving at passing cars like a big kid.

A car skidded into the gas station and Donny accosted the anxious-looking driver with a business card.

Nervous laughter peeled out of my mouth. How ludicrous *and* wonderful Norb and Donny were for whoring themselves out for me. I was deeply touched and teary.

With my hand on the door handle, my heart swelled to ten times its size. Well, maybe three. I was the Grinch!

I spun around and yelled at the top of my lungs. "Thanks for all your help, guys!"

The Steeltown Avenger saluted and John Travolta waved without looking, as he was busy chatting up another potential customer stopped at the red light.

Without Donny the Village would be a bore. *I'd* be a bore. I wished I had his spirit of adventure and risk. He must have inherited that from his parents, who'd had the guts to cross the ocean and start a new life in Canada. *Yours did, too, John, so nice try!* I wondered if my parents' DNA would show up in the next generation, because it had definitely missed mine.

I used to think I had no idea why Donny and Norb put up with me, but now I knew why. It was the L word. And thinking it made me uncomfortable. I took a deep, steadying breath, and admitted to myself just how lucky I was to have life-long friends.

I charged up the stairs. The hallway was dead.

My studio door was ajar. I figured Donny had unlocked it and had forgotten to hand me the keys.

I was expecting a horrible turn-out, certain I'd be stuck teaching my first class with Norb and Donny and a homeless guy they'd dragged in with promises of smokes and booze. Surely, no one else would be interested in dance lessons taught by a middle-aged, has-been loser.

As soon as I stepped inside, I froze. The walls closed in.

Wearing a tight leopard print leotard, her massive breasts threatening to explode over her low neckline, was the only woman I'd ever had sex with other than Sophia. *Shit, what's your name?* I'd been so friggin' drunk!

I forced a smile that probably looked like a grimace. Air wooshed back into my lungs. *Please don't remember me!*

"Johnny Pappas, it's me, Lyra!"

Fuck!

"Lyra," I stammered. "Of course, Lyra. Long time. How are you? What brings you here?" Hot waves of guilt pounded me.

"Duh," she said skeptically, "dancing, what else?"

"You like to dance?"

She laughed. "You know I do, Johnny. Don't you remember that night at the Blue Ball when you swept me off my feet, busting out the Gene Kelly moves?" She flung out her hip emphatically.

Please don't do that.

I laughed nervously. "How did you know I opened a dance studio?" I went over to a row of chairs against the wall to dump my jacket and tie on my dance shoes. My mind raced, searching for a solution to this effed-up situation.

Whatever had attracted me to her in my drunken state no longer existed. Sure, she was a good-looking woman, but I felt nothing for her, only scorching guilt.

Practically reeking of hot sex, Lyra sashayed over to me. I swallowed nervously. She watched my face knowingly. I was just glad that no one else was here to witness this nightmare.

"Easy peasy, lover," she said. "I was on the internet looking up old flings and found you on your website promoting a free dance lesson. And I thought to myself, if he's as good a teacher as he is a sex-machine, then bring on the Salsa, baby!"

"A sex-machine? My website?" *Donny, you didn't! I never asked you to make a freakin' website! It's all your fault Lyra's here. You've turned my first class into a nightmare!* I clenched my jaw.

She smiled coyly and ran a long, red fingernail down my arm. "I remember you oh so well, my sweet Greek lover."

I gulped. "You do?" I glanced at the doorway to make sure no one was there to hear this. "How long has it been? Five? Six years?"

"Yeah, three, four, five, six, whatever. All I know is that our night was one of a kind. Not something a lady easily forgets." She kept stroking my arm like it was something else.

I swallowed the basketball-sized lump in my throat.

She whispered into my ear. "Remember how things got so hot in the men's washroom we nearly blew off the stall door?" She whipped her head backwards and cackled like a whorehouse witch. The hairs on my neck stood up.

The men's washroom? But I did remember now! It was all coming back! My desperation to feel *something* good that night, to have one moment of forgetting Sophia. *Someone shoot me!*

"Sorry, Lyra, I was really drunk that night. I wasn't myself."

She slipped her arms around me and smooshed her massive breasts against my chest. I didn't know where to look. Hot shame burned my face. I wondered if she'd gotten breast implants—I couldn't remember them being that enormous.

If my past literally coming back to haunt me wasn't bad enough, things suddenly got even worse.

"Looks like you have some customers, Johnny," Lyra said, sounding like she didn't care one bit.

Agnes and Sheena were standing at the door, eyes wide.

Fuck me!

Sheena cleared her throat and pressed a tight smile on her face. In her sing-song voice, she said, "Sorry, are we interrupting?"

"No, no," I said. "Not at all." I tried to pull away but Lyra wouldn't let go.

"Uh, Lyra, this is Sheena and Agnes," I gestured. I was pretty sure my heart had stopped.

Lyra just smiled and nodded. She was ruining everything! I squirmed, trying to break free from her octopus grip.

"How do you two know each other?" Sheena asked, a cheeky grin lifting a corner of her mouth. She was clearly enjoying this.

She chaired her bag and slipped off her coat. She was wearing a pair of black high-heel shoes, pink tights, a baby-blue wet-look mini-skirt, a tank top with spaghetti straps, and a plastic turquoise necklace. A pink bow stuck out of the explosion of bleach blonde hair. She would have fit right in an 80's Madonna video.

While Lyra was sizing up Sheena and Agnes, she had relaxed her grip, so I quickly slid away.

Get this horror show over with and shut down the business, I told myself. *Then go back to the Olympia with your tail between your legs you delusional piece of skank-banging shit!*

"Okay," I said, forcefully clapping myself into a pleasant mood, "let's get this show on the road!"

Then, because apparently things could get worse, *he* made an appearance.

"Right, Johnny!" Archie Love shouted. "Let's get crackin'. I'll show you how to cut a rug!"

He shucked off his coffee-stained parka and dumped it on a chair.

He was wearing a Mr. Mugs t-shirt. The coffee shop's owner apparently believed that the best way to bring in customers was to depict a brown coffee mug enjoying a smoke. Archie refused to step foot into Tim Hortons, claiming it was run by some corporate mafia.

"Are you sure you're up for this, Mr. Love?" I asked, hoping his answer would be no. "Dancing can be very strenuous."

Right then Donny and Norb tumbled through the door.

Donny stopped dead in his tracks. "Dad?"

Archie scoffed. "Aye, son, I'd knew you'd be here. What are you doing, dressed like John Revolta?"

Donny looked riled.

"Ach, take a chill pal, laddie. I was on my way home from Mr. Mugs and I saw you two Nancies parading about with your clapboards. What are you two donkeys up to, anyway? Halloween's months away!" He pointed at Donny's sign and scoffed again. "Well, anyway, I knew what you'd tried to say, free salsa *dance lesson*. So, I said to myself, 'Archie, this is your chance to meet a sexy new wife'. So here I am." He rubbed his hands together in delight.

Donny's face was beet red. "You're married, Dad. To *Mum*, remember?"

"Ach, quit your bletherin', lad. I'm just here for a wee bit o' fun."

"Whatever, you crazy bastard," Donny mumbled, shaking his head, moving as far away from his father as possible.

"I heard that."

"Good!" Donny said.

I followed behind Donny. "I didn't ask you to build me a website," I hissed.

"OK, OK, I'll take it down if you like. I was just trying to help."

He actually looked contrite. And of course it wasn't his fault Lyra had found the website.

I really was trying to be a better man, so I clapped him on the shoulder. "Thanks for making it. I bet it looks great."

Donny smiled guardedly.

Then people started flowing through the doorway. I had to clamp my jaw shut. Three geeky guys I recognized from Norb's shop paraded through the door. The first was the yellow cardigan guy with Buddy Holly glasses. Behind him came the skinny guy in shorts he'd obviously purchased in a kid's clothing section, and the last was short and apple-shaped, with cheeks like a feverish baby.

They were followed by Tank and her nana, I presumed. Norb had told me she'd sometimes show up at his shop to take Tank out for lunch. She was shorter than Sheena and her brunette hair was a pixie cut, buzzed at the sides like Tank's. According to Norb, she was also a real firecracker. Next in were two well-groomed gents in matching tights and George Michael t-shirts. Then there was Lily from Mike's Sub Shop, and a young brown woman with long shiny hair and a non-descript boyfriend. "Hi, I'm Yasmin, and this is Doug!" she called from the doorway.

A rugged dude with a cop moustache kicked off his oil-stained work boots and strutted onto the floor. In his plaid shirt and tight jeans, he looked like he was going to break into "YMCA". I wondered if he'd lost a bet. We all stared as he busted out fifty push-ups.

Then three of my former Lyle Dance Academy dance students arrived. The little room was starting to get crowded.

"Hey everybody, I'll start warm-ups in a few minutes," I announced, on auto-pilot. Rugged guy stood up and cracked his neck loudly.

I went to the door and peeked down the hallway to see if anyone else was coming.

Lyra was swinging her arms side-to-side, leering at me. I forced a crinkly smile then went to the window and pretended to check the parking lot for latecomers.

As I turned back to the class, something bright and fluffy caught my attention. Heels off, like some 80s punk ballerina, Sheena arced through the air and performed a graceful grand jeté. *Holy shit!*

The rugged guy was now doing the splits. Norb was eyeing him, clearly getting ready to join in.

"Go easy during the warm-ups," I said nervously. "We don't want any pulled hamstrings before we start."

Sheena finished a cartwheel. "Sorry, John," she offered. "I'm not very good at going easy."

I was in awe of her. Had she been this good at The Blue Ball? I couldn't remember. She had a graceful, unorthodox style.

What a sweet piece of shortbread! my heart cried.

"Keep your tongue in your mouth now, Johnny," Mr. Love guffawed, grinning a row of nicotine-stained teeth. He was working on a decent box-step.

I ignored him.

Donny snorted in amusement.

The geeks were awkwardly watching everyone else warm up.

"Where's the free salsa?" the guy in the kids' shorts asked. "The sign said free salsa."

"Oh, that was my mistake," Norb said, finishing a wobbly pirouette. Now I'd seen it all. In fact, we were *all* seeing way more than we wanted to. Norb's tights were...tight.

"Nope, the Steeltown Avenger *never* makes a mistake," Buddy Holly chimed in. He dovetailed his hands on his hips. "You owe us free salsa, dude."

His friends nodded in agreement and they glared at me.

Norb bit his lip. "Fellas, there is no free salsa, but let me make it up to you. The next edition of *The Steeltown Avenger* will be on me!"

The geeky guys high-fived each other, way more excited than anyone ought to be about a comic book.

I knew it was time to whip this motley crew into shape. The rugged guy gave me the stink eye, silently demanding his free lesson *now*.

"Okay, folks, spread out, give yourselves lots of room." I ran them through some gentle warm-ups. Then I put on "Toro Mata" by Celia Cruz and danced a basic salsa set for them. It felt so good to dance, and the music lifted my spirits right up. And when I finished, there was cheering and applause. I found myself smiling, for real.

"OK, so begin with your feet together. On beat one, step forward with your left foot, on beat two shift your weight to your right foot...relax your hips...keep your hands centered so your energy flows more easily. Small steps..."

I couldn't decide if Archie Love had decided learning salsa wasn't for him or if he just hated instruction—he kept dancing the box step, albeit a sexy senior citizens' version. I caught him leering at Lyra's breasts but was shocked when she winked back at him. *Gross!* But I had to give Archie credit. For a man his age, he *was* a smooth dancer.

Other than rebel Archie, everybody followed direction as best they could. But experience had taught me that half these well-meaning people wouldn't return. They'd either realize they didn't like salsa dancing, or it was too hard, or they weren't coordinated enough, or they didn't have the money to continue, or it wasn't the sexy singles club they'd hoped it would be.

Ironically, sometimes the uncoordinated stuck it out the longest. And for those with two left feet, dancing was better than being stuck at home alone, so I always did my best to encourage these people. I knew from experience that loneliness sucked.

Buddy Holly was lumbering back and forth like a robot, his eyes locked in a thousand-yard-stare. The apple-shaped guy stumbled over himself because he'd been fixated on Lyra's cleavage. It *was* hard not to fixate.

Lyra had nailed the steps. She was a natural, obviously comfortable with her body, swaying her hips provocatively. I felt queasy, remembering our sexual encounter in that filthy bathroom stall.

Norb was now dancing on his tippy toes. He was hard to watch. His face was a shiny orb of sweat.

Although Tank and her nana were pretty good, I found Tank a little annoying. She kept chewing her gum and snapping out bubbles. The gents in tights were stereotypically very good. I couldn't tell if they were partners, friends, or identical twins. Regardless, they seemed to be enjoying themselves.

And Sheena, well, she was amazing.

When I asked everyone to partner up, things got even more weird.

Lyra latched onto poor Norb. I watched him utter a silent apology to Morag, what he always did whenever another woman got near to him. As always, his face went tomato-red.

Oddly, the men outnumbered the women today. As a result, the apple-shaped geek partnered up with Buddy Holly. Donny, grimacing, partnered up with the third one. At first, his partner looked offended, but after a while he seemed to think he'd found a new friend.

Lily from the sub shop joined with Sarah, one of my Lyle dance students.

As I ran them through the steps, I saw Archie in a standoff with his new partner. Like UFC fighters, he and the rugged guy had squared off, sizing each other up. I wondered if Archie had already insulted the guy. Was I going to have to break up a fight?

I couldn't wait for this night to be over!

"Right, Push Ups, let's get it on," Archie conceded, finally. "But just so you know, although I'm straight as a caber, I'm also not afraid to touch a man."

The rugged man belched. Was he drunk? "Let's do this, bro," he agreed, and then they were off dancing together like no one's business.

As they circled around the room like bulls in a china shop, Archie spared no one from his blunt remarks. "Aye, you're doing great, sweetheart," he called out to Lyra. "Next time, you and me, right?"

She winked at him, and Archie beamed. Then Norb backed onto Archie's toes.

"You call that dancing, Norbert?" Archie said. "You're dancing like a wee girl. Man up, lad!"

Everyone stopped and stared at Archie, then me. The gents in the George Michael t-shirts scowled, pissed at him. I'm pretty sure they wanted me to kick the old dinosaur out of the class.

Tank marched up to Archie and got up in his grill. Fire blazed in her eyes. "What did you call Norb, old man?" she cried.

"Oh, who do we have here? A *punk rocker*?" Archie hooted at his own joke.

Norb tried to shoo Tank down, but she wasn't having it.

"You're a sexist pig!" Tank roared. Her fists came up. She looked like she could take Archie in a fight.

"Woah!" I cried, quickly jumping in between them. Nana had glued her hands firmly to her hips, looking like she was ready to tag-team Archie.

Donny rushed over. "Dad, you can't say stuff like that anymore!"

"Apologize, Archie," I ordered, "and no more comments like that, or I'll ask you to leave. Got it?"

"Ach well, when you put it that way, I'll gladly shut it. No skin off ma' nose." He laughed at his own humour, and went back to happily box-stepping with the rugged man who seemed unfazed by Archie's drama.

Tank went back to her nana. "Old bastard," she grumbled.

"Oh aye," Archie said. "Old, but not *deef*. So watch your tongue, Punky."

"Dad!" Donny cried.

Tank took a step toward him, hands fisted.

Mr. Love pretended to shake in terror.

What a shit show!

"Archie!" cried a familiar voice at the door. "That's no salsa! You're doing the bloody box step! And if you think you can take that wee girl in a fight, you're daft."

It was Esme! Donny must have told her about my class. She was dressed in grey track pants and an old grey parka. Her pink dolly hair was bouffed up, and for once she wasn't smoking a fag.

She was using a huge walking stick that looked more like a wizard's staff. She looked like she was planning to beat Archie with it. There were people in this room who would gladly help her.

Archie's face flamed as he released the rugged man and jabbed his index finger at his wife. "I'd rather have married Cruella De Vil than you!"

Everyone stared in disbelief at the Village champs of Public Arguing.

"Eff I was Cruella," Esme said, "I'd have surely made a coat out of you by now, Archie!"

"You'd never catch me, Gimpy!" he said, tilting his chin defiantly.

"Archie," she said coyly, suddenly reversing direction, "I've just baked a batch of Empire biscuits with extra icing."

He perked up.

"C'mon, I'll drive you home and put on a fresh pot of tea."

He licked his lips. His mind was working overtime. "Aye, after class, Esme," he said, returning to his partner. "I can't let down the Marlboro man."

She looked lustily at the guy. "You've landed a real catch, Archie."

Archie grumbled under his breath.

She smiled at me. "Sorry to interrupt, Johnny."

"Nice to see you, Mrs. Love." Thank God she'd interrupted a potential brawl.

She caned out the door. My students looked like they'd barely survived a terrorist attack. I was almost sure that had been the Loves' shortest public argument. They usually ripped into each other for a good thirty minutes. Donny had told us their record was just under two hours at the Price Chopper, when the cops had arrived at the grocery store and finally put a stop to it. Perhaps old age had finally sapped their fighting spirit and short bursts were all they could manage.

I ran the group through the set a few more times, to reset the good mood. At the end of class, I thanked everyone, told them to see Donny about class times (since he seemed to know more about my business than I did), and reminded them to wear loose clothing next time. Everyone filtered out the door, but Agnes and Sheena lingered.

And then I did a weirdly juvenile thing. Like some Grade Eight kid hot to impress a girl, I tap-danced, twirled, then went up and over a chair, tilting it backwards and landing it smoothly on the floor like Fred Astaire in *Let's Dance*.

Sheena and Agnes quietly stared.

"Way to go, Gene Kelly!" I didn't recognize my new fan, but the man standing beside him was Barry Supinder.

"I love Gene Kelly!" the man repeated as he crossed the floor towards me. He peered at me through orange, oversized grandpa glasses. He extended his hand. "Dirk Singh, Bollywood film director."

Barry had mentioned him the other day. I shook his hand, wondering if the night could get any weirder.

Sheena and Agnes were obviously impressed. Sheena mouthed "good luck" to me, then gathered up her things.

"Well, not Bollywood yet," Barry said, coming in beside Dirk. "But soon, we hope."

"You are just what I'm looking for," said Dirk. "Barry was right about you. You're right out of the Golden Age of Hollywood. I'm so impressed!"

"What's your movie about?" I asked, feeling flattered.

"It's about a woman who must choose a suitor, when, all along, the love of her life has been right in front of her!"

I nodded distractedly as Sheena left, gone without so much as a smile. My heart sank. Then Dirk was yammering excitedly about his project. Donny and Norb stood at my elbow, hanging onto every word.

But no matter how hard I tried, I couldn't fully take in the amazing things Dirk was promising me. And they *were* amazing, as Donny later reassured me. All I could think about was Sheena, my heart dancing nervously.

Chapter 15

PACING IN MY BASEMENT dance studio, I psyched myself up to follow through on Steps 2 and 4.

Heart pounding, I dialed Sheena's number. I was about to hang up when she answered.

Before she could speak, I blurted, "Hi, Sheena it's me, John!"

The silence was deafening.

"Hi, John," she said, hesitantly.

"Uh, sorry to bother you so late." I hoped she couldn't hear the tremble in my voice.

"Ach, no bother. Is everything okay?"

"Yes, of course. I, uh, wanted to thank you for coming to my class. And to apologize for my behavior at Tim's. Um, I'd wanted to make a good first impression and I totally blew it. You didn't deserve that."

"I appreciate that, John."

Another pause.

"I should probably get going," she said. "Tomorrow, I start my new job so I'll need my beauty rest."

"Right! Of course, your new job!" Idiot! I should have asked her more about it at the coffee shop, instead of going on about myself. "That's exciting!" I said as cheerily as I could.

"Did I tell you Donny also got Agnes a job at Jimmy the Barber's?"

"Seriously?"

"Aye, Jimmy's says it's high time he hired a woman. And he really wants to help out a fellow Glaswegian."

"Wow, times are changing! But you might want to tell Agnes to watch out for Jimmy. He's quite a womanizer."

"Is that so? Well, back home, men are terrified of Agnes. So Jimmy better watch *himself*. Maybe you should warn *Jimmy*."

"Ha! Maybe I should. Have you worked as a travel agent before?"

"Oh aye, I've done since I was eighteen. It's all I know."

"Good for you." Gathering my courage, I cut to the chase. "Sheena, do you think you could give me a second chance and let me take you out to dinner?"

"Not yet, Johnny."

Her loaded and quick response surprised me. "Not yet?" Knowing I probably wouldn't like the answer, I asked anyway. "Do you mind if I ask why?"

She sighed. "I don't think you're ready for a relationship, yet."

Old anger stirred. "Not ready? How do you know I'm not ready?" My old wall slid up.

Her tone was firm. "It was sweet of you to call, John. But I really need to go to bed early. I have to make a good impression tomorrow. I especially don't want to let Donny down, after everything he's done for Agnes and me."

I swallowed the bitter taste of disappointment. "Right, I totally understand."

"Good luck with your dance school, John. I'm sure you'll do great. You really do dance like Gene Kelly."

I fake-chuckled. "So, I guess you're not coming back?"

"Sorry. Donny said you could really use help getting started so we agreed to pitch in. But to be honest, Agnes and I aren't into Salsa dancing. We're hardcore 80's girls."

"Oh, okay, no problem. And thanks again for the two of you pitching in."

"Good night."

"Good luck tomorrow," I said, but she'd already hung up.

Not ready for a relationship? If I were being honest with myself, she was right—I wasn't ready. But at least I had tried tonight, so that was a good start, wasn't it? But my ego was bruised. Failure burned in my belly.

Compelled to wreck myself, I bolted upstairs. I returned with the box of pain.

Just to add a celebratory note to the rejection, I turned on my disco ball and the dance floor lights.

I slid in an 8-track Bee Gees Greatest Hits cassette into the stereo. I blasted "Staying Alive" through the speakers.

Then I dumped all of Sophia's letters onto the dance floor. Dots of glitter ball light spun over them.

I picked up the one I called Letter Number 2 because this was the second one I'd let myself read in seventeen years.

What's wrong with me? Why can't I finally say goodbye?

"Fuck it!"

Hands shaking, I read the letter.

May 2, 1985

Dear John,

I can't believe we're getting married in three months! Mom is freaking out with excitement. She's invited all the relatives. Trust me, Johnny, they're going to love you!

Mom loves to tell everyone the wedding will cost $60,000. She says that's the price you pay for the best Greek wedding Hamilton will ever see. And of course, as tradition demands, your parents will pay the bar bill. Teehee!

Ma asks if I'm in love with you, and all I can say is, I don't know what else to call it Ma, so I must be! Haha!

Me and the girls are having a blast in Fort Lauderdale. Elaine and Marta have met a couple of hunks and seemed to be hitting it off. Of course, those days are over for me, but I'm still having fun, if you call fending off rich guys cruising in Ferraris on the beach fun. Ha! If they only knew how good I got it, Johnny, right? Wink wink!

Greeks rule!

Sophia
XO

"*Greeks rule?*" I repeated, quietly. "*I don't know what else to call it?*"

I felt a wave of pity for young John. In my youthful inexperience, I had failed to see the truth. Her spell on me had been so powerful that she could have cut off my legs and I'd still have found a way to walk to the ends of the earth for her. My love had been blind!

I leapt up to my feet.

Even her sign-off had been lukewarm. Not *Love, Sophia*. Nope. Just a childish "xo"!

How could *I*, Johnny, Smarter-than-half-of-Hamilton Pappas, have been so fucking blind? How could Sophia marry me, if she didn't love me? What kind of monster does that? Tears ran down my cheeks.

Her letters to me held the same painful truths. Sophia hadn't loved me, not in a deep, meaningful way. But what confused the hell out of me was the way her eyes had twinkled when she'd gazed at me, and the great sex we'd had—like Salsa-dancing in the bedroom.

So, what had changed? What had I done to turn her off?

No one should ever marry someone they don't love, I thought. *That's beyond cruel.*

I dragged my hands down my wet face.

Maybe it wasn't Sophia I really wanted. Maybe what I was really craving was the dopamine rush of being in love. So, if that was true, why not start over and fall in love again? What was I waiting for?

My brain switched gears.

Hopefully Lyra didn't show up to class again. If she did, I'd have to make it perfectly clear I wasn't interested. What must Sheena think of me, after seeing me with Lyra? I didn't want to know. Thinking about Sheena got my heart throbbing, but I wasn't having it. I'd already been through enough pain tonight, so I made myself focus on Dirk Singh's crazy movie offer.

I was still in a state of shock over it. Why had he chosen me—humble waiter, Village nobody, crackpot, unemployed boozer, dirty bathroom-sex slut—to dance in his feature-length film?

Of course, the answer was easy. The Grand Schemer himself had convinced Dirk! For better or worse, Donny had made things happen. Again. Or maybe this Dirk guy was a nutbar, too. Seeing I had nothing to lose, I decided to give it a shot.

And if my Bollywood career blew up before it left the ground, at least I could tell myself I'd had the guts to make myself vulnerable and risk failure. If Norb could face The Screw, then I could dance.

I buried my face in my hands. Life in the Village was now full-on insane. The Screw? Shadow? Humpty Dumpty Village Vigilante? Norb on psychedelics? And now me, Greek-Boy-Bollywood-Gene-Kelly?

If the people of this neighbourhood really knew what went on here, they'd pack up and hit the road. It was Crazy Town!

I stared up at the slowly rotating disco ball.

It was now obvious Sophia had married me—a handsome, stylish Greek man—to placate her Greek parents. Maybe a seventeen-year-old with no real-life experience could make that mistake, sure, but a twenty-three-year-old?

Although I had no respect for her, I had loads for her parents. After arriving in Canada, they'd built and run three successful restaurants, and could easily have bought a beautiful house on swanky Mountain Brow Boulevard, overlooking the escarpment, but instead had opted for a humble bungalow on Lunchbox Street.

Sophia loved to talk about three-car garages, European sports cars, and in-ground swimming pools, and yet she'd settled for a humble waiter and a blue-collar bungalow. That must have killed her.

I bitterly studied the burnt photo of us cutting our wedding cake. Was my beautiful bride smiling in joy, or just for the camera?

I whipped the photo against the floor and ran upstairs. I grabbed a bottle of Johnny Walker Black out of the liquor cabinet and swigged. The whiskey set a fire in my throat. I hated how mean it tasted, but that didn't stop me. I *needed* mean.

Chapter 16

I was driving to see Dr. Hotz, my old psychotherapist.

For over two years, I'd done everything in my power to go it alone, but I couldn't anymore. I needed help.

Shockingly, my dance studio was already breaking even, an amazing feat for a new business. I was teaching three times a week, with class sizes hovering around twenty. Lyra had poutingly accepted the news that I wasn't interested in a relationship, especially one involving filthy bathroom sex, though she hadn't completely given up on me and would occasionally blow me random kisses, which I always ignored. But I have to admit, it was embarrassingly comforting to my battered ego.

Norb and Donny still insisted on hustling my business out on the cold street. I'd thanked them again and again, but couldn't convince them to stop making fools of themselves out there on my account.

That morning, despite a gruesome hungover, I'd driven to Brampton and rehearsed my over-the-top scene with my friendly co-stars, Dev Banerjee and Sita Chaudry, in a make-shift studio in the back of an abandoned furniture warehouse. Dev played suitor Gary Kumar and Sita played a free-spirited young woman Kiara Agarwal.

The movie was called *All Along*. I was cast as a Greek suitor, Achilles Stiliadis, and was in a final dance-off competition with Gary, both of us trying to win Kiara's love.

The dance choreographer, Arjun, taught me a genius blend of Bhangra and western dance moves inspired by the movie *Singin' in the Rain*. He also taught me Indian hook steps, and I was loving the new challenges. Dev was a true master of the *Bharatanatyam* dance, which was energetic and graceful, so this was going to be one wild dance scene.

Dirk told us the set in the main part of the warehouse was almost ready and next time we'd rehearse there. Shit was getting real, as Tony would say.

Dirk was ecstatic I'd signed on. He fully believed that casting me in his movie would impress the studio big wigs in Mumbai and help secure him a distribution deal. So, he was definitely delusional.

Recently, I'd been working hard on Steps 2 and 5. Dancing in a movie was definitely a joyful experience, albeit hard. And I also knew it was courageous for an old guy like me to get out of his comfort zone.

The buzz of the lights and activity on the set had energized me, and I'd felt like a young dancer experiencing his first show biz break. That is, until I drove home and could barely pry my aching body out of the car. Once I'd hobbled into my house, I'd popped an ibuprofen and groaned on the couch for two hours.

Most days I drank to get drunk. Except when I had to teach or rehearse and then I waited until I got home. If I didn't have to go anywhere, I didn't shower or shave and lived in my underwear. I survived on instant coffee, chocolate-covered almonds, whisky, ice cream, pizza, and tins of soup. I'd come to enjoy sleeping off hangovers the way some people enjoy the bitter taste of aspirin.

Two years ago, after three sessions, I'd felt Alice Hotz wasn't telling me anything I hadn't already gleaned from reading psychology books and Dr. Google—all the Cognitive Behavioural Therapy stuff was free online—so I'd stopped going. Another reason was her exorbitant fee, a hundred-and-fifty bucks an hour!

Today, I seriously hoped one session would do the trick. It'd better, at that price.

But instead of driving to my appointment, I drove downtown to the corner of Wentworth and King Street and parked behind the Olympia. I'd been putting off talking to Dad. His opinion of me mattered, and I couldn't shake the worry that he'd see me as a coward for bailing on him. Would he be angry? Disappointed in me?

This time I felt different going through the back door.

As always, Dad was in his office, swamped with paperwork. Despite his big ears, he was a handsome man. Like Uncle Leonard, he had old silver screen charisma. I knocked on the door frame. He peered at me over his black reading glasses and waved me in. I stayed right where I was. *Coward!*

"So," he said mildly, "my prodigal son returns." He leaned back in his old desk and crossed his arms against his chest.

He's protecting himself, I realized. I didn't like the thought that my father felt he had to protect himself against *me*, his son.

Instinctively, I crossed my arms, too. "Prodigal son. Is that what you think I am?"

"Aren't you?"

I sighed. "Maybe, maybe not."

Dad scowled. "You look terrible, Johnny." He shook his head, then relaxed his face.

"I know."

"Uncle George is on his last legs." He stared at me expectantly.

Deep breath. "I'm sorry, for everything Dad, I really am. I'll be back soon, I promise."

"Don't make a promise you can't keep." His tone was neutral.

I couldn't believe Dad was so calm about everything. I'd expected him to freak out on me.

"I want you to speak to Uncle Leonard."

"Uncle Leonard? Why?"

"He has something important to tell you." He crinkled his nose.

"Since when?"

"Since now."

"I haven't seen Uncle Leonard, in what, seventeen years?"

"He still asks about you." He gave me a meaningful look. Seeing Uncle Leonard was important, apparently.

"I'm still waiting for you to yell at me, Dad."

He leaned forward. "I love you, Johnny, you know that, and so does your Ma, but you can't just walk out on the business. You're not just another waiter, you're part-owner and *future* owner. If you don't want to work here anymore, fine, but you have to give notice. You just can't walk out."

"I'm really sorry, Dad, I've been depressed—"

"I know you have," he said, softly. He tightened his expression. "You go see Uncle Leonard. Today. He's expecting you." He bent his head to his paperwork. Our conversation was obviously over.

As I walked back down the hall, he shouted after me. "And take a shower, Johnny! You stink!"

Chapter 17

AS I BOOTED UP THE stairs to the sixth floor of the medical arts building at Augusta and King Street, the little boy inside me felt huge relief knowing his Dad didn't hate him.

With just a minute to spare, I hustled out-of-breath into Dr. Hotz's waiting room. She opened her door and invited me into her office.

"Nice to see you again, John," she said. We both sat in matching beige easy chairs.

Through the tall wood-framed window beside her, sunlight shone and softened the white walls.

The doctor was in her late fifties. She was kind of a plain-looking woman. What made her stand out was the occasional way her smile lifted the corner of her mouth—her moon smile, as I'd come to think of it—and the intelligence in her eyes.

I crossed my legs and nervously bobbed my pointy shoe. Me and my fucking fancy-pants shoe, I thought. *What's up with me, anyway? Maybe I should stab myself with it.*

Dr. Hotz was silently nodding at me.

"How's the forgiveness going, John?"

I sagged a little. "Not great, to be honest. I gave up trying a long time ago. It was exhausting. One day, I forgave a hundred times! Can you believe that? And guess what? That night I still went to bed angry. Surprise, surprise."

"That must have been really hard on you."

"Yep, it was."

She went silent, giving me time to open up. I did. After all, that's why I'd come here today.

"So, my obsession with Sophia has recently spiraled out of control."

She kept nodding, slowly. "Last time, I asked about your triggers, and you said you weren't ready to talk about them. Are you ready now?"

I fidgeted, curling my toes until they cramped. Exploring my sick mind and heart with another person was brutal. But I was desperate.

"My number one trigger is *the moment*. When I feel down, I dredge up Sophia's memory and make myself feel worse. And when I'm feeling good, or great, I do the same thing. I must be a masochist."

"You deserve better, John."

"Damn right I do!"

And then she was nodding again. *How much per nod, Dr. Hotz? Twenty bucks?*

"Being aware that you do this to yourself is a great first step to healing," she said.

"But here's the thing," I said. "I don't purposely dredge up her memory. Sometimes it just happens. Like sneezing or getting a sudden itch."

"So, I hear you saying that you don't choose these painful thoughts?"

"You know I said that, and I know you're re-framing what I just said. I know your techniques, Dr. Hotz. No offense, but coming here was obviously a bad idea. You couldn't fix me last time and you won't this time. So, once again, a hundred and fifty bucks down the toilet!"

She smiled her moon smile.

I cast my gaze downward. "Shit, I'm sorry. As usual, I'm not handling this very well."

"The key is to catch your negative thoughts before they expand—"

"Or blow them up with an atomic bomb!"

"I was thinking—"

I knew I was being rude cutting her off so much but I couldn't help it. I was frustrated and irritable. "You asked me to read *The Four Agreements*, by Don Miguel Ruiz. It was very good, but then, you know, like every other self-help book, I eventually stopped reading it and I forget what the hell it was even about." I crossed my arms against my chest. "Maybe I need a frickin' lobotomy. Know any brain surgeons?"

She smiled faintly.

"Guess not," I said. I was feeling agitated again, like I was losing more of my mind by just being there.

"Have you tried the techniques we discussed?"

"Sort of. But I made up my own checklist. So far, *they're* helping. Oh, by the way, I walked out on the family business."

She raised her eyebrows a little. "How come?"

I told her.

I got the predictable nod in response. *Always fucking nodding! You already know what you're going to say Hotz, so spit it out!*

"John, would you be open to trying a low-dose antidepressant? I think that might be of great help to you."

I felt ambushed. *Me, a candidate for meds? Donny sure, but me? No fucking way!* "Thanks, but no thanks. And I'll definitely pass on the buffet of side effects."

"Medication combined with CBT often gives good results."

"Aaron Beck," I said, smugly, "the inventor of CBT."

I could tell she wouldn't be distracted from her goal.

"Aren't you going to ask me about my nightmares?" Maybe *that* would throw her off.

"Yes. Tell me about them."

"Nightmare exposure and rescripting. Number 6 on the CBT checklist. I remember it well."

She just looked at me, waiting.

So, I told her about my recurring nightmare, where I suddenly find myself inside Sophia's parents' house without her knowledge.

"What's your main emotion in the dream?"

"Fear."

"Of?"

"Rejection, I think."

"From now on, when you experience fear, I'd like you to replace it with love."

"Obviously, not during the nightmare."

"Right. When you're awake. Or any time you catch yourself about to re-traumatize yourself. Loving someone who has hurt you can be freeing," she said. "It can help you move on."

"Yeah, easier said than done."

"Sending her your love will also help free you from her perceived control over you."

"*Perceived* control?"

Dr. Hotz's moon-smile vanished. She'd seen the anger in my face.

I pitched forward. "I have a meeting with Sophia on February 22 at 11 a.m. and she's going to hear, in *great* detail, the massive harm she's caused me. Perceived control? Send her my *love*? You, dear Doctor, have got to be kidding!"

She was cool as a cucumber.

And I was trembling.

"She's the one that divorced me without an explanation. She should be sending me *her* love, not the other way around!" My heart was thumping. "What kind of person does that? I'll tell you who—a horribly cruel person, that's who, the frickin' Devil incarnate!" I pounded my fists on the arms of the chair, enraged.

Dr. Hotz finally looked concerned. I wondered if she'd tell me to leave. I wouldn't have blamed her.

I held up my hands in surrender, and slumped back into the chair, ashamed.

"I'm sorry. I'm sorry."

She was perfectly still. "Will you be hiring a mediator?"

"Uh, no, we're going to work it out the old-fashioned way, just the two of us, face-to-face."

She looked concerned. "I strongly suggest hiring a mediator. Emotions can run very high in these situations. A mediator will help facilitate the best possible outcome for both parties involved. By the way, I *am* a court-appointed divorce mediator."

"I didn't know that."

"What are you hoping to gain from this meeting?"

"I want her to hear why, exactly, she left me. And for her to hear in vivid detail how much she hurt me."

"I can definitely help with that. Basically, my job is to create a safe space for both parties so they can air their grievances, constructively. And when things go sideways, and trust me they will, my job is to get them back on track."

I stared at my madly bobbing shoe as I considered her offer. I quickly realized having a mediator would allow me to get everything off my chest without completely flying off the handle and potentially blowing my one chance for closure. "Okay, I'll get back to you on that."

"Good." She paused. "If you're open to it, next time I'd like to discuss your letters."

I had told her about them the last time I saw her, but at that point I still hadn't read them. "Sure," I lied, not so sure I'd share them with her. I was still processing them.

She asked me a few more questions about the big meeting, and then we discussed my progress with Cognitive Distortion Item #12, *Fallacy of Change*, the one where I was convinced I'd be happy once Sophia was forced to face the truth that I had been the love of her life and she'd made a huge mistake leaving me. Intellectually, I knew my thinking was delusional, but my mind wouldn't let go.

Dr. Hotz suggested more coping mechanisms, but I was so consumed by emotion I'd barely heard her. Abruptly, I got up to leave.

"Just one more thing before you go, John. And next week we can discuss what it means to you. And what it might mean in terms of Sophia."

My jaw tightened. "I'm not a little boy who needs a homework assignment." I scoffed.

"Go ahead," I said, impatiently, "I'm listening."

She moved past me, set her hand on the door handle, and faced me.

"Often, we are unreliable narrators of our own story."

I repeated her words aloud. "Who said that?"

"Wayne C. Booth. He was a literary critic. He coined the term 'unreliable narrator' in 1961 when he wrote a book called *Rhetoric of Fiction.*"

"Hmm, okay, I'll think on that." I was dubious. Fiction writing? Literary critic?

She opened the door.

"Take care, John."

I silently walked out.

If I'm an unreliable narrator, I thought, as I headed for the elevator, *then maybe you are too, doctor. Maybe everybody is!*

In the main lobby, I was cursing Sophia for fucking my head up so badly that I had to pay a shrink hundred-and-fifty dollars an hour. When I saw her, the first thing I'd do is dump all my bills at her feet.

I imploded with the realization that my wounds had never healed. CBT, my ass!

And meds? Me? *Pfff!* Sophia was the one who should be on meds!

By the time I got into my car, my anger had cooled. Dr. Hotz was right about hiring a mediator. I couldn't be trusted to stay calm in that meeting. And if I couldn't stay calm, I might not get my answers.

So I called and hired one. Her!

Chapter 18

UNCLE LEONARD LIVED downtown on King Street, just west of Wentworth Street North, in the second-floor apartment of a building he and Aunt Iris had owned since the fifties. On the ground floor they'd run the very successful Parthenon Bakery.

A decade ago, ALS had claimed Iris's life. Leonard had been in his seventies at the time and had found it too hard to run the restaurant on his own. Now the rented space was a Jamaican roti spot.

Unlike my Dad and Ma, they hadn't moved up the escarpment to get away from the hustle and bustle of downtown life.

I drove along the poorly-lit alleyway behind their building and parked next to the old, dilapidated garage. Memories of happier days flooded back.

Ma and Pops used to take Amara and me here after Christmas Eve mass to be with our cousins and aunts and uncles. We'd always had a great time.

But now, as an adult, I felt strange being here. Where had I last seen Uncle Leonard? Maybe at church? The last Sunday before I'd quit going? I remembered missing Aunt Iris's funeral because I'd had the flu. I couldn't remember if I'd sent a card.

I scanned the alleyway to make sure I wasn't about to be mugged. I knocked on Leonard's door several times. It was a heavy steel door, practical and industrial-looking.

No answer.

Was he home? Maybe he was hard of hearing?

"Is that you, Johnny?" a muffled voice cried.

"Yes, Uncle Leonard, it's me."

"Door's open, come on up."

Door's open? In this neighbourhood? Are you crazy?

There were twenty-four stairs in total. At the top, I was breathing hard. No wonder the old guy was still alive, I thought. Those stairs would keep you young.

Uncle Leonard had vanished into the kitchen to make coffee. The apartment was a 1940's time capsule. Above a chair on the wall was a framed poster of Fred Astaire and Ginger Rogers in *Barkleys of Broadway*. There were some black and white framed photographs of famous dancers and actors and old Hamilton architecture. A big blue vase was brimming with sunflowers.

Another wall hosted a bank of mirrors. On a blue table beside them was a stack of old vinyl records and a stereo, and in the far corner an old-school weight bench.

I couldn't believe how neat the place was.

Had it always been decorated this way? Had I been too busy having fun with my cousins to notice? Or too young to care? Looking at it through adult eyes now, it seemed like the living space of an artist.

"I haven't been here since I was a kid," I called into the kitchen. "Was your place always this nice?"

"After your aunt Iris died, I had a total re-do." He still had a strong Greek accent.

When he entered the living room carrying a tray of espresso and biscuits, something clicked in my brain.

As Norb would say, "my Spidee senses were tingling!" I was pretty sure that my Uncle Leonard was gay.

He set the tray down on a table beside me and opened up his arms for a hug. "Little Johnny!" As we put our arms around each other, familiarity came flooding back.

He hooked his thumbs behind black suspenders. He was wearing a snug white t-shirt and black pants. He sized me up and tutted. "You look so much like your Dad."

He was incredibly lean and fit, so unlike Dad, whose idea of fitness was taking a two-hour nap and eating a tray of baclava. Leonard looked more like Freddy Mercury, if Freddy were short and Greek.

He crinkled his nose at my body odour, but that didn't break his smile.

"Sorry," I said, "I'm not at my best lately."

"No problem, Johnny. We've all been there, one time or another."

"You look really good for an old guy, Uncle Leonard," I joked.

He laughed, his thin moustache arching above his lip. His eyes were blue like Dad's.

"You look like you just stepped out of *Dancing With The Stars*," I said, trying to be kinder.

He smiled broadly. "That's a huge compliment, coming from a trophy winner like yourself."

"Ha! Well, that was a long time ago."

"You and Amara were talented, no doubt about it. Speaking of dancing, your Dad tells me you've opened a studio."

"Unfortunately."

Something stirred in his eyes. "Sit," he ordered, gesturing.

He faced me from the other end of the red velvet couch.

The din of rush hour traffic out on King Street was muffled.

Leonard sipped some coffee and rested the mug on his thigh. "When your Dad told me you'd walked away from the business, he asked me to tell you a story he's very familiar with, and I thought that if you agreed to come here, I'd also tell you another story. But before I begin, nephew, let's be clear on one thing." He leaned forward. "It's not my intention to change your mind on anything, so please understand that. Okay?"

"Okay," I said hesitantly.

Back in the day Uncle Leonard had been hipper than the other Dads. He'd been metrosexual long before it had been a thing. Had I inherited his fashion gene?

His charisma lit up the room. "My first story, Johnny," he said, "might surprise you, even shock you." His eyes widened. "After your Mom and Dad moved to Canada, he broke up with her."

"What?" Shock raised goosebumps on my scalp. This wasn't the story I was expecting!

"At the time, they'd been living together *in sin*", he said, miming quotation marks, "in a small apartment on James Street North. Our parents would have disowned your Dad if they'd known. They were very religious."

"Wow, I didn't know any of that. So why did Dad break up with Ma?"

"To be an actor," he grinned.

"An *actor*? *Dad*? Are you messing with me Uncle Leonard?"

He laughed. "I guess he never told you."

"Guess friggin' not," I said, sarcastically.

"Yeah, he acted all through high school and later in community theater. He was talented, and he was so desperate to make it. To say he was crazy about acting would be a huge understatement. He was *mad* with it. Of course, your Ma, like most Greek girls of that time, was very practical and wanted him to settle down and start a family, but he wasn't ready for that. Not yet."

"So, Dad left Ma to be an actor?" I was having a hard time taking in this new, bizarre information.

Uncle Leonard sighed. "Basically, your Dad left your Ma to chase a dream."

Dad? Mr. Sensible? Mr. Conservative? Mr. Doting Husband? Now, *Mr. Asshole*? I didn't want to think of him that way, but how could I not? He'd ditched Ma!

"How did he make out?" I asked, tentatively, knowing he couldn't possibly have made it or I'd have surely known.

"Well, he landed small parts in local plays. His big and only break was a speaking part on a Kraft cheese tv commercial. They paid him a whopping thousand bucks, which was pretty good dough in those days. But after that, his luck ran out." He smiled ruefully.

"A *cheese* commercial?" I said, flummoxed. "Okay, my mind is officially blown."

"Shocking, right?"

I felt a twinge of disappointment. "Why did Dad dream so small? Why didn't he try his luck down in Hollywood? You can't make it as a full-time actor in Hamilton."

"Your Ma was never far from his mind. He couldn't quite leave her." He slipped a cookie into his mouth.

"How did he support himself?"

"Odd jobs. And always the night shift, so he could audition during the day. He once told me he'd worn a groove in the highway, driving to Toronto for auditions."

"So, he *did* dream bigger than Hamilton."

"He did."

"How long did he act for?"

"Three years."

"Really? That's a long time to stick with something that wasn't working, especially for someone like Dad who obviously needed to succeed. I'm shocked he ever tried to do something so unlike him."

"Ah, but if you knew him as a young man, you'd known it was *just* like him."

"So, what made him finally quit?"

He sighed. "Lydia. He wasn't happy without her. He had a few flings, but no one could replace your Ma. She was and is still the love of his life."

I was glad to hear that. "How did they get back together?"

"Fate. They bumped into each other at the old Chicken Roost restaurant on King Street, and your Dad apologized, and six months later they got married, started a family and opened a restaurant. Bada-bing-bada-boom, as they say."

"Why didn't Dad ever tell me any of this?" But I knew why as soon as I'd asked.

"Your Dad's a very proud man, Johnny, as you know."

"He is." I sighed. *So am I.*

"And you're a chip off the old block, huh?"

"Afraid so."

His smile faded. "So, my second story." He hesitated. "Now don't judge me, Johnny."

"I won't, Uncle Leonard. I know. You're gay. It's okay." I shrugged.

He looked startled. "Is it that obvious?"

"Honestly, I only figured it out half an hour ago."

His face was serious. "I loved your Aunt Iris, truly, and she was my best friend, but I just couldn't bring myself to come out. We had a business, we had kids, and announcing to everyone that I was gay would have gone down in the Greek community like a lead balloon! And I couldn't abandon her like that."

"That must have been so hard."

He gazed at his hands in his lap. "I'm ashamed to say that I wasn't always faithful to your Aunt Iris, and I've asked God to forgive me for that. So, after she passed, I decided to be the true me—I stopped going to church and started a new life. Since the kids had grown up and the family get-togethers were few and far between, it was easier to re-invent myself."

"Geez, I'm so sorry."

He shrugged.

"Did Aunt Iris have her suspicions?"

"If she did, she didn't say. She was a beautiful soul, and I loved her in my own way. I always had great respect for her."

I was slowly digesting this new info.

"So, then a year ago, things really started to turn around for me. I re-decorated. I fell in love, this time with a man. My old life exists now only in photo albums."

I thought about his sons. "How did Constantine and Alex take the news?"

"Not well, to be honest. Alex wouldn't talk to me for five years. And Constantine tried his best, but it was very hard on him."

"That must have been a painful time for everyone."

"It was, but all that's evened out. We all get along well now."

"Alex is a firefighter, right?"

"Yes, and Constantine's a police officer. Both boys are married with kids. Alex lives in Toronto, and Constantine's down in Grimsby."

"Nice. I wouldn't mind seeing them again. We had lots of fun as kids."

"I'll tell them you were asking for them."

He sipped his coffee. "Your Dad asked me to tell you his story. He hoped it might help you make an important life decision of your own."

Dad's love for me was pouring through Uncle Leonard! I felt like crying.

"But I told you *my* story to inspire you. See, it's never too late to come out of the closet, Johnny. I should know. So, run your dance school. Teach others. Share your joy with them. Build a life you will love." He toasted me with his cup. "There's more to existence than waiting tables."

We were interrupted by a phone call.

"Mmhmm...lovely. See you in an hour, hon." He hung up and smiled at me. "Allan's on his way over. We're working on our routine for the High Tones Dance Recital. Think Fred Astaire and Ginger Rogers."

But my mind was already someplace else. "Sounds great," I said, getting up. "I need to go, Uncle Leonard. There's something I need to do."

He patted me on the back.

On the way out, I stopped at the door. "Thank you for sharing all this with me. I appreciate it so much." I had a lot to think about.

"Maybe you and Allan would like to come to my dance studio some time?"

"Sure, that sounds wonderful. You'll really like Allan."

"I'm sure I will. How angry is Dad with me?"

Uncle Leonard pursed his lips. "Not angry, Johnny, surprised yes, maybe a little shocked, but not angry. Not the way he was with me when I came out."

"Brutal."

"It was. But that's in the past. Your Dad forgave me, in his own way."

"Salsa for Seniors!" I urged, trying to lighten the mood. "You and Allan! I teach Monday and Thursday evenings and Saturday mornings!"

"We'll be there! But after the recital. We have to conserve our energy. We're not spring chickens anymore.

We hugged and off I went, feeling lighter than when I'd first arrived.

Chapter 19

LIGHTER, THAT IS, UNTIL the red neon Irondale Bowling sign came into view. Then my old familiar feelings came knocking.

Sophia and I had bowled there with our church league. She'd always been the life of the party, laughing and high-fiving everyone. Anyone would have thought her the happiest woman alive.

Fool me once, shame on you: fool me twice, shame on me.

Obviously, shame on me.

The thought of going home to an empty house was too much to bear, so I parked and headed past Norb's shop to the Blue Ball.

I slunk into a darkened booth furthest from the sex bathroom.

For a Tuesday, the place was hopping. A women's bowling league was crowded around the dance floor. Some of them were up dancing.

Not only was it three-dollar tall boy night, it was also request night. Donny's DJ guy, Brucie, was playing Loverboy's song, "Turn Me Loose." He recognized me and shot me a peace sign, a Donny move, for sure. I wondered if he belonged to Love's Incognito group.

Waitress Trish approached me. "Disco Johnny, dancing solo tonight, are we?"

"Disco Johnny?" I groaned. "That bad, huh?"

"Let's just say that we don't usually see that kinda dancing in this joint. It was pretty different. What can I get you?"

"Three Moosehead tall boys, please. Ice cold, if possible."

I downed the first beer in one go. The blue-collar crowd around me got me thinking about Sheena, of course.

How much education do you need to be a travel agent? Grade Seven? Oh, the old snobbery was asserting itself tonight.

Sophia had a Masters' Degree in Business Administration from Queen's University. She spoke proper English. Her clothing had always been tastefully subdued. In her sunglasses, she'd looked like a European model to me.

Then I thought of Sheena's extraordinary blue eyes, and my gut jellied. *No! Not happening!*

As a farewell gesture, I ordered and downed four shots of Glenfiddich in rapid succession.

Sheena's words from the other day rang in my head. What exactly did she mean by "not yet"? Was she saying that I wasn't ready to date her? Or her me?

As all that alcohol took hold, liquid courage flooded my heart.

Maybe I should call her for clarification. Or I could apologize for misleading her into thinking I was in any way interested in her.

Or simply tell her I wanted be friends. But that was something a naïve teen might say when he broke up with his girlfriend, so no. Although I really could use a new friend.

I was looking for any excuse to call Sheena, obviously.

Comfortably numb, I dialed her.

And that's exactly when the front door swung open and in paraded Jimmy the Barber like a prize peacock. Tonight, he had a different squeeze. She was a real looker, in her early twenties, with shapely legs, large breasts, and spikey high heels. How did he do that? They sashayed up to the bar and ordered drinks.

Suddenly, re-thinking the phone call, I think I hung up.

I could only imagine how many ladies he'd brought here over the years. No doubt it was the same set-up—drinking, dancing, then back to the barber shop for a blow-dry special.

I sank further back into the booth, praying Jimmy wouldn't notice me. I was sober enough to know I wasn't fit for small talk.

I ordered more beer, then against my better judgement rambled over to the DJ and requested Donna Summer. Then I proceeded to knock it out on the dance floor to "Love to Love You Baby".

Jimmy and his squeeze joined in. Half way through "Night Fever", the room and the glitter ball suddenly canted, it seemed to me. Nausea puckered my gut. Somehow, I found my way to the bathroom and barfed my guts out, the same stall where Lyra and I had had our unholy coupling.

As vomit pissed out my nostrils, all I could think about was my sordid encounter. The shame was almost as bitter as the puke.

Then I did something really, really stupid. I staggered out to my car, cranked the engine, and swung out onto Steel Street. On the way home, I got pulled over and charged with impaired driving. The police impounded my vehicle, slapped me with an 800-dollar towing fee, and suspended my license.

The next morning, I woke up in the Barton Street Jail horribly hungover and feeling lower than a cockroach.

I signed the necessary paperwork and cabbed home. I made the mistake of guzzling an entire can of ice-cold apple juice. My empty stomach rebelled, but this time all that came up was bile.

I checked my alarm clock. 8:15 am. After an hour of trembling, wakeful nausea, I finally, thankfully, passed out.

But then, not long after, I wakened with a start. Someone was pounding on my front door!

"This better be good!" I moaned, lurching down the hall.

Chapter 20

IT WAS NORB, AND HE was smiling like a shiny golden Buddha, bearing gifts of hot coffee and sweet donuts. Apparently, the Buddha didn't have much to say.

I waved him in and closed the door. If he wasn't such a caring friend, I would have slammed the door in his face for showing up unannounced.

My stomach lurched and cold chills made my whole body shudder. A massive pulse throbbed in my right temple.

I crashed on the couch as he untied his boots and set down his care package on the coffee table.

Sadly, I had a clear memory of myself last night with the other losers in the drunk tank, breathing in the stink of body odour and urine. More than a few of us had shamefully pissed our pants.

I hated myself. I vowed to never drink again. I prayed I could actually keep that promise. It didn't seem too likely.

"What are you doing here, Norb?" I managed to say. "I don't remember inviting you." *Cultivate your gentleness. Yeah, yeah.* All at once I broke out into a cold sweat and that's when I knew I officially had the worst hangover ever.

Norb plopped down in the reading chair across from me, grinning.

"You called me last night from the bar," he wheeze-laughed. "Remember?"

He was happily chomping on a Boston cream donut. Goo squirted onto his chin but he didn't seem to care. I still couldn't get used to him without his goat-beard, the one Patricia had snipped off.

"I called you from the bar? Sorry, man, I don't remember doing that. I was hammered."

"No kidding." Norb held out the donut box as if gifting me with treasure.

I waved him off. "Don't do that Norb! The sight of food makes me sick right now."

"Sorry, buddy." He fished out an Apple Fritter and took a bite. "Yeah, you said that from now on we were going to hang out every day. And you said that of all the buds I'm your favourite." His smile was so hopeful.

Sheepish, I found the steam to say it. "You *are* my favourite, Norb." I cleared my throat. "Well, all my friends are. Anyway, I was drunk and overly sentimental and I shouldn't have drunk-called you. My bad."

He looked a little disappointed, so I offered up my latest shame as a kind of gift.

"So, uh, Norb," I groaned, "last night I got pulled over for drunk driving."

His jaw dropped and revealed half-masticated donut. "Reee-lly?" He edged forward. "Holy cow, how hammered were you?"

"Very. The cops threw me in jail and impounded my car."

He made prayer hands. "Geez, John, that's fuzzin' awful." He bit his lip. "Did they suspend your license?"

I hung my head and stared at the floor. "Yeah, for a year, I think. I have to go to court." I hugged my knees. "Mind if we don't talk about this anymore. It's giving my hangover a hangover."

"Sure, Johnny, no problem."

"So, was there another reason you're here?" I said. "Besides my drunk call?"

"Actually, I'm here of my own volition."

"Volition? Gee, Norb, I didn't know they used big words like that in comic books." I was being cranky, but I couldn't help it.

"Aw, you'd be surprised." He plucked an old-fashioned glazed out of the box and downed it in two bites. "I like to learn at least one new word a week."

"Good for you, buddy." I thought about taking some ginger tablets for my nausea, but the distance to the medicine cabinet felt insurmountable.

That is, until I made the mistake of fixating on Norb's big, gummy tongue lolling around his donut-stuffed mouth, and had to run to the bathroom to puke one last time.

Afterwards, I found Norb finally cleaning the goo and icing off his chin. He was half-way into a cruller, totally unfazed by my vomiting. In his younger days, he used to gag at the mere thought of vomit. Life had for sure toughened him up.

"Volition," he said, gesturing with his donut, "super-awesome word." His eye-bulbs were practically glowing. "Hey, I know a guy that can help you, John, on a deep spiritual level."

"Like, one of Donny's *guys*? No thanks."

"No, no, it's the same guy I mentioned to you at Wing Man, Dr. Ferguson. He's super legit. A real psychiatrist. And he's trained in mindfulness and trauma therapy."

"Yeah?"

"Scout's honour."

"You know psychedelics are illegal, right?"

"Yeah," he said, sheepishly. "But maybe they shouldn't be."

"Well, either way, Norb, I'm out. And I need to go back to bed." I sat on the edge of the couch, waiting for my dizziness to subside.

"Do you know what the psychedelic community calls the doctor?"

"No Norb, I don't. Throw me a bone. Then please leave."

"Mushroom Mike!"

"Mushroom Mike?" I said, flatly. "Wow, what a professional-sounding name."

Norb chuckled. "Pretty cool, right?"

Although milk-and-cookies Norb had already told me he'd tripped on mushrooms, I still found it hard to believe. This was the same guy whose idea of getting high was consuming an entire box of Cocoa Puffs cereal.

"How many times have you tripped, Norb?"

He squirmed like a kid caught with his hand in the cookie jar.

"I've lost count," he said guiltily.

"What! That's not good, Norb! What if you end up like Joe Franco's brother? Remember? He blew his brains out on acid and got schizophrenia? He still lives at home, you know. I see him outside the Village Variety, picking up cigarette butts off the sidewalk. He's practically homeless."

"Terry Franco," Norb said. "Yeah, very sad story." He sighed. "I know you're concerned for me, John, and I appreciate that you are, I really am. But like I told you at Wing Man, I was desperate and, to some degree, I still am. And schizophrenia doesn't run in my family, so fingers crossed I won't get it." He looked like the saddest puppy dog ever.

"I know you were desperate, Norb, and I know how much you miss your mother. She was a great lady."

He closed the donut box. "When Mutti died, I got steaming mad at God, and I started yelling at people for no good reason, and that was really hard on Morag, and then I got insomnia. And for the first time ever, I got really, really depressed. And I'd never been depressed before that."

In that moment Norb was more human to me than ever. And for the first time I could really see why and how good people might turn to drugs to numb their pain, or, in Norb's case, heal.

"Taking them was Morag's idea. Her co-worker's husband died in a horrible car accident and the woman swore tripping improved her depression and anxiety, so I thought I'd give it a try. The first time, Morag tripped with me so I wouldn't be alone."

"Morag tripped, too?" I was incredulous. This was certainly the week for shocking revelations. "Wow. I'm shocked. But good for her, and you...I guess."

"Johnny, I know how hard it's been for you after all the bad stuff with Sophia. How you never really got over her, you know? And I want to help you."

"So, is this guy a real psychiatrist?"

"Bona fide."

"And what's his actual role? In the mushroom tripping, I mean."

"He administers the dose. And the people who take it are called psychonauts."

"Psychonauts?" I laughed. I remembered our conversation at Wing Man. "As in psychedelic astronaut?" I was amazed that Norb would ever know something like that.

"Cool name, right? Yeah, so Dr. Mike, aka Mushroom Mike, calmly acknowledges your experience without judgement. When Morag and I tripped the first time, he suggested somewhere comfortable, so we chose our king-sized bed. If you like, you can play soothing music, so we chose ambient music. And we covered up with our favorite cozy blanket."

"So, what was it like?" Despite my doubts, I felt intrigued.

Norb looked thoughtful. "Freaky, but good. I saw happy entities, and lots of bright colours, but the best part was how spiritual I felt afterwards. I started forgiving God for taking Mutti away. And I realized that death is just the beginning, and not something to be feared." A sweet smile perched on his face.

Norb was radiating so much love, I swear his skin was glowing.

Suddenly, *I* felt high. Embarrassed, I glanced down at my phone.

There was a voicemail message waiting.

"Sheena!" I said out loud. "Shit!"

Norb gave me a three-finger Scout salute. "I'll leave you to it, then." He sauntered to the door and pulled on his boots.

"Thanks for the donuts and coffee," I said. *Do better than that!* I swallowed my pride. "And thanks for thinking of me, Norb. You're a good friend." Why did it have to hurt to be nice? "A *great* friend!" *Ouch.*

After one more salute, he was out the door.

Anxiously, I stuffed a maple glazed donut into my mouth. I'd been so immersed in Norb's story that I'd temporarily forgotten my hangover. Now it was back with punishing vengeance. Maybe sugar would help.

Paranoia spin-cycled my innards. Had Sheena called to tear a strip off me for drunk-calling? Had I said anything inappropriate? No, I seemed to remember hanging up in time.

I listened to the message. "Hi, John, it's Sheena. Call when you get a chance. Not urgent. Ta."

After ten minutes spent pacing, I finally marshalled my courage and dialed. Six rings later, she picked up.

"Hi, John," she said cheerfully. She didn't sound pissed off.

"Sheena, did I call you last night? If I did, I'm sorry."

"Last night? No, you didn't call me."

"I didn't? Oh, good, I mean, well, I thought maybe I did, but then maybe I hung up." I chose not to tell her I'd been drunk. It would only make her think less of me.

She giggled. "Er, listen, I'd like to invite you to a wedding. As a friend, of course. Donny said you could use a night out."

"Did he, then?" I said, sarcastically. "So, who's getting married?"

She laughed. "You're kidding right?"

"No, who?"

"Your cousin, Zoe, silly. On February 21. But you knew that, right?"

"Yes, of course," I half-lied. I'd known but had put it out of my mind.

"So, what do you think?"

Guilt pricked my conscience. "Sheena, I'm sorry, but I don't do Greek weddings *or* churches anymore." Since my divorce I'd declined four Greek wedding invites.

"Why not?"

"Long story," I sighed.

"Well, that's too bad," she said. "but I totally understand."

I was pretty sure Donny must have told her my story by now. "Who the hell told you Zoe's getting married?"

"Donny," she said merrily.

A pain grew in my forehead as if Donny had pressed a gun there. "Of *course,* he did. And how the hell did *he* know?"

"Well, he knows a mechanic guy who fixes cars on the cheap, and your mum mentioned your cousin's car kept breaking down, so he put them in touch with his guy. Zoe and her fiancé wanted to personally thank Donny, and when they met him, they liked him so much they invited him and Allison to their wedding!" Her enthusiasm was unbelievable. "And, of course, Donny, ever the one to push the limits, asked if Agnes and I could come with dates and Zoe said sure." She paused. "But if you don't go to Greek weddings anymore, John, I can ask someone else."

Move forward, leave the past behind, Pappas!

"Okay, I'll go," I said, abruptly. I just knew I'd regret it, but what the hell? I'd been to jail. It couldn't get much worse, right? "Where is it?" I'd binned the invitation the same day I'd received it.

"St. Demetrius Church. Reception at Carmen's Banquet Hall."

Both places had hosted my wedding! Forget it!

I exhaled long and hard. "I'll go to the reception only," I said, carefully.

"Aye, okay. The reception it is."

"I can't pick you up. Sorry, another long story." A shameful story. She didn't know I'd lost my license.

"Just how many long stories do you have?" she said, laughing.

"Too many."

"Aye, I bet. Well, one day maybe you'll tell me one of them."

Something warm and comforting nested in my heart.

I may have been turned off by Sheena's loud hairdo, her chipped pink fingernails, and her cheap platform shoes, but not by *her*. I *liked* her. A lot.

"So, what's new?" I asked, nervously, wondering how long I'd zoned out for.

"There's no time for what's new, Johnny lad," she said, cheekily. "I'm off to work. See you at the wedding."

"But that's four weeks away—" That was too long to not see this vivid woman.

"Ach, don't worry, Donny says time flies in the Village."

She hung up before I could vent about Donny's interference in my life.

Cultivate Your Gentleness.

Whatever!

I half-acknowledged that Donny was trying to help. And maybe it wouldn't kill me to go to a Greek wedding, after all, although it would no doubt trigger me.

I began wracking my brain for a way to back out without hurting my chances with Sheena. Why the hell had I agreed? *Stupid! Stupid! Stupid!*

But while I sat there, agitated as hell, the living room started to spin like scene changes in the old Batman tv series—alcohol withdrawal!

Some time later, I came to, face-down on the carpet. My chin throbbed. I touched a gash there and came away with blood. I must have smacked it on the corner of the coffee table on the way down. A huge blood stain threaded the white carpet and the cover of *Your Sacred Self,* which had tumbled down with me. What else could go possibly go wrong?

Lots, actually.

Dirk Singh called in a panic, wondering why I hadn't shown up for rehearsal. How could I have forgotten? It was on set! His movie was the only thing keeping me sane. I apologized profusely and offered to drive to Brampton right away then remembered I didn't have a license or a car. He'd told me not to bother but cheerily reminded me that time was money. I gave him my word it wouldn't happen again. "But if it does feel free to kick my ass," I half-joked. "Not funny," he said, and hung up.

I considered heading over to Steel Street to jump in front of a moving car, when two potentially life-saving words blazed inside me head.

Magic Mike.

I was frozen in indecision.

Could Dr. Mike do for me what he'd done for Norb?

Was tripping the cure?

Or was it the final hail Mary before I killed myself?

I gulped. This suicide self-talk was escalating, and that was a bad sign.

Imagining Norb feeling suicidal and alone, holding a gun to his head chilled me to my marrow. The blood in my head throbbed with oceanic hiss. I went numb.

Be like Norb, an internal voice said, *see Magic Mike.*

And if he can't fix you, then kill yourself.

I bawled like a kid.

Chapter 21

In the intervening days, I cleaned the house, taught dance, isolated myself, and thought of ways to kill myself. What I didn't do was call Dr. Mike.

Today was game day at the Irondale Collegiate parking lot, home of the Hamilton Hammer's Ball Hockey League. It was overcast and teeth-chattering cold, the sky icy breath. Wind swept snow pellets across the grey pot-holed tarmac.

All I really wanted to do was go back home and drink Ben Wiley out of my mind. I was filled with dread of what I'd say or do when I saw Sophia's husband, who was going to ref our match today. But I couldn't let the Village Idiots down. Winning today's ball hockey game was crucial to keeping our playoff hopes alive.

Experience had taught us how to navigate the ice patches in the parking lot, and I loved to use them to my advantage by dance-sliding on them. Sometimes I'd slip and fall, but so did everyone else.

"Stay cool," I mumbled to myself. "Don't say anything stupid or insulting to this do-gooder-wife-stealer. Keep your head down and play your game." I grit my teeth. How had I not known he was living under my nose all these years? At some point had he been bowling in the lane beside me? Hanging out at Tim Hortons two tables over? Had he been a guest at my fucking wedding? And not only that—he wasn't even Greek!

Worse than all that, Wiley was better-looking than me and way more muscular. *And* he was super cheery and upbeat. Everything I wasn't. Sophia had definitely scored the perfect man!

Although I'd often wondered what her new man looked like, I wished I hadn't actually met him. I was burning with jealousy.

Courage, Pappas! You can do this!

Up until Christmas, the Village Idiots had floundered. We'd since fought our way into ninth place in the standings. But only eight of the twelve teams qualified for the playoffs, so we had to win every game until May.

Tony was league President and keeper of the white rink boards which he stored in his garage. That morning, along with our team mates Jeff McGrory and Roderick "Whitey" McCleod, we'd packed them into Tony's pick-up truck and set them up in the parking lot.

Another guy on our team, Pete "Bucky" Rainford, was an old buddy of Donny's from elementary school and liked to ride a unicycle while making strange whistling sounds. No surprise that he was one of Donny's side buds. Bucky was our top goal-scorer, so we accepted his weirdness—most of the time.

At each end of our parking lot "rink", behind regulation-sized hockey nets, we'd set up tall wide ones which slung back missed shots and kept our games moving by reducing the time spent chasing balls across the snowy school field.

We paid the league refs twenty-five bucks a game. They loved the game as much as the players.

Regulation play was four per team with three subs. Bucky and Whitey were on defense, and Donny played left wing and I played right. I'd worn my lucky dance shoes, which were easily as slick as freshly sharpened skates. The guys loved to tease me for wearing "disco skates", but it was water off a duck's back, because you can't argue with success.

Today we were facing the Machine Shop Psychos. They'd been buds since high school and, like Tony, worked the trades. They were tough, talented, and in second place. Their captain, Danny Scabbard, was tall and lanky, his chin scarred up from a lifetime of scraps. He was missing a front tooth and his hair was big and puffy like a fluffy dandelion head. He and the rest of the Psychos wore orange and black jerseys, a tip of the hat to the notorious Broad Street Bullies from the infamous 1970's Philadelphia Flyers. I wondered which one of us they'd hurt first.

Norb was oblivious to them. He'd transformed into his eighteen-year-old self. His long green toque had a red pom-pom that flew through the air like a giant pimple.

Like his old-timey hero, Toronto Maple Leaf goalie Johnny Bower, Norb swung his stick against the goal posts, fell on his pads, bounced back up, stretched his neck, shimmied in and out of the net, crouched, pincered his catching glove and whacked his stick against his pads. "Bring it on!" he cried.

Bucky was riding his unicycle and practicing slap shots on Norb, while Whitey was deep into knee bends. I was too fixated on Ben Wiley to warm-up. I even hated his name. It was sickeningly gentle.

Donny set his boom box on the hood of his car. Before ball drops, he inevitably cranked up the song "Big League", by Tom Cochrane. It always fired everybody up. Donny had once tried to switch things up by playing one of his original tunes; Scabbard had taken a slapshot and busted the boom box into a thousand pieces. Donny made sure to never make that mistake again.

"How's the movie business?" Donny asked me, taking a shot on Norb.

"Oh, you know, Donny, show business is everything they say it is."

"You're being coy, John. I know that trick. C'mon, spill."

"Well, then you also know that I probably won't tell you because you'll blab to everybody and I'll end up being some ridiculous YouTube laughing stock like poor Norb. So no thanks."

He laughed me off. "Johnny Pappas! Ye of little faith!"

"Ha! Prove me wrong," I challenged him.

He just shrugged me off. "I'll find out sooner or later anyway. You know I will."

I scanned Princeton Drive but saw no sign of the refs. Butterflies danced in my stomach. I really had no idea how I'd react when I saw Wiley. I was new at this.

"Nice shoes, Disco," Scabbard shouted.

"Damn right they are! You can admire them more when I glide right past you!"

He laughed vengefully.

After all these years, the guys on the Psychos still scared me, but especially Scabbard. The thing is, I felt so raw and angry these days, especially knowing Wiley was going to ref our game, that I secretly hoped Scabbard would kill me with a slapshot before he arrived.

"Yo, tough guy!" Frank Butters cried. He'd just finished blasting a shot through his goalie's five-hole and that had given Frank an idea. "Is it true Greeks like it up the five-hole?" he guffawed.

Oh, how Frank loved to get under my skin. And when he did, I gave as good as I got. "Do they, Buttered Frank? You tell me. You're the one that loves pumping pucks through five-holes."

He started towards me, gripping his stick like an axe. "Sounds like Johnny Pappas needs a tune up!"

Frank was a muscled-up shorty with a Napoleon complex. He had been notorious for ramming kids' heads into gym lockers. But I'd always danced out of harm's way and that royally pissed him off. I think he was still trying to get back at me for that.

He'd gotten practically everyone else I knew, except for Tony. Everyone knew well enough to leave him alone. Tony was naturally big and strong, and although tender-hearted, he could be bulldog-mean. Half way through Grade 9, he'd once warned Frank to leave us alone. That one warning had been enough.

I was about to insult the size of Frank's frank, always a popular dig, when a shiny new BMW zipped into the parking lot. "Fucking Yuppie!" he scoffed at the driver. I was grateful he'd found a new target for his anger.

As pissed off as I was with Frank and life in general, I didn't really want to fight him. With my luck, I'd end up in Henderson Hospital or back at the jail.

The driver of the car was the guy who'd replaced me. For the sake of the team, I knew I should focus on Wiley after the game, but who was I kidding? I wasn't a saint!

Wiley was obviously rich, maybe due to his combined income with Sophia or from an inheritance. And I was just some single, plod-along middle-class wage earner, basically a Greek Peter Pan working for scraps for his parents.

Insecurity burned my gut.

Man up! Introduce yourself! He won, you lost! Shit happens!

Instead of being mature and reasonable, I began hammering Norb with blistering slapshots.

"Easy, John!" he cried, rubbing his bicep with his glove hand as he left the net.

I kept shooting, more furious than ever.

"What's your problem, man?"

I ignored him, in a ridiculous, anxious temper.

Before I knew it, Wiley was at the imaginary face-off circle, dropping the orange ball. And Donny had "Big League" blasting.

I played opposite Scabbard. He loved to axe your stick with his and steal the ball almost as much as he loved to miss and hack your shin. He had the most penalty minutes for roughing and had game misconducts for fighting. Other than his hair going white, he hadn't changed much since high school.

Donny was using his new Lannie McDonald hockey stick, a wooden one he'd bought to replace the original. He won the face-off and flipped the ball perfectly onto my stick. I hopped around Scabbard, deked Butters, and fired a hard wrister towards the top shelf of the net.

The ball flew over the goalie's glove!

The Village Idiots cheered.

"How do you like my dance shoes now, Scabbard?" I asked, doing a nice little shuffle and heel click to rub it in.

He and Butters glared at me. I suspected they were planning to bash in my head, but I grinned at them to show I wasn't afraid, although I sure as hell was. Then, to show them I wasn't afraid of *anyone,* I stared down the wife-stealer, who was all smiles, chumming it up with the other ref. His good looks tweaked me. My insecurities boiled over. I predictably made myself imagine him having sex with Sophia. *Why? Why? Why? Stop!*

Wiley blew the face-off whistle. Scabbard and I positioned ourselves across from each other at our respective wings. He was staring daggers at me. All the Psychos were. Butters started laughing maniacally. I was screwed.

Tony had subbed in, and on his way to the face-off he leaned into me and whispered. "Drop the cocky act. Scabbard *will* hurt you."

I nodded. But what I was really thinking was that I *wanted* Scabbard to hurt me. New pain to forget the old.

A moment before the other ref dropped the ball, Scabbard hissed, "Do you take it up the ass, Greek boy?" He grinned a one-toother at me.

"You oughta know!" I hissed back.

The ref dropped the ball at the exact moment I lost it.

I was John Travolta/Mike Tyson swinging a knock-out hook at Scabbard's squabbie but Scabbard easily dodged my telegraphed punch. In a flash, he'd tied up my legs with his stick and dumped me onto the tarmac. The impact spiked pain through my shoulder and sent all the air out of my lungs. Wiley blew the whistle.

The Psychos were laughing their asses off.

My team body-blocked Scabbard from finishing me off. But that didn't stop him from circling me, daring me to stand up so he could.

I jolted to my feet.

Wiley and the other ref jumped in front of Scabbard. Wiley made a cutting motion with his hand against his shin. "Three minutes for tripping!"

A question mark crinkled Scabbard's face. He flipped his palms out in bewildered exasperation, as if totally innocent. *That old chestnut*, I thought. *Fuck you!*

Fueled by angry courage, I dropped my gloves, but instead of going after Danny, I went after Wiley. I had lost all sense.

"Hey, motherfucker!" I cried, getting up in his face. "Do you know who I am? I'm Sophia's ex, that's who, John Fucking Pappas, the one she dumped for you. So, yeah, there it is, so thanks for ruining my life, you wife-stealing fucking asshole!"

Ben Wiley stepped back, looking flummoxed.

Everyone had gathered around, clearly confused by what was happening. But let's face it—drama is fascinating.

All the chickens—divorce, abandoning my parents, being too scared to chase my dreams, ruining my date with Sheena, never standing up to the high school bullies, and losing my driver's license while under the influence—had come home to roost. It was a Festival of Failures.

"What are you talking about?" Ben said, totally bewildered-looking. "I don't know any Sophia. I'm not even married, man."

"Don't you teach at Hill Park Secondary School?" This wasn't how this confrontation was supposed to go. I gave Tony a pleading look.

"Yeah? So?" Ben said.

"My cousin Loretta's a custodian there," Tony said, tentatively. "She said you're married to Sophia Andonis, formerly Pappas?"

"No, I'm not." Ben shrugged. "I have a sister named Sophie. She's a mail carrier with Canada Post. Your sister heard wrong. You've definitely got the wrong guy."

Tony's face went red. He threw up his hands and blew air in exasperation. "Loretta! *Again* with the wrong info! What the frig is wrong with that woman! I should have learned my friggin' lesson by now."

Donny started to laugh. Even Norb cracked a smile.

Often we are unreliable narrators of our own story. Dr. Hotz's words haunted me.

"Loretta?" I said, remembering that it had been Tony's sister who'd mistakenly thought she'd seen Steven's gravestone down in Jordan, Ontario. And now she'd done it again, convinced that Sophia had married a teacher named Ben Wiley.

Loretta was the unreliable narrator! Tony should have known better! I should have known better!

Norb and Donny cried "Loretta!" in unison. It was a relief to be able to blame someone else, after all.

There was a lot grumbling and slurs from the Machine Shop Psychos.

"Sorry," I said to Ben. "I thought you were my ex-wife's husband." I felt like such a fool.

"No worries," he said, which was very big of him.

"Sorry for throwing the punch," I offered grudgingly to Scabbard.

"Not a bad swing for a faggot dancer." Anything resembling an apology from Danny Scabbard or any of the other Psychos would have been a miracle, so rather than fighting back, I decided it best not to look a gift horse in the mouth. I was relatively unhurt, after all.

My adrenaline dump left me unsteady on my feet.

Ben blew the whistle and it was game on again.

But my heart wasn't in it now and the angry energy I'd had when I thought Ben was Sophia's husband was gone. I went through the motions, praying for the game to end, so I could go home and never wake up.

Donny scored a goal and so did Whitey, and in the last seconds of the game, Tony hit the bottom corner with a tidy snap shot. But those shining moments weren't enough. We lost ten to four.

The only good thing was that Norb had broken a personal record. He'd made eighty-five saves. He was as happy as a school kid on a snow day and sweaty as an arsonist trapped in a burning building. No one remarked on the fact that the rest of us had let eighty-five shots on goal through.

Chapter 22

If it hadn't been my turn to buy coffee, I would have ended it under the street sweeper passing the coffee shop. Next time I would.

Like I used to do as a kid, I dumped sugar from the dispenser into my Coke and drank all of it, praying for a diabetic coma. Norb was watching me carefully.

"Shit. Sorry about the whole Loretta thing," Tony said. "I really thought she had it right this time." He'd taken an early afternoon break.

"She was close," Norb said, brightly.

Donny glowered. "Close my ass." He was clearly fed up with Loretta's ineptitude. We all were. He faced me. "Did Sheena call you?"

"Maybe," I said defensively.

"I *know* she called you, bud. She told me." He sighed. "Listen, I think it's great you're going to Zoe's wedding. It'll cheer you up."

"You know I don't go to weddings, anymore. But I agreed to go to the reception, although I'll probably bail."

"You *better* go," Donny said.

"And why is that?"

"Because Sheena likes you, you big dope."

My shoe bobbed under the table. "And how do you know that?"

"Ah, John, have you not seen the way she looks at you?"

"No, I haven't. Listen, she's not my type. And you can tell her that. Better she knows that now, before she gets hurt."

"Hey, that's pretty harsh," Norb squeaked. "Sheena's really nice."

"*Life's* harsh, Norb," I said. "Sorry to—" I was going to say "break it to you" but stopped. Who was I to tell Norb about the harshness of life? He was already well-acquainted. He'd lost his Mom. "Sorry, Norb."

"It's okay, buddy. It's true. Life can be harsh, I guess."

"What I mean to say, Norb, is that sometimes it's hard to get over a woman you've loved, besides your Mom."

Norb stared out the window. Normally I would have assumed he was day-dreaming, but then I saw the hurt in his eyes.

"I hope to hell Norb doesn't mourn his ass off for seventeen years like you have," Tony barked. He wired into a Boston cream donut.

I knew Tony wasn't that angry with me. He was simply frustrated he couldn't fix me.

Norb looked at Tony in alarm.

"Don't worry, Norb," I said, "you won't mourn for seventeen years. I'm obviously a special case."

"Special in the head," Tony grumbled.

Norb smiled goofily. I was relieved. He was going to be okay for another day, even if I wasn't.

Donny hadn't been following the conversation and was totally immersed with something on his phone.

An attractive dark-haired young woman entered the coffee shop. She reminded me of Sophia at nineteen. Tight jeans hugged her amazing figure.

At least once a day, I saw a young woman who reminded me of Sophia. How could a man still be so hot for a young woman who wasn't that young anymore? Really, young Sophia didn't even exist.

I felt a breakdown coming on. Both my legs were pumping now and I'd broken out in a cold sweat. I jumped up so quickly I jerked the table and sloshed the coffee out of everyone's cups.

"Where the frig do you think you're going?" Tony said. "Slot cars at my house, then dinner. Remember?"

"I'm not up to it, Tony," I said, staring at the mess. "Sorry guys. Next time's on me."

"Can Norb and I come, instead?" Donny asked Tony.

By the look on Tony's face, Donny had his answer.

Norb laughed nervously. "Heck, I couldn't go if I wanted to. Morag and I are having Karl over for Sunday dinner, and it's my turn to mash the potatoes and carve the roast beef." They'd made a point of including Karl in family life as much as possible, since Mutti's passing.

Donny was glum. "And I guess I'll be home having dinner with Allison and Stewart."

His eyes suddenly lit up. "Tony, we should race at your place every week and order pizza and watch the Leafs on tv." Basically, what I'd said to Tony that time in his basement.

Donny nodded at each of us encouragingly.

"Sure," Norb said, hesitantly.

"We'll see," Tony said. He looked at me. "Angelina was really looking forward to racing her Uncle Johnny. She says you're the best."

"Uncle Johnny?" Norb said. "Wait, are you guys related?"

"No, Norb," Tony said, "we're not related. You know we're not."

"Right, of course not. Obviously not." And then, for some reason, he laughed like he'd just cracked a hilarious joke.

"Tony," I said. "I'm super hungover. Next week, for sure. I promise."

"Okay, bud, next week."

"And please tell Angela and Angelina I'm looking forward to seeing them."

"I will."

But then I felt super guilty adding Angelina to the long list of people I'd let down. I fled towards the door.

"Where are you going, John?" Donny said. "Are you okay?"

"Just fucking great!" I cried. Then I was outside, running homeward down Flux.

Even the nasty stitch in my side couldn't stop me.

Chapter 23

The GO bus's wipers juddered against the windshield. Heavy snow whipped through the headlight beams. A storm had slowed traffic to a crawl and it was taking much longer than usual to get home from Brampton. A phalanx of snowplows angled across the road ahead of us.

As the bus crested the Skyway Bridge, you could just make out the far side of the Bay, where the steel factories spewed smoke and hellfire. Once again, I was reminded of Tolkien's Mordor.

If the maligners from outside of Hamilton would take the time to see beyond it, they'd for sure see our city in a better light.

Beside me a punk was reading NOW magazine. He had a bright red mohawk and stank of weed. He scowled at me before I could say a pleasant "hi".

I'd spent my time on my headphones listening to the movie's soundtrack, visualizing my dance routine with Dev. Arjun had worked us hard. My legs were still vibrating, and my groin was aching from the harness. Next to Sita, I'd felt like a total beginner. She really was that good.

Earlier today, I'd made up my mind to tell Dirk I was quitting. There was no way a middle-aged man should be dancing in a movie. But Arjun's energy, the professionalism of the crew, and the lavish set had re-invigorated me. Despite myself, I was feeling inspired.

Dirk had pleasantly reminded me that movies, no matter how great, aren't always picked up by Hollywood *or* Bollywood, so I should prepare to have both my hopes dashed.

I'd told him not to worry, as I was a master of all things broken—hearts, hopes, sanity. Like a maharishi, Dirk had pressed his palms together and smiled gently at me.

I'd wondered how in tarnation (one of Norb's favourite cuss words) Dirk had thought he could cast a middle-aged white guy from

Hamilton in a Bollywood movie. But as soon as I'd read the script, I'd realized the role was an everyman role, that my skin colour was irrelevant. And when I'd danced with my young co-star, Sita, I'd *felt* that.

Each time we finished a run-through, the cast and crew clapped enthusiastically, chanting, "Gene Kelly! Gene Kelly! Gene Kelly!" And Sita would bow to me and I'd be so embarrassed.

Sitting in the darkened bus, I had lots of time to think, unfortunately.

When Ben Wiley popped into my mind, I felt almost sick with embarrassment. I decided to frame my outburst as a lesson on how *not* to act, if I ever met Sophia's real husband.

I imagined the looks on Frank Butters' and Danny Scabbard's faces, if they ever saw me dancing on the silver screen. I would pay to see that. Those assholes would have to reconsider their contempt for me!

Speaking of assholes, it dawned on me again that I'd been a drunk driver and lost my license.

Me, Mr. Clean, who *loathed* drunk drivers! I deserved contempt, after all. Without a license, I had reverted to a fifteen-year-old, riding the bus and going backwards in life, a classic Donny defect.

My phone rang and, of course, it was you-know-who. I was almost afraid to answer it. But, remembering that if it wasn't for him I wouldn't be dancing in a feature-length movie, I picked up.

"I'll keep this short." Donny sounded enthusiastic. "Today, Allison and I were taking Stewart for a walk along Concession Street and he pointed at something super amazing in the window of Bert's Antiques shop. And you know what he said?"

"No, what?"

"He said, "*Uncle Johnny!*" His first words, I swear! So, we seized the moment, carpe diem and all that, and we bought it for you, *in the moment,* a sign from Heaven. Wait 'till you see it brother. You're gonna freak out!" He was actually out of breath from his buzz over this.

Uncle Johnny? First Angelina was calling me that and now Stewart? I wasn't sure I could get used to it, but I did find it touching that my friends wanted their kids to think of me as their Uncle.

"That's really nice, Donny. So what was Stewart so excited to see?"

"It's just a wee gift, nothing too special. Swing by Saturday after class and Stewart will give it to you. He'll be so happy."

"Donny, you know I'm not up to socializing."

"No worries brother. Knock, we'll open the door, gift you, and then on-your-way-John-Day. Promise." He was talking rapidly. He sounded like unmedicated Donny. *Shit.*

"You okay, Donny?"

"One-hundred percent. I'm just friggin' happy for you, that's all."

Happy for me? About what, exactly? My life was still a pile of crap, as far as I could tell. "Fine. I'll be there. But no tricks. Understood?"

Stewart was crying in the background. "Gotta go. See you Saturday!"

I sighed wearily. I just knew Donny had something more up his sleeve.

But then, strangely, my spirits lifted. A "wee gift" from Stewart would be nice and memorable. More than likely it was something his dad wanted for me, but I'd play along.

Find your courage like Norb and Donny did.

So, I used Canada 411 to track down two people who'd been close to Sophia—her childhood best friend and Maid of Honour, Liz Littlewood and Gerti Braun.

As soon as I got off the bus, I dialed Liz's number.

A woman answered.

"Liz?"

"No, this is Billie. Who may I ask is calling?"

"John Pappas."

"Just a second."

Did Liz have a sister? Or was she gay?

There were some muffled conversation, then, finally, Liz got on the phone. "John Pappas? Married to Sophia Andonis?"

"Yes, that John," I laughed nervously. I was shaking with nerves and pacing the parking lot.

"Long time, John. How are you?"

"I'm good," I lied. "You?"

"Fine," she said carefully.

"Sorry to be calling you, Liz. I just want to ask you a couple of questions, if that's okay."

"Uh, sure. Is Sophia okay?"

"As far as know. I haven't seen her since she divorced me...a year after we were married."

There was a notable silence. "Oh."

My pulse quickened. "Liz, I'm hoping you can shed some light on the real Sophia. Looking back, I realize I never really knew her."

"The real Sophia? Why don't you ask her yourself?"

"Her lawyer said she wanted no contact. So, I've honoured that." Another awkward silence.

"Yeah, uh, John, we haven't been in touch since the wedding."

Well, this *was* unexpected. "Really? Mind if I ask why?"

"It's kind of a strange story," she sighed. "You knew we were besties up until Grade Nine, but like a lot of kids we grew apart. Fast forward, what? Nine years? And she's suddenly on the phone, asking if I'll be her Maid of Honour. She was so enthusiastic I couldn't say no."

"That's weird."

"Yep. But I'm glad I did it. Your wedding was a blast. And I was glad I got to know Sophia again, even if it was just for a little while."

"Cool."

"In a way, her wedding was the final chapter of our friendship, and we went back to being strangers again. Not long afterwards I came out and married the love of my life." I heard Billie say something to Liz.

"Oh, well, congratulations on the marriage *and* coming out."

"Thanks."

The flow of our conversation was encouraging, so I dug deeper, aware I might be very sorry if I did. "Were you surprised Sophia married me?"

"Not from what I saw of you. You were friendly, and you were a good-looking, talented, hard-working man, so, no, I wasn't surprised. Sophia wasn't the only one who thought you were a catch. Lots of women at the wedding did."

"Really? They must have been drunk," I said, trying to laugh it off.

"I don't think so."

"Well, uh, did Sophia ever express any doubts to you about marrying me?"

"No, though we weren't as close as we'd once been, of course. But what stands out for me was that Sophia was always going on about how handsome you were and how you had the nicest family, that kind of thing. Nothing that would have suggested she had doubts, at least none that I can remember."

"Did you think we'd make it as a couple?"

She laughed wryly. "Why wouldn't I? Life was going to work out for all of us, right? Young people! So naïve."

I'd caught onto a niggle in her voice. "Liz, is there something you're not telling me?"

She was silent for a moment. "I don't know, John, you're a good guy, but—"

"Please, Liz, tell me. I need to know." Ugh. I sounded so pathetic and desperate.

"I'm okay," she whispered to Billie. "John, you still there?"

"Yes. Please. Go ahead."

She sighed. "Before the wedding Sophia told me a secret. It had been building for some time. And she asked me not to judge her or tell anyone. She said no one else knew and she made me swear not to tell. *A forever promise*, to use her words. So, I haven't. And I won't."

A forever promise? I thought, sarcastically. *Yeah, I know what happens to those.*

I prepared myself for more pain. Had Sophia loved another man? Had she been having an affair?

"John," Liz offered, "when you were with Sophia, right away I knew who you were."

"How? You barely knew me."

"You were a big-hearted romantic. Everyone knew that about you. You wrote Sophia poetry and when you danced with her, you held her in your arms like a precious doll. Anyone with eyes in their head could see how much you loved her."

My cheeks were burning with embarrassment. "I really did wear my heart on my sleeve, didn't I? I'd forgotten I was that far gone."

"Sophia crushed your heart and it never healed," she said gently. "Now you're a broken-hearted romantic like my Billie. She never got over her ex either. She's *still* working on it."

"Great," I said sarcastically, "so it's a lifelong curse." I let the weight of what Liz had said sink into me. "Please tell Billie she's not alone, okay? I totally get it."

"I will. Just so you know, she sees a counsellor and that helps her a lot. Have you considered one?"

Admitting this out loud was like ripping out my fingernails. "Yes, yes I have. In fact, I'm currently seeing a psychotherapist."

"Good for you. And by the way, John, you're not crazy. You never were. You're just in pain."

I breathed out the rest of my nervousness. "Thanks, Liz, I really, really needed to hear that." Powerful, unnameable emotions made me convulse once. I stemmed the tears behind my eyes. *Don't embarrass yourself!*

"John, I'm glad you called and I really hope you find some closure. You deserve it. I'm sorry I couldn't tell you more."

"Thanks, Liz, and thanks so much for listening to me."

"You're welcome. So, good night, and good luck."

"Thanks, you too."

Although I'd felt good knowing I'd learned something about myself and that I wasn't alone in my unhealed heartbreak, the feeling didn't last for more than five seconds.

It had been building for some time, Liz had said. Maybe just not an affair. Had Sophia dumped me for another woman? But our passionate love-making didn't jive with her being full-on lesbian. Bisexual, then? Who knew?

And Liz Littlewood from middle school was gay? Not that I was truly shocked. It seemed everyone was gay these days. So much societal change in my lifetime, I thought. And on top of that, all the changes in my friends and their lives.

But I hadn't changed. I was perpetually stuck back in 1987 searching for pieces of my broken heart. *Idiot.*

I huffed it along Hunter Street towards the bus stop on James. My breath fogged like a mushroom cloud.

Sophia's typical reaction to my love poetry had always been a giggle, followed by a swift peck on the cheek. "Aw, that's so sweet Johnny. You have a way with words," and then she'd laugh, as if I'd just told her a stupid knock-knock joke.

She had no idea how hard I'd worked on those poems. I'd weighed each syllable, re-written and perfected the stanzas, so she'd precisely and exactly see just how much I'd loved her.

Feeling low, I hailed a cab up the Mountain to McDonald's and ordered three Big Macs, two chocolate milkshakes and a cherry pie. I ate so fast I hardly tasted my meal.

At the table beside me, an elderly man knocked over his cup and coffee splattered all over the floor. He leaned stiffly down past his walker but he couldn't quite reach, so I picked up his cup, binned it for him, and went to the counter to order another. When I came back, a staff person had finished mopping up.

"Thank you," he mouthed to me. His thin lips parted as he wrapped his ancient hands around the hot cup. His skin was like soft, wrinkly paper.

He was so frail and vulnerable, I had to look away. "You're welcome," I said, sitting back down.

What was his story? Was he widowed? Divorced?

Now fretting that I'd end up a lonely old man, I downed my last Big Mac and called Gertie. She answered on the first ring.

"Gertie? Gertie Braun?"

"Who's this?" She sounded pissed off, her voice husky and curt.

"Are you the Gertie Braun who used to work with Sophia Andonis at the McDonald's at Molson Boulevard and Mohawk Road?"

"Maybe." She clammed up. Probably thought I was a scammer.

"My name is John Pappas. I was married to Sophia Andonis."

"Mm-hmm. Sure," she said, dripping sarcasm.

"I was hoping I could ask you some questions about her."

"Why would I talk to you? You could be a serial killer, for all I know."

"What? Of course not! I'm just a normal guy. Honest."

"How do I know you are who you say you are?" she grumbled. "I never heard of any John Pappas."

"Well, I certainly remember you." I waited.

"*Hmph*. Go on."

"You had short, permed, blonde hair and blue eyes and your catchphrase was "Top of the day sir, how can I help you?" And you wore a McBurglar pin on a red golf shirt, even when it wasn't fashionable. And sometimes you'd sneak out back and have a puff."

"Yup, that was me." She softened. "But I don't know why you're calling me, Mr. Pappas. I haven't seen Sophia since she was a teenager."

I told her my divorce story. "...and all I ever wanted was closure."

"Phew, that really sucks."

"Right? So, yeah, any info would be helpful."

I listened to her light up a smoke.

"Hey, now I remember you! You dressed like John Travolta and you and your sister were always dancing it up in the foyer, even after we threatened to kick *youse* out, not that we would have." She puffed. "You two kids had the moves."

I laughed out loud. I'd forgotten about that.

"Sorry I was such a pain," I said, not sorry at all. In fact, I wish I'd held onto that youthful confidence.

She took another drag and pressed on. "Sophia was an excellent employee, hard-working, obedient, smart, and punctual. I treated that gal like she was my own. All the staff did. Basically, she grew up at MacDonald's."

"Were you at our wedding? I can't remember."

"We were invited, but Bernie and me had already booked our twenty-fifth down in Orlando, so we couldn't make it. I was really sorry I missed it."

"Um, so, Gertie, did Sophia ever mention me?"

"Well, she talked a lot about her fiancé, and I'm guessing that was you."

"It was."

"You know, Sophia was impressive. By the time she was twenty, she'd made part-time manager and back in those days that was a big deal."

"For sure. I remember her telling me that." It seemed to me that Gertie was avoiding answering my question.

"Anything else?" she asked.

I grimaced. "Did you ever hear Sophia say she loved me?"

She scoffed. "Mr. Pappas, what kind of question is that? If she did, I sure as hell can't remember. And don't you know that trying to make sense of the past is a fool's game? Anyone who's lived long enough knows the past is full of shit holes." She paused. "Go get your answer from the horse's mouth. The Sophia I used to know will tell you straight."

Shivers ran down my legs and back. Gertie was right. As much as I was dreading it, my upcoming face-to-face with Sophia was the only answer to my pain. Only ten more days until I stormed the beaches.

"You're right. I'll call her. And thanks for putting up with my silliness in the foyer, Gertie."

"You had a lotta talent, Mr. Pappas."

"I did?"

"Did you go on in dancing? As a pro, I mean?"

"No, not really."

"Why the hell not? You were young. Only fools and cowards don't follow their dreams."

The McDonald's Oracle of Truth had spoken.

I brightened. "Well, maybe it's not too late for me. I'm working on a dance scene in a Bollywood movie. It's a small part, but it's spectacular. And I've also started a dance school called Saturday Night Dance Academy."

"There you go! Bollywood, eh? Never too late."

I wondered if the Gerties of the world dreamed? And if so, how big?

"Thanks for taking my call, Gertie. You're a good soul."

"Aw, you're welcome."

Gertie Braun had inspired me! For about five minutes after our call, I felt revitalized.

Then my newfound energy fizzled out.

Why did thinking about Sophia always make me feel so raw?

Years ago, I'd found her address online. I'd never set foot near her house. But *oh* how I'd wanted to catch a glimpse of her and how often I'd almost gone there. Thank God I'd had the good sense not to. At least I'd never become a stalker!

No sir, I had never turned my rage and grief on to my ex-wife. Instead, I'd turned it all inward. I'd basically poisoned myself. That was the excuse I told myself, when I did what I did next.

Chapter 24

The blue sky smirked at me. And the yellow house mocked me.

On the west Hamilton Mountain, I'd found a park bench on swanky Scenic Drive, directly across the road from Sophia's house. It was kind of a Spanish Colonial, with its arching doorway and clay tile roof. It was a pleasant change from the boring three-car garage castles surrounding it. A BMW was in her driveway. She had so much more now than *I* ever could have given her.

A silver Mercedes whizzed past.

I *knew* I shouldn't be here. It was stupid. Dangerous. Masochistic. But I just couldn't help myself. To my credit, I had *not* used Donny's number for Patricia from his Incognito Group—not yet, anyway. However, I *was* sitting across from my ex-wife's luxurious home wearing a cheesy fake beard, sunglasses, a ball cap, and a trench coat that would've made a flasher proud.

"I'm tired of being a coward," I mumbled, staring down at my old black Converse shoes, the very ones I'd worn when I was young and in love.

Normally, I wasn't jealous of rich people. But being there that day made me feel vulnerable and small. I'd never wanted the kind of job necessary to afford this lifestyle, one Sophia had clearly needed and gotten, but now that I was here, I felt shame. If I'd made better money I might still be married to Sophia.

I imagined her behind the second-story window on a king-size bed, naked and entwined with her husband, joyously orgasming. The thought made me nauseous.

Should I ring the doorbell? Who would answer? What if it was her husband? Then I'd be forced to compare myself to him. What did a rich guy have that I didn't? (Besides a big house and money *and* my ex-wife?) Plus, he was probably handsome as hell.

What if Sophia was the one to answer the door? I imagined her reaction, "Hit the road, psycho, or I'll call the cops!"

Something dark and terrible filled my veins like toxic ink. Tears slid down my face. I turned around and stared at the black steel fencing that curved along the roadside, at the edge of the escarpment. As if propelled by a supernatural force, I spun off the bench and swung a leg over the rail. The sheer drop was dizzying. I felt as if I were floating out of my body. What had happened to the young man who had fallen in love with Sophia Andonis? What had happened to Johnny Pappas? I didn't feel like anyone at all. I was numb beyond belief.

How had he ended up such a fucking coward?

My other leg sent itself over.

Then I was floating, falling, praying, screaming, and that's the last thing I remembered.

Chapter 25

IN THE HENDERSON HOSPITAL Emergency Room, the cops said I'd been hugging the tree for dear life. I couldn't remember that.

A rescue crew had roped down and pried me out of a huge oak tree jutting out of the rock face. It had literally saved me from plunging to my death. Turns out it I'd only fallen three meters. But it felt much worse.

My chest was raw and sore from impact. The X-rays showed I hadn't cracked my sternum or my ribs, so I was grateful for that.

Tylenol 3 had made my chest pain bearable. And I was on Xanax which made everything seem like a movie—someone else's tragic story, not mine. Definitely not *mine*.

The intern had asked me an exhaustive list of questions about my attempted suicide. Well, even in my drugged-up state, I insisted that I'd never deliberately harmed myself. I must've slipped while bird-watching. It was obvious she didn't believe me, but didn't have enough evidence to keep me so she was forced to discharge me.

After I got in my front door, I began shaking like a leaf and sobbed uncontrollably.

I really had tried to kill myself, hadn't I?

I managed to call Dirk to let him know I couldn't make rehearsal. I'd had a little fall but, not to worry, as my dancing legs were uninjured.

He'd been very concerned for me and had told me to rest. "We need our Gene Kelly in tip-top shape!"

The only good thing about that day was that I climbed into bed sober.

And alive.

Chapter 26

SATURDAY, FEBRUARY 14, Noon.

It was Valentine's Day, of course.

Breakfast was instant coffee: black, like my mood.

My boots crunched in the icy snow as I went east along Flux toward Donny's house. The sun hurt my eyes and my chest still ached. A nice black bruise had come up.

Donny's house was 29 Coke Street, just like Ken Dryden's hockey jersey number.

I was grudgingly going there. The alternative was another trip to Sophia's address, and God only knew if there'd be an oak tree to catch me this time.

Parked cars jammed the street. Donny's newlywed neighbours, the Kostarevwas, were having one of their infamous all-day pot parties. You could smell it all the way down the street.

Saturday in the Hammer, I thought sarcastically. *Yeehaw.*

Donny had recently announced he could no longer tolerate the reek of dope smoke. "Those youngsters and their goddamned skunkweed," he'd say, half-jokingly. In our younger days, he used to love the smell of dope smoke and partaking. Personally, marijuana had never been for me.

It was just as well Donny didn't toke anymore, what with his meds. As it was, he wasn't as careful as he ought to be. He'd once confessed that sometimes he played with his medication dosage so he could have some control over the side effects, although he knew he shouldn't.

However, fully or partially dosed, Donny was just Donny, and that was fine by me.

But did his neighbours know he was crazy? How could they not? The entire Village had recently been subjected to his attempts to make himself famous.

Unlike the fifties-style bungalows on my street, the ones here were ranch-style, their brick much nicer, and worth about fifty grand more. Despite his rapid job changes and money-losing schemes, Donny had beat the odds and found a way to live here. How had he done that? Quite honestly, I figured that Fate had rammed a giant horseshoe up his butt!

I knocked on their door, planning to politely accept Stewart's gift and then get the hell out of there.

When Donny whipped opened the door, instead of being royally pissed off at him for basically extorting me into coming here, I was moved to tears.

He was holding Stewart. Behind him, everyone I knew roared, "Happy, Birthday John!"

I was stunned. Feelings of unworthiness burned inside me.

As I came in, Norb hugged me like I'd just saved the planet.

"You tricked me, Donny!" I scolded over Norb's shoulder.

All my buds' parents, my parents, my friends and their wives, Tony's kids Frankie and Angelina, and even Karl, were all stuffed inside Donny's front living room, their champagne glasses raised to me.

Everyone belted out "Happy Birthday" which somehow morphed into "He's a Jolly Good Fellow". My actual birthday wasn't until Monday, when I'd planned to get shit-faced, alone.

I felt tears on my face. *Damn it!* I was a regular crybaby these days.

"Ach, lad, it's okay," Archie Love said, patting me on the back. "You're amongst friends and family."

Archie Love? Kind? To me?

Esme came over and did her best to hug the cynic right out of me. I felt the urge to run, of course. This was all too much, after the previous day's trauma.

Tony had wedged himself between me and the door. His expression was bulldog-stern. "Not happening, Johnny-boy. Not leaving. Not yet."

Donny grinned at me. He was clearly in his element.

"Donny, you, you..." I couldn't choke out the rest of my words, whatever they were.

He shrugged.

Angelina had wrapped her arms around my waist. "Happy Birthday, Uncle Johnny!"

Tony patted me on the shoulder. As if that was a signal, my friends grabbed me and aggressively hustled me past balloons and streamers and stampeded me down the back stairs and out the door onto snow-caked grass.

They shoved me up makeshift wooden steps onto a platform and then into a huge wicker basket. Karl stood beside it, shouting, "Shazammy-zam-zam!"

"What the fuck is this?" I cried.

Wearing aviator glasses, Donny fell in beside me and so did a spry elderly man wearing an old-timey brown waistcoat and pink bowtie. Above us floated a red-and-white hot air balloon.

My heart melted, but now I became breathless with fear. I was about to die or perhaps freeze to death in a hot-air balloon accident on a wickedly cold day. I'd lost all control and I everyone knew I couldn't *stand* losing control!

I lunged for the little door in the basket, but Donny deftly strong-armed me, yanking my hat down over my face. By the time I tore off my hat, "Up, Up, and Away" blasted out of Donny's boom box so loud I had to cover my ears.

"Lift-off!" he cried to the old man, who opened up the burner. Hot air surged up into the balloon.

"Stop! I'm afraid of heights!" I shrieked at our ancient pilot.

"Don't worry, son! You'll get used to it!" he cried. We started to rise.

Terrified and desperate, I somehow forced myself to peer over the basket. "Someone stop this!"

But not only was Donny laughing his ass off at me, everyone on the ground was cheering and oblivious to the fact that I was scared out of my mind.

Everyone waved goodbye to us. Dorothy sailed away. I gripped the edge of the basket for dear life, quickly realizing I was stuck inside a floating death trap with Donny and the Wizard of Oz.

Next, Donny played, "I'll Be There" by the Jackson Five.

"You bastard," I said, punching his arm hard. "You know I love that song! Are you trying to break me? You're the one that needs help, you know that?" He calmly smiled off my death-stare as the wind whipped his curly hair. He gazed out at the view, peaceful and happy.

And now, with his big heart he'd chosen to give his hurting friend the ride of a lifetime. My heart melted. I was overcome with gratitude.

Sailing on a cold winter wind, Up Up and Away from the Village, I realized I'd never loved a friend as deeply as I did Donny Love in that moment.

"C'mon, Johnny. You're missing the best part! Just stand up here and look at this panorama!" Donny pulled me up from my panicked crouch, draped a blanket around me, and slung an arm over my shoulder.

I suddenly sobbed.

"Why are you doing this for me, Donny?" I shouted above the howling wind. "I don't deserve this! I've been a lousy friend!"

"Because I love you, John. We all love you. And we're concerned about you! And you're *not* a lousy friend. So don't say that."

"Oh, before I forget," he said, pointing to the old man. "This is Gavin, our pilot." I nodded at him.

I gripped a guy wire and peered further, over the edge.

Far below us were my pin-prick loved ones, making me wonder if they'd ever really existed.

"This must have cost you a fortune!"

"Not as much as you might think!" Donny said, the wind stretching his hair over his scalp. "I know a guy. I got a good deal."

"Hey, is it even legal to launch this thing from someone's backyard?"

Donny just shrugged.

I got all teary again.

"You're a good friend, Donny."

We gazed down at his neighbourhood and the grid of streets below. To the north, the lake glinted a beautiful shade of blue. Donny turned back to me. "Hey, good news, mate! Yesterday, I sold nine hundred copies of *Making Steven Famous*. I bet Steven bought them, but I'll never know, although it's something he'd do."

"Wow. That's a lot of books."

"I know, right? The dough will definitely come in handy. I've decided I'm going to surprise Allison with a mini-vacation."

"She deserves it!" She *really* did. "Hey, why don't you email Steven and find out if he bought them?"

"Naw. He never responds. I gave up emailing and texting him months ago."

"Hey, look!" He was pointing downward. "Irondale!"

Our old high school was a brown dot below us. And I could just make out the plaza where my dance studio was. From up here, everything looked less significant. A man could escape from his pain up here.

There was a propane heater at our feet, to keep us from totally freezing to death.

Then Donny produced a bottle of champagne, popped the cork and filled flute glasses.

"A toast," he said, "to friendship!"

I was happy to listen to his playlist of old treasures like Bacharach, The Association, and Brazil 66, get buzzed, and stare dreamily at the morphing clouds as we sank back down towards Donny's house.

Always the King of Risky, Donny grabbed a guy wire and leapt up onto the edge of the basket. If it had been anyone other than Donny, I would have been terrified he'd plunge to his death, but he always seemed to dodge a bullet. Well, so far, anyway. It also helped I was half in the bag and had poor judgement.

I raised my glass. "To you, Donny!"

"To us!"

We raised our glasses and drank some more. The champagne was potent stuff.

"Music fixes me, John," he slurred, half-drunkenly. "But you know what else fixes me?"

I played along. "No, what?"

"Helping the people I love. Helping them helps *me*. And *it* makes me happy."

"Good for you, Donny," I said, slurring a bit, myself. "Maybe I should try that."

He swung down and lunge-hugged me. But I couldn't reciprocate. Despite feeling warm-fuzzies, all I could manage was a few pats on his back.

He hugged me some more, then leaned against the basket.

Something very adult pressed out of his face, and I could see that my old childhood buddy, the Peter Pan who'd returned home to Hamilton with his tail between his legs, had grown up a lot.

"I love all you fucking guys!" he slur-cried. "I always did!"

I raised my glass. "To love, Love!" How buzzed were we? And how full of shit was I? Talking about love was easy, but giving it was *not*. As we sank closer to the ground, my old bitterness and grief were seeping back. And to top it off, Dionne Warwick was singing "I just can't get over losing you/And so if I seem broken and blue/Walk on by, walk on by"!

"Donny," I slurred, "you're purposely playing this music to make me feel something, so I'll talk about my emotions, aren't you? And yet you know how that would be torture for me. So let's call this what it really is, okay? Extortion!" Oh, I was mad now.

But Donny was unfazed. He finished off his glass.

I looked down over the basket. "And I have witnesses!" To show him I was serious, I threw my glass against the floor and it shattered past his feet.

"Guilty as charged, Your Honour," he roared dramatically. "Let the punishment fit the crime!"

"Fuck you," I muttered in resignation.

Of all my friends, he was the most intuitive. When he'd catch me falling into a rabbit hole of my own making or notice my mood tanking, he'd say, "John, Sophia's not home." And I'd say, "Right. Sorry about that." And then I'd pretend to be okay, although I never was and he knew it.

Well, today he'd morphed from psychotherapist to sadistic D.J.

For the final ten minutes, Donny jerked my heartstrings with highly emotional tunes: "Both Sides Now" by Joni Mitchell, "It's too Late," by Carol King, "You're My Best Friend," by Queen, and then he gut-punched me with "You've Got A Friend," by James Taylor.

"You evil prick!" I'd roared at him, tears hosing my cheeks. I randomly told him to eff himself, half-hearted in my anger.

Did he not know that music and a hot-air balloon ride and a birthday party were not enough to heal a man's withered heart? The fool was trying so hard for me.

By the time the balloon touched down, I was emotionally drained and weak-kneed from champagne and crying. I should have felt lighter but didn't.

Tony and Norb helped me totter down the steps. Allison was there with Stewart in her arms. He offered me a *Grease* movie patch, one you could sew on a jacket. "Thank you, Stewart," I said, "that's very kind of you." He smiled shyly and plunked his thumb in his mouth.

"You wouldn't believe all the cool stuff at the antique shop," Donny said. "Stewie really wanted you to have that."

We both knew Donny had used Stewart as a pawn to trick me into coming here. But it *had* been a hell of a ride. And despite being the miserable old Scrooge that I was, I knew I was loved.

Chapter 27

I was trudging south on Steel Street to do the unthinkable. Norb had given me a big, pre-appointment pep talk, repeatedly telling me not to be scared. I wasn't—I was *terrified*.

It was a brutally cold night. The bus shelter in front of the Blue Ball was empty and the roads were basically the same. Most *normal* people were warm at home.

I felt a sudden, unhelpful ache for the Olympia. I shoved it aside and trudged faster.

I'd hired Norb's therapist, Dr. Ferguson, for two-hundred dollars, to guide Norb and me as we tripped in the comfort of his childhood home where he and Morag had moved after his mother's passing. I'd have paid more, I was that hopeless.

I'd told Norb any room in the house was OK, except for his old basement man-cave. Secretly, I was afraid I'd hallucinate loin cloth Ted Nugent out of his poster and he'd fire an arrow through my skull. Norb had agreed and said we'd use his bedroom, instead.

I prayed psilocybin permanently shrank my bad thoughts to pinpoints, the way sailing above Hamilton in the hot-air balloon had. If getting high didn't reduce my depression, I promised myself I'd see Dr. Hotz until she fixed me. If necessary, I'd re-mortgage my house to finance the costs, and more than that I'd try any pill she suggested until we struck gold.

Shame daggered my chest. How low had I sunk?

What scared me most about getting high was losing control. I hated that. Would I vomit? Cry? Scream?

What if I started tearing my hair out? Or got so paranoid I killed Norb? Or what if I developed schizophrenia? I shuddered, stunned by how desperate I'd become.

A teenager gassing up at the Shell station made me think of myself at his age gassing up my first car, a Honda Civic. Before it had died an early death, I'd kept a worn copy of *A Tale of Two Cities* in the glove box. It had been my favourite novel and it suddenly dawned on me now that I'd become a living embodiment of the brilliant, cynical, alcoholic lawyer, Carton, who was tortured with self-loathing and his unrequited love for Lucie Manette. Though I wasn't brilliant, I *was* cynical and tortured, and I *was* an alcoholic.

At the novel's end, hours before his execution, Sydney trades places with Lucie's husband, Charles Darnay, to give his life for Lucie's sake, the only woman he could or would ever love.

My heart skipped a beat. Would I be willing to do that for Sophia? A beat later I had my answer. "Damn right I would!" I spit. But immediately, I knew that this thought was not the sign of a healthy mind. Dickens wrote *fiction*.

On the sidewalk behind me came a shuffle-tap.

My pulse thumped in my ears.

I spun around, ready to defend myself.

But it wasn't a criminal or a cop. It was Pot Shop Bob in his black Beatle boots.

His long, spindly legs angled in front of him, pulling his torso along the conveyor belt sidewalk. Part praying mantis, part Old Testament prophet, he strode with purpose, staring right through me.

Meanness swelled up inside me. I pictured Bob heading home to his happy dope house for dinner after a hard day selling bongs and roach clips to impressionable teens, a practice he should be ashamed of.

I hurried on before he could do whatever nasty thing it was a mantis did to its prey.

I thought about my meeting with Sophia, only three days away! My fears struck out from behind shadowy bushes and across snow-capped lawns towards me, wielding razors. What if seeing her was a life-altering mistake? What if I ruined my only chance to get answers by clamming up? Or what if I screamed sad, jilted, adolescent shit, and blew my one and only chance to get answers so I could finally move on?

Should I make her feel like a piece of shit, so she'd know how it felt? Or should I tell her I'd love her until the day I died? Or that she'd completely ruined me? Worse thought of all, what if I flew into a rage and Dr. Hotz had to call the cops?

I tried to counter my anxiety with positive thoughts. On the movie set, Dev and I had locked in—our dance routine was taking on a life of its own, and my dance studio business was actually making some profit.

But then a real a doozy of a thought blew up inside my head:

You've spent seventeen years mythologizing Sophia and making her real inside your jail-skull. You've imprisoned her there! Sophia hasn't ruined your life. You did it to yourself, asshole!

A dizzying wooziness levelled me. I felt like I was going to pass out before I made it to the safety of Norb's house. I'd freeze to death on a snowbank. For a man who'd ruined his own life, that seemed like a fitting way to die.

The night sky spun in my eyes. My legs buckled. But for some reason my landing was soft—Bob was under me, holding me like a dancer dipping his partner.

He towered over me. He was easily six foot five. A mystical aura seemed to encircle his head. Maybe it was just the glow of a streetlight.

"Thanks," I croaked.

I broke away and staggered toward Norb's house.

Surprisingly, my heart opened a crack. Bob had saved me from smashing my skull on the sidewalk. Maybe he really was a guardian angel. "Thanks, Bob!" I cried over my shoulder. But I didn't look back, because, angel or not, Bob gave me the shivers.

And then I was at Norb's front door and he was practically naked, ushering me inside.

Chapter 28

"NORB, WHAT THE HELL?" I said. "Are you wearing a diaper? And are you greased up, or is that sweat?"

"Aw, you're a joker, Johnny," he laughed in his reedy voice. "I like to feel free, you know? So I only wear my tighty-whities in the house."

Great. My second thoughts were having second thoughts.

I pulled off my snowy shoes and he led me through the living room. Norb's body glistened like a big sweaty Buddah.

"Also, I inherited my Aunt Heidi's genes. When we were kids, she'd get so darn hot and sweaty cooking the Christmas turkey she'd have to put on her Christmas bikini, and she was always fanning herself. She was a riot."

I just tried to smile and nod. This was weird, even by Norb standards.

The old sarcastic urges fought for a foothold inside me, but I wouldn't let them.

"Well, Norb," I said, trying my best to be kind, "since you *are* the Steeltown Avenger and fighting Hamilton scum *is* an exhausting job, you should re-charge any way you see fit. If that includes near-nudity, so be it."

"Yer darn tootin'," he wheeze-peeped.

We padded down the carpeted hallway which was lined with Morag's and Norb's wedding pictures.

"Morag's staying overnight at her girlfriend's so we can have uninterrupted, psychedelic guy-time."

"Cool," I said. The fewer witnesses to this fiasco, the better.

"Morag is the best, right?"

"The best, Norb, definitely."

Norb had a king-sized bed, with two comfortable brown leather chairs set up at the foot. I guessed one was for Dr. Ferguson.

Norb dimmed the overhead light, low-keying the room. "Are you ready to transcend into the fourth dimension?"

"The fourth dimension?" I tilted my head. "Any dimension will do, Norb, just not the one I'm currently in."

The doorbell rang.

"Coming!" Norb cried. He trotted down the hallway, his underwear sagging dangerously low.

It was actually a nice bedroom. The walls were soft spring-green, reminding me of Easter eggs. More wedding photos and old-timey pictures of her parents and grandparents lined Morag's dresser.

A crocheted afghan covered the bed, probably one Mrs. Reingruber had knitted.

I felt safe here. My anxiety dissolved. I was ready to hold hands with the Steeltown Avenger and heroically transcend.

This was going to be the third biggest risk of my life. The first had been getting married. The second was the folly of still hanging out with my old high school buddies.

Footsteps on the carpet runner. *Dr. Ferguson I presume.*

Behind Norb came a skinny man who was so tall he had to duck his head under the door jam. He straightened up and looked in my general direction without making eye contact. "Hey, man. Bob Strangelove." His voice was low and soothing, a deep baritone. He extended his shovel-sized hand. Reflexively, I shook it.

"Head—that is, uh, Bob? What are you doing here?"

I scowled at Norb.

He knew how I felt about head shops, proprietors of head shops, and stoners, especially ones that couldn't remember meeting me ten minutes ago, no doubt because of short-term memory loss. "Bob, don't you remember me? You just stopped me from smashing my head against the sidewalk. Also, we met at Home Hardware that time. Donny introduced us."

There was a flicker of recognition in his lizard eyes. "Oh, that was you?" He laughed. "Sorry, man. I save a couple of guys a day. After awhile, they all look the same."

"So," I said, "you just happen to be there when a guy is spinning out and then you save him?"

"Brother, you'd be surprised how many people are spinning out these days. I'm also kind of helping taxpayers by reducing 911."

"That's very noble of you, Bob." It was hard to remain polite. *He must be one of Donny's guys.* He'd said *brother.*

"And why are you here, exactly?" I asked, eyeing Norb, who'd flopped down on the bed, absolutely unconcerned.

He rolled onto his side. "Dr. Ferguson came down with the flu today, so Bob has offered to facilitate our journey. I knew that if I'd told you that earlier, you wouldn't have come."

"You're damn right I wouldn't have!" I cried. "Taking mushrooms is serious stuff, Norb— for me, anyway." I glared at Bob. "If I knew there wasn't going to be a doctor involved, I never would have signed up for this."

"Totally understandable," Bob said.

"Whatever," I muttered, but he kept right on smiling.

Norb looked like he'd just found his prize in a Cracker Jack box. "John, Bob is a psychonaut veteran. He has a mindfulness certificate from the Hamilton Buddhist Center. He's also a registered nurse and works alongside Dr. Ferguson to guide psilocybin patients all the time. The doc basically recommends him to everyone."

"Why would a registered nurse work at a head shop? That makes no sense."

Bob crossed his arms. "Brother, here's how it went down. After twenty-three years working shifts in the West Fifth Psych ward, I burned out. I knew that working in a pot paraphernalia shop wasn't exactly a lateral career move, but at least the hours were humane and I could help people in a different way."

He saw me looking quite skeptical.

"And I quickly realized that many of my customers were struggling with anxiety and depression and trauma. So, when they're ready, *if* they're ready, I refer them to Dr. Ferguson."

I just stared at him, feeling cynical.

"And maybe this is hard to believe but, as a result, many of them no longer use booze or hard drugs." He was looking pretty animated now.

"*And* they no longer have a terrible fear of Big Daddy," he said, triumphant.

"Big Daddy?"

"Death." Bob's face went back to stillness. "Are you afraid of dying, John? It's OK if you are. I mean, it's the ultimate mystery, right?"

"Dying? Well, I am *now*, Bob! Did you bring a gun or something?"

"I'm really sorry I didn't tell you Dr. Ferguson wasn't coming," Norb piped up.

I glowered at Bob. "Sorry, Bob, but I need a medical professional, not a guy who sells roach clips and bongs. No offence." I shook my head at Norb. "You should have fucking called me. You *knew* this situation would piss me off."

Bob leaned against the wall. He was very calm, like Gandalf on Valium.

I, on the other hand, was anything but calm now. "Enough of this shit, I'm out of here!"

I was half way out the door, when Norb jumped up to intercept me. "Please don't go, John." His voice trembled. "Look, I'm still having a hard time accepting Mutti's death and I could really use a good friend by my side."

When I turned and saw him so naked and vulnerable, I found I couldn't say no. But I was doing this sober.

• • • •

THIRTY MINUTES LATER, having drunk mushroom tea from his Superman mug, safe and secure under his afghan with Bob and me in the room, my good friend had begun charting the deep waters of his mind.

He tossed and turned and moaned, his eyes shuttered. Whenever he was agitated, I held his hand the way Bob had instructed me.

The love pouring out of Bob as he validated Norb's experiences buffaloed me. I promised myself I'd never again judge people by their appearance, or their line of work or their drug of choice.

The more I re-assured Norb, the less self-conscious I felt. I spoke to him in increasingly soft and loving tones as I acknowledged, without judgement, what he was experiencing. Whenever he'd cry out for Mutti, I'd re-assure him and gently rub his back. Sometimes Bob would quietly shake his head and I'd know to say nothing. At one point, Norb was giggling like a baby in his crib, staring up at the ceiling. I figured the stucco swirls were performing a comedy routine just for him. He reached up, then clenched his own wrist and began shaking his hand like a rattle.

Six long hours later, he was giving me a bear hug. "Thank you so much, Johnny. You kept me safe, and I'll never forget that."

"No problem, buddy," I said "Anything for my friend."

All at once, I was hit with overwhelming exhaustion. "I better be going," I yawned.

"You really are a great friend, John," he called after me, as I padded down the hallway.

"So are you. Goodnight, Bob. Sorry for giving you a hard time."

"Tootles," he called from the bedroom.

Out on the porch, I spotted a baggie.

Candy? It was full of coloured pills. *Yikes! Nope. Definitely not.* Some were stamped with LSD happy faces.

It must have fallen out of Bob's jacket pocket. But instead of going back inside and berating him for using drugs (selling them?), a dark urge made me stuff the baggie inside my sock and head home.

Chapter 29

No other guy my age was insane or desperate enough to allow his Ma to orchestrate a meeting with his estranged wife. Only a Mamma's boy would have allowed that. Was *that* why Sophia had dumped me?

The clouds in the sky hung like half-hearted apologies. My boots spat slush as I clomped north on Steel Street towards the Andonises' house.

I mentally leafed through the moldy, dramatic scripts I'd written and stored in my head over the years. But now not *one* of them fit this situation—there were way too many variables!

My anxiety was ballooning. I couldn't stop drumming my thighs.

The night before at my dance studio, Lyra had become re-enamoured with me. All evening, she'd ogled my crotch. For the first time ever, I knew how a woman might feel. It really was a sickening feeling.

Esme had shown up and Archie had accused her of sleeping with the mailman, proclaiming vehemently that Donny wasn't his real son. When Esme heard that, she threatened to call the police to drag Archie to the psych ward for "a long overdue assessment". The other students were mesmerized by their drama.

I'd cancelled my weekly slot car session with Tony and Angelina, was a no-show for our ball hockey game, bought new clothes, and worked out like a fiend. Sophia would see how just how hot and sexy I was and completely regret dumping me.

Then my resolve crumbled and I'd hit the junk food and red wine with a vengeance. I'd paced so much I'd practically worn a groove in the living room carpet. I kept calling Ma to make sure the meeting was still on. By the fifth call, she wanted to come over to check on me, but I put her off.

On my way to rehearsal, the bus had hit a traffic jam, making me an hour late. For the first time ever, Dirk was upset with me. I hated myself for letting down such a good guy like that. I promised myself I'd catch the bus two hours earlier next time.

But the rehearsal had gone well. In fact, it had been mind-blowing. I couldn't believe the lavish set. Dirk had re-mortgaged his house and borrowed money to make his movie. It was a make-or-break effort. There was so much to look at—dancers, costumes, set design—I could barely focus on the stunt coordinator as he strapped me into a harness and reminded me of our safety protocols.

I rehearsed my scene with Dev and Sita at least thirty times. Dirk had stopped the rehearsal twice to check that I was okay. I assured him I was fine, although I knew I barely was, and he looked skeptical. I'd spent the next week hobbling around with a pulled groin. And I'd had massive bruises on my biceps from swinging on a pole and my left shoulder was an aching mess. More than once, I wondered if I was too old to be doing this shit.

Bent out of shape, I'd called and pressured Dr. Hotz into seeing me right away, so I could show her Letter #3. Going through it with her, I saw things in that letter I'd never seen before. Then I'd felt even worse than I had after reading the first two. I begged Dr. Hotz to swear she would not miss the big meeting the next day. She promised, but I couldn't relax.

Now, plodding towards my doom, I realized I'd stopped breathing. I gasped and tried to calm myself.

A bus heaved past, spraying slush against my pants. "Shit!" I flipped the driver the bird, but he was long gone.

Fuming, I swatted the slush off. I was also wearing a black woolen double-breasted winter coat, a grey cable-neck sweater, and a pair of brand new black polished dress shoes. I'd shaved and was wearing Ralph Lauren Polo cologne, the same scent I'd worn when Sophia and I had dated. In fact, it was the same bottle. I hadn't used it since she'd dumped me. *Maybe you were in love with my cologne, Sophia. And me? Well, not so much.*

When I turned onto Lunchbox Street, there was the Andonis house up on the left. It was just as I'd remembered it. Very little about their tidy red-brick bungalow had changed. I slowed to a halt. My heart began to throttle.

Several cars were parked half way into the snowbanks on either side of the street.

Sophia's brother Atticus had done well for himself in the construction business so I guessed the black BMW belonged to him. Although we didn't have much in common, we'd chosen to get along. I assumed the silver Lexus belonged to Dr. Hotz. Further up across the street was an idling blue Mercedes. A man's head poked above the driver's seat. Was he Sophia's rich husband? I was suddenly enraged.

Fuck you buddy! Damn right I'm going to confront your wife! And what are you going to do about it, huh? Nothing, that's what! So stay the fuck where you are if you know what's good for you!

Impulsively, I whipped a snowball and it exploded against his rear bumper. The man spun around in his seat and jerked opened his door to get out but changed his mind when a pick-up truck skidded up beside him.

Tony? He rolled down his window and scowled at the driver. The man shrank back and quietly shut his door.

Tony climbed his truck up onto the opposite snowbank. Had he somehow known Sophia's husband would be here? But if he had, that would mean he'd known the place and time of my meeting. And then I spotted Donny and Norb crammed into the truck beside him. While I watched in disbelief, Norb passed Donny some popcorn. *What the frick!* It was like my life was some kind of drive-in movie to them! But I had no time to think about that now.

A woman hurried down the driveway of a neighbouring house and got into the Mercedes.

Not Sophia's husband! I breathed a sigh of relief. I would let myself feel guilty about the snowball later.

The boys gave me a hearty thumbs up. To show my supportive, pain-in-the-ass friends just how pissed off I was at them for prying into my personal business, I flipped them a Tony special, the classic Italian salute.

Then I was up the porch steps, knocking on the Andonises' door, my heart thumping in my ears. I felt myself floating, separating from my body like elastic. The sensation reminded me too much of my fall (leap?) over the escarpment.

I fought the urge to bolt.

Dr. Hotz opened the door. Instead of inviting me in, she quickly stepped outside and closed it. She was wearing her coat and boots. She had a strange look on her face.

"I'm so sorry, John, but Sophia cancelled. She said she'd fully intended to come but at the last minute suffered a panic attack."

What? Sophia had a panic attack? In all my scenarios, I had only ever pictured *myself* as the effed-up one.

"So now what?"

"That's up to Sophia."

"Isn't it always!" I blurted.

The doctor went silent, waiting for me to calm myself.

"So, is she willing to re-schedule?"

"She didn't say. She left me a voice mail and when I called back she didn't pick up."

The door creaked open. Standing there were Mr. and Mrs. Andonis, my old in-laws. I hadn't seen them since the divorce. Time had not been kind to them.

"We're so sorry, John," said Mrs. Andonis, her accent as Greek as ever.

I could see pity in Mr. Andonis' eyes, which were the same colour as his brown cardigan.

I felt sorry for them, too, and I pleasantly surprised myself by taking the high road. "Thanks for agreeing to set up the meeting. It means a lot. I know I should have gotten over Sophia years ago and I'm sorry that I haven't." I sighed. "And to be honest, seeing you now, I realize I never got over losing you, either. You were both so good to me."

"We've miss you, too," Mr. Andonis said. "You were a good son-in-law." He gave me a sad smile.

Mrs. Adonis shook her head. "Sophia owes you an explanation. What she did to you was cruel, Johnny, for sure, and the way she did it, too. But she won't listen to me or her father, and for that I'm so sorry."

She bear-hugged me. Stunned, I found myself squeezing her back and then we both started crying. Atticus appeared in the doorway, wearing a black and gold Hamilton Tiger-Cats jersey. He was as big and strong as I remembered him.

"Hey, John, long time." He leaned over and gave my hand a firm handshake. "I'm sorry today didn't work out. You know I got no problem with you, bud. I never did."

"Thanks, Atticus," I said, snuffling. "Same."

I'd expected the Andonises to be cold and indifferent and to scorn me for not being able to move on with my life; instead, they were kind and compassionate. To say I was relieved would be a gross understatement.

I knew enough not to stick around. What would be the point? I was no longer their son-in-law.

I wiped away my tears. "Thanks for being so incredibly understanding. And don't worry, I won't ask for another meeting." I nodded at Dr. Hotz.

Mrs. Andonis avoided my gaze. Mr. Andonis opened his mouth to speak, then snapped it shut. Obviously, there were things they wanted to say but couldn't. What the fuck was Sophia's deal, anyway?

Before I could lose my temper, I left, heading for Tony's truck.

Tony swung his Ford up to the foot of the driveway. Donny offered me his spot in the seat and climbed into the cargo bed.

The Andonises gave me a sad wave. For a single year, back in 1987, they'd been my extended family. Knowing I'd never be a part of their lives broke my heart all over again.

Squeezed in between Tony and me, Norb handed me a tissue. In a sweet and melodramatic gesture of empathy, he had cued up "Love Hurts" by Nazareth. Tony looked grim. But Donny leapt up to his feet in the cargo bed and air-guitared my pain.

But I didn't cry. The dark urge inside me was growing. Then, it flexed, as if to say, *Not yet John, there's something you need to do first. After that, there will be time enough for crying.*

Chapter 30

I'D REVERTED. ONCE again, I was the young fool guzzling liquid courage in Donny's basement on a Friday night before a school dance, while Archie and Esme were off at Irondale Lanes, bowling with their church league.

Except now, I was drinking alone, in my living room, in an all-too-familiar pattern.

And instead of pacing myself with beer, I'd hit the gin. Two hours later, seriously buzzed, I'd ordered a cab.

February was an odd time for a Greek wedding, but according to Ma these nuptials were of the shotgun variety. Zoe was six months pregnant! When her parents had found out, they'd freaked and squeezed in a date before Lent, in case the baby arrived early. Lent was traditionally a forty-day black-out period for weddings.

The traffic was busy on Steel Street. As the cab sped south, snow ticking against the windshield, my thought process went like this: *I made the effort Sophia I hired a mediator and I included your family to make you feel safe but you didn't have the guts or common decency to show once again completely disrespecting me and this time also your family and now thanks to the piece of shit coward you really are I realize just how much better I am without you how much better I am than you and how lucky I am to have a date with a Scottish woman who although she looks like she stuck her finger in a socket and then fell into Cyndi Lauper's wardrobe is nothing like you!* Then I found myself speaking out loud. "Are you happy, now that I *hate* you, Sophia? Great! You fucking win!"

"Woah!" the cabbie flinched. "Everything okay back there?"

"Sorry, I didn't mean to say that out loud."

He frowned and shook his head at me in the rearview mirror.

I sank back into my seat. Clearly, I hadn't gotten past the anger, yet, despite my efforts.

On a positive note, I'd been showering regularly, drinking less (today didn't count), and had brought new energy to my dance classes.

I'd also pushed Dev to work harder, and had cleaned up my pigsty of a house. I'd had my parents and Amara and her family over for dinner. I'd scored a winning goal in hockey and had returned to the Olympia two nights a week to help Uncle George wait tables.

On a negative note, the previous Saturday I'd lost my cool at the mall. Donny had convinced the mall administration to let his Incognito group do a March Break children's performance.

They'd dressed up as Shrek, Teenage Mutant Ninja Turtles, Fred and Wilma Flintstone, Teen Titans, and all four Teletubbies—Tinky Winky, Dipsy, La-La and Po.

Donny had somehow conned me into dressing up as Barney, the purple dinosaur. He was the McDonald's Hamburglar. Normally, I wouldn't have gone for it but I was desperate to escape myself. He had caught me in a weak moment.

The kids sat in front of the huge fountain in the centre court as we juggled, performed magic tricks, and made animal balloons. We sang the Barney theme song and did silly dances and clapped and cheered along with the kids.

But the heat in the costume was getting to me. I was sweating like a pig. The Harry Nilsson song "Without You" was burning a psychotic loop in my head.

Just as the show ended, a mom chasing her bratty daughter around the fountain barreled into me. "Sophia!" she screeched. "Get back here right now!"

Hearing that name added fuel to the fire inside me. I charged towards her and blocked her with my purple paw. She looked enraged.

"You bumped into me and you didn't apologize!" I huffed at her from inside my giant head, my voice muffled and strange. "What kind of mother are you? Are you teaching your daughter to be rude and pushy like you?" The shoulder harness slipped a bit, and the head suddenly tipped forward of its own accord.

The woman lurched backward in terror.

Things got suddenly really quiet around the fountain.

Two young, zealous mall cops ran up and grabbed me by my purple arms. I yanked away from them and all three of us lost our balance. I landed on the top of the pile.

Then I was blindly lumbering down the mall, my massive tail swinging behind me.

In my desperation to get away, I wasn't thinking too clearly. I managed to avoid several benches and garbage cans, but my luck ran out. I crashed into one of those firetruck strollers, almost upending it and the kid inside. The mother shrieked at me.

A gasp went up from onlookers. "Hey, asshole!" a guy roared at me. From somewhere on my left a little voice shrilled, "I hate you, Barney!"

Through the mesh in Barney's mouth, I could see that the beefier of the two security guards was gaining. Somehow, I made it to the parking lot. In the distance, the Kenilworth 21 bus was pulling into the mall terminal. I ignored the screeching of tires as I lurched out in front of traffic.

The driver may have given me a weird look but at least he forgot to make me pay. In my shame, I couldn't bear to take the head off and have people look me in the eyes.

So I rode the route home like the big purple ship wreck I was.

• • • •

THE CAR HAD ARRIVED at the Astoria Banquet Hall. Sadly, my gin buzz was fading, and along with it, my bravado. I was about to open the door when anxiety paralyzed me.

"You, okay?" the driver asked, turning around to stare at me.

"No, no I'm not."

I hadn't seen most of these people since my wedding.

What was there to talk about? Would they ask about Sophia? Did they know about the divorce?

Powered by nothing more than stubbornness, I dragged myself out of the cab.

Chapter 31

I WAS A WALKING NUMBSICLE.

Just head to the bar, keep your head down, find Sheena and Agnes, and stick to them like glue. I steeled myself, praying no one would notice me.

"Welcome, John," said a female greeter.

Busted!

Bristling, I looked up.

"That's me," I said, barely meeting her gaze. I didn't recognize her, which was a relief. *The groom's side of the family?*

But in the Greek community, word would spread fast. Everyone would know that sad, angry, jilted Johnny Pappas had finally come out of hiding after his painful divorce, and that everyone should be very careful what they said around him, because he'd become a super-sensitive, cynical, sarcastic hot-head—all of which was absolutely true.

"Coat check is that away," she pointed. "And don't forget to sign the guest book."

"Yeah, thanks." I kept my head down and scuttled away.

The foyer was lovely. A beautiful staircase with gold handrails swooped down to meet the marble floor, and gauzy fabric draped the floor-to-ceiling windows. *Yeah*, I thought, *I remember being here. It was the best day of my life. Until it fucking wasn't.*

I deadened my gaze and walked briskly past the guest book to a polished oak cocktail bar and ordered a double whiskey on the rocks. I downed it and ordered another, praying I wouldn't meet anyone I knew. At a Greek wedding, that's about as likely as flying pigs.

I felt a few people staring at me and my face reddened. Once the wedding party arrived and formed their reception line, I'd duck into the washroom and sneak into the Grand Hall later.

I'd half-imagined I'd wear a track suit, just to thumb my nose at the institution of marriage. Instead, I'd opted for the sharpest suit I owned. I looked pretty good, which kind of defeated the whole "melt into the crowd" strategy. If I were being honest with myself, I wanted to look good for Sheena.

A quick glance told me the place had filled up quickly, everyone dressed to the nines. Young and old exchanged hugs and kisses, and kids chased each other. I knew I should feel hopeful for Zoe and whatever-his-name-was, but I just couldn't. My faith in marriage had long since ossified.

And then it happened! Of course, it did! Just as Ma and Dad and Amara and husband Greg spotted me and were on their way over, an explosion of energy blasted through the front door. A slurry Scottish voice crowed, "Let's get this party started!"

It was Donny, channeling his dad, brandishing a triumphant fist and whooping it up as if the Glasgow Rangers had just defeated the Celtics. Allison and Agnes were with him, and they were all in a jolly, half-drunk mood.

Donny's eyes were pinballing—he was in wildcard mode! *Shit!* You could hear a pin drop. Six groomsmen, the size of the Tiger-Cats' defensive line, hustled toward him, but quick-witted Donny caught the play and *Houdini-ed,* ducking out of reach.

Like a carnival barker, he lifted an invisible megaphone to his mouth and addressed his audience. "Sorry, folks! All good, just excited to be here! I promise I'll tone it down from now on!" He saluted the groomsmen. "As you were, gentleman!"

The times Donny had squirmed out of his self-inflicted faux pas were too numerous to count. He could be charming.

Laughing, he led Agnes and Allison to the coat check. Allison was obviously pissed off by his outburst. The groomsmen went back to the bar. They were more interested in partying than bouncing some middle-aged nut bar.

In a few minutes, Donny and the girls blustered up to the bar and gave me big hugs. Agnes looked great. She was wearing a dusty blue lace wedding dress with short sleeves and a shiny white cowboy hat and boots. She was channeling serious Stevie Nicks. I looked around for Sheena.

"You, okay?" Ma asked, coming up behind me and rubbing my back the way she had since I was a kid.

"Yeah, yeah, Ma, I'm good." I gave my folks a lop-sided smile.

Dad wasn't fooled. He knew why I was half-drunk. He ordered red wine for himself and Ma. "Slow down, Johnny. You got all night."

"It's all good, Dad," I slurred. "Not to worry."

With my friends and parents there, I now felt protected. Slowly, I began to relax. I willed myself to take a deep breath and then exhaled.

Turns out my posse's arrival had green-lighted me to my other relatives, who suddenly popped out of the crowd like whack-a-moles. Various aunts, uncles, and cousins hugged and kissed me, genuinely happy to see me.

They asked me all sorts of questions about my studio, but no one mentioned Sophia or scolded me for deserting the family biz. Relief made my legs weak.

And then I realized how much I had missed them, my huge extended family.

Uncle Leonard slipped through the crowd and introduced me to his partner, Allan, who was just as handsome and distinguished as I had imagined he'd be. The two of them were wearing GQ-level suits. They were a sophisticated-looking couple.

Then I was greeted by Zoe's parents, Ma's sister Kiki and Uncle Dimitri and their kids Luke and Helena. Dad's sister and her husband Christopher came up next, followed by Constantine and Alex. But all the hugs and kisses were cut short when I saw her.

"Johnny," Ma said. "Oh my Lord, what's wrong?"

We all stared at the stunningly beautiful, sophisticated woman across the room. Time froze. Just for a moment.

Gone were the electrostatic hairdo, the knee-high platform boots, the mini-skirt, the fake eyelashes, and the heavy-handed make-up! A classy sheath the colour of an emerald highlighted her small, shapely figure. Delicate high heels showed off her trim ankles. Her hair was now a thick, honey blond wave, splashed across her shoulders.

My heart began to pound deep in my chest.

"Sheena," I croaked. Love soughed through me like a warm breeze.

Sheena eyes stayed locked on mine. And what I saw in them was love.

An electric sun grew in my belly.

"Johnny," Ma whispered into my ear, "she's so beautiful. Who is she?"

Donny clapped me on the back. "That, Mrs. P, is Sheena Stirling. Johnny's date."

Agnes squeezed my shoulder.

I found myself across the room and in front of her. She opened her mouth to speak, when suddenly the emcee announced. "Ladies and gentlemen, I present to you the bride and the groom, Zoe and Daniel Ioannou!"

Heads turned. Reluctantly, I took my eyes off of Sheena's face. Cheering and whistling erupted.

Through the main doors, the bride and groom and their wedding party of twelve sailed in. *Wow!* My cousin Zoe was all grown up now, and she was beautiful and she was married!

The groomsmen started chanting, "Daniel". One nervy guy wolf-whistled Zoe, and that got a few laughs.

The wedding party formed their reception line at the hall's main doors. Inside the dining room, a Greek band started to play, kicking off the fun.

This was going to be a great night, I thought, drinking in Sheena. A really great night.

She slid her arm through mine and we lined up to congratulate the happy couple.

"You look lovely, Sheena," I said. *Lovely* seemed inadequate, though. She looked like a completely different woman.

"So do you." She winked. "I didn't know George Clooney was Greek."

I laughed. "And I didn't know you needed glasses."

"I don't," she said meaningfully. "Definitely not."

The warmth in her gaze gave me goosebumps.

After the meet-and-greet, we all found our assigned table, conveniently next to the dance floor. Donny arrived with a tray of ouzo shots for the table. He set a shot glass in front of each us and then spun his tray on his fingertip like a circus juggler. It was a trick he'd picked up during his waitering days at Yuk Yuk's Comedy Club, back in his twenties.

"Yamas!" he cried, and we all downed our shots. The familiar licorice taste burned my throat.

The tables were covered with white linen with long-stemmed glassware and white candles in beautiful floral arrangements. In each corner of the dance floor, vases of white roses topped short Doric pedestals. There was a massive chandelier and soft purple light fanned up the walls. The hall looked stunning and very romantic. I snuck a peek at Sheena again. She was an angel in the soft light.

The emcee was announcing the arrival of the wedding party as they entered the hall.

Cheers and clapping erupted as they all took their seats at the head table.

Dinner was a grand affair. A seafood salad starter followed by grilled lamb skewers, rice, moussaka, and, for dessert, baklava with a side of vanilla gelato, followed by more red wine and ouzo.

The band began playing, "*Simera Labi O Ouranos*".

Zoe and Daniel burst onto the dance floor and twirled. Then the immediate family, including Amara and me came up, joining hands for a circle dance.

Although Sophia and I had danced to this same song at our wedding, I refused to be triggered by it. I was here to celebrate Zoe's wedding, not wallow in self-pity, and from the moment I'd seen Sheena tonight, I had known that I wanted to marry her. I prayed she felt the same way.

Drummers pounded their way onto the dance floor and accompanied the *bouzouki* player and the violinist. Next, the bridal party danced the *Kalamatiano*, then the groom and groomsmen the *Hasapiko*. The entire room surged with dancing.

The emcee was grating on my nerves so badly I wanted to punch him out. He wouldn't shut up! He kept talking over the performers, providing a play-by-play, like some rookie hockey announcer.

Then I wanted to kill him. He'd made a "special announcement" that Amara and I were going to perform. The crowd went wild for us.

I turned to my sister. "Is he out of his mind, Amara? We haven't danced together since we were kids!"

But the cheering had drowned me out. Everyone remembered how good we'd been.

And they were probably so drunk they wouldn't care if we made fools of ourselves.

As soon as the band lit into the theme from *Zorba the Greek*, Amara tried to drag me onto the dance floor, but I dug in my heels. Donny got everyone chanting, "Johnny! Johnny! Johnny!"

"Come on John!" Sheena cried. "Everyone's rooting for you! We're all your friends here."

Maybe it was the ouzo talking, but she was right. I was amongst friends. Just as we had in the good old days, Amara and I held hands and paraded onto the dance floor. For a split second, I remembered my sister at twelve, lean and attractive with long legs and dark curly hair like mine. And I remembered Johnny Pappas at fourteen—full of vitality and in seventh Heaven on the dance floor.

Our audience cheered and clapped along. As the tempo picked up, we laughed and found that magical, effortless responsiveness to each other that we'd had in those days of studios and dance competitions.

Then the guests spilled onto the dance floor and everyone was doing the Zorba.

Uncle Leonard took over with Amara so I could dance with Sheena. She flavoured her Greek dancing with a little bit of Highland Fling, which inspired Donny a little too much.

He was so buzzed, he'd began wildly cartwheeling and walking on his hands, which, for a guy his age, was actually quite impressive. However, his swinging feet almost knocked Ma in the head.

Dad scolded Donny and he finally had the good sense to simmer down.

If only the loud-mouth emcee would stop being so annoying, I could have completely enjoyed myself.

"Hey, buddy!" I shouted. "We don't need a play-by-play, okay? It's not Hockey Night in fucking Canada!" Ma glared at me.

But the emcee ignored me and continued his commentary. I could tell the guests and even the musicians had also lost their patience with this asshole.

Ma came over to me. "Johnny, for Zoe's sake, please don't make any more scenes. And watch that language!"

I decided to behave myself.

"Now, by special request," the emcee cried, "'More than This' by Roxy Music." The band launched in, sounding amazingly good.

Sheena slipped into my arms. She *fit* me.

"You picked this tune, didn't you?" I asked her.

She just raised her eyebrows at me and smiled enigmatically.

"What a great song," I said. Then I made a mistake. Too much alcohol! "You're so beautiful, Sheena. What happened to your crazy 80's look? I barely recognize you tonight."

A dark cloud crossed her face, and she chose her words carefully. I could tell she was trying to rise above my unintentional insult. "Sometimes I dress up to have fun. And sometimes to forget." She leaned deeper into me.

I was about to ask her what she was trying to forget—heartbreak?—when she said, "We all have a story, John. But for now, let's enjoy the moment, okay?" She gripped me more tightly.

"Sorry, Sheena. Alcohol has made me an idiot tonight." I held her close and we swayed together for a few moments.

Finally, she bit her lip and shook her head. "Alright," she said, almost to herself, as if she'd just decided something. "Two years ago, my husband Glenn passed away."

I crumpled inside. "Oh Sheena, I'm so sorry."

She continued to dance with me, but her thoughts were somewhere else now.

"Glenn was the love of my life." Her voice was soft.

My heart panged for her. "Is that you why you came to Canada?"

She pursed her lips. "Aye, everything in Glasgow reminded me of Glenn. And when Donny suggested I come to Hamilton for a fresh start, I jumped at the opportunity." She looked up at me, smiling in a determined way.

"Good for you." I tried to lighten the mood. "You know what some Canadians call Hamilton?"

She shook her head.

"The arsehole of Canada."

"Now, John," she said cheekily. "Armpit, maybe, but never an arsehole."

"Ha!" I laughed. "You're definitely related to the Loves. That's something Donny would have said."

"A nutbar, but definitely the best cousin ever," she said.

I couldn't disagree.

I was poised to ask her more about Glenn but she shushed me. "Now, let's just dance, okay?"

I felt my back go up. Sophia used to shush me. It was like she thought only nonsense came out of my mouth. I'd forgotten about that, about how it used to infuriate me! How could I have buried that memory?

But my anger had no chance to take hold, because then Sheena smiled the most beautiful smile. Her teeth weren't the stereotypical Scottish ones, rotted by sweets and stained by smokes. They were white and even and pretty. I just wanted to kiss her sweet mouth, all over again.

I had new, mad respect for Sheena—by moving to Canada, she'd taken a radical first step to move forward in her life, to move past a real tragic experience.

I'd only experienced a divorce—almost two decades ago!—and I hadn't taken any steps at all to get past it.

I could learn a lot from this strong wee lass, and if it was true that good things come in small packages, then lucky me!

I drew Sheena closer. Her soft hair was against my chin.

Heat like warm water coursed through me.

I was falling for her, hard. But then, out of nowhere, that dark urge inside me grew and grew and grew. Why? Why did I have to go and destroy everything? I turned the best time I'd had in years into a dumpster fire.

Apparently, I downed tequila shots with Donny and gave Zoe's new husband, Daniel, a financial analyst, bullshit business advice. But I did remember heckling the emcee. I used colourful language and threatened to call "the DJ police".

I remembered smashing several dinner plates on the dance floor and yelling "Opa!"at the top of my lungs before the wait staff stopped me. Sheena had been right into it. She was like a rabid animal, flinging her hair wildly. I was in awe of her. But Agnes had a sharp word with her and that slowed her down some. I totally recognized Sheena's frustration and joy. She was me and I was her.

Then the band led by the bouzouki player slid onto the dance floor to perform the song "Emeis Oi Trees Ston Kafene" and of course the emcee ruined the moment. Over the music's smooth voice, he bleated into his microphone. "Good times, great oldies!"

"Seriously, buddy?" I cried. "You're a wedding emcee not an AM radio DJ! Smarten up!"

Seeing that I was triggered, Daniel squeezed my shoulders. "I'll have a word with him after the dance. Okay? But for now, I *dance!*"

He grinned at me, signalled the band to change the music, tore off his jacket, and proceeded to dance the *Zeibekiko*. He spread his arms wide and spun, jumped and stepped with passionate intensity. Guests left him shots on the dance floor, and he'd periodically pick one up and down it.

In my drunken, disrespectful state, I crashed his one-man-party and joined him.

"Let's give it up for Johnny Pappas!" the emcee interjected, "The winner of the 1975 Kiwanis Dance Festival!"

"Shut up!" I cried. "You're ruining the song!"

He gave me a cavalier wink and a couple of pistol fingers, and that's when I *really* lost my shit.

I broke through the crowd and leapt onto the stage. I wrestled the mic out of the emcee's hand. He looked terrified.

"Johnny's gone loco!" I heard Amara cry. My parents stood at the edge of the dance floor, aghast.

The music stopped. Everyone stared in absolute, stunned silence. Perfect!

"What's everyone staring at?" I cried. "I am your new Master of Ceremonies! That asshole is fired! Now, let's keep this fucking party going!" And I let out a raucous whoop.

From the far end of the dance floor, the groomsmen charged towards me. Donny charged from the other side. Obviously, he was hoping to save me from making a complete ass of myself, which struck me as ironic, because that's all we ever tried to do with him.

Everything good that had happened that evening had officially melted like a Salvador Dali painting.

"Seventeen years ago, Sophia Andonis divorced me!" I roared. "And you know what? She never told me why! But *someone* here knows the reason! Oh yes, someone knows. But did you ever get up the courage to tell me? Put me out of my misery? No! Oh, poor Johnny Pappas, if you bump into him, don't mention Sophia. He's crazy now. He sees a shrink. Damn right I see a shrink, and yeah I'm fucking crazy now! And here I am at another bullshit wedding because in the end what's the fucking point of getting married? Huh? There is no point! That's the reality! It will only end in heart-crushing, soul-destroying divorce!" The pain on Zoe's face was terrible to see. "I'm sorry, okay, I'm *sorry*, Zoe! Your marriage will probably be OK."

"And, you Sheena," I cried, pointing at her. A murmur went up from the crowd and Agnes threw her arm over her friend's shoulder. "You need to stay away from me, you hear! I'm damaged, I'm no good for you, and I couldn't love again if my life fucking depended on it!"

Before I could utter one more regrettable word, Donny wrestled the mic out of my hands. I fought the groomsmen like a cornered rat, kicking and punching and tearing as they raised me up like a trophy and hustled me across the dance floor.

Outside, they tilted me onto my feet, which was gentler treatment than I deserved. But, of course, I just swore at them, raging and ungrateful.

I staggered along the curving driveway down to the snow-crusted sidewalk. Donny caught up and tried to give me my winter coat, but I shrugged it off and kept walking.

"Piss off, Donny!"

"John, I'm not leaving you alone. I'm going to walk you home."

"Get out of here, Love!" I shouted.

But he continued to trudge along beside me, so I spun around and right-hooked him.

Thank God for both of us his Peter Pan reflexes kicked in and he dodged my blow.

"I can't believe you tried to punch me," he yelled.

"Keep following me and I'll kill you!" I was shaking with rage and sobbing, lurching along.

When I finally let myself look at him, he had gone. Strangely, that just made me more angry.

By the time I'd reached the Village, I was huffing and puffing, a far cry from the fit high school senior who'd taken fifth in the city cross-country finals. A stitch knotted my side, and although my face was frozen, my body was soaked with sweat.

I reached into my trouser pocket and dug out Bob's goodie bag. The black urge inside me pumped through my veins.

I dry-swallowed *all* the pills. It was time.

Chapter 32

WHEN I BROKE THE GLASS in the side door of Tony's garage, the alarm system blared. *Shit!* My heart hammered. I reached through the gaping hole and let myself in.

I flicked on the lights and found the garage door-opener button. The door slid upwards but then stopped abruptly. *Double Shit!* Tony had deadbolted it a foot off the floor.

The overhead motor heaved and whined. I turned it off before it could burst into flames or something.

I scoured Tony's rolling tool box and workbench for bolt cutters but came up empty-handed. *Triple Shit!*

I had to act quickly before the drugs kicked in! I used Tony's sledgehammer to bash the deadbolt.

I tore a pre-written cheque out of my wallet and slapped it on the work bench. "Seventy-two thousand, Tony. My life savings. Shit, I hope you forgive me."

The last time I'd been over to Tony's house, I'd snagged his spare car keys off the hook beside his front door. I reached into my pocket and ran my fingers over them now.

The Camaro was the same one he'd used in our face-off against The Screw, that night outside the bowling alley. It was a totally bad-ass vehicle. I nodded respectfully at the red-lettering on the hood: "Italian Stallion".

I cranked it awake. I revved its powerful engine. It roared like a lion!

I found the garage door remote in the glovebox. The door shuddered and groaned, opening only two-thirds of the way. I jammed the stick shift into Drive, matted the gas pedal, and blasted the car out of the garage door in a fury of twanging, sheering metal. I could only imagine what the garage door had done to the car roof.

I parked behind the Rexall Drugstore. Grimly, tearfully, I waited for Bob's goodies to blow my mind.

Beyond the chain-link fence, the neighbouring houses were shrouded in darkness. The people inside had no idea what I was planning.

Some of the drugs had felt like wafers, some aspirin, and others dry bits on my tongue.

I'd consumed them all without compunction.

There was still time to stick my finger down my throat and puke up the drugs, but I refused to. *No more tortured mind! No more pity-party!* There was a painful lump in my throat. *Please, God. No more.*

To be perfectly honest, my suicide plan wasn't that original. I'd ripped it off from a poor Grade Nine kid named Terrence Martin. He and his buddy Robbie Gizarre had driven their souped-up yellow Ford Mustang over the Hamilton escarpment on the first Saturday of October, 1976 and plunged to their deaths.

Rumour had it they'd each taken seven hits of LSD while listening to Judas Priest's song "Better by You, Better Than Me," and that Robbie hadn't wanted to die, but Terrence was driving so fast that Robbie couldn't bail.

The following Monday, over the intercom, our Principal Mr. Randall had expressed his condolences to friends and family. He hadn't mentioned the word *suicide* but we weren't fooled. That event had profoundly impacted all of us. There's nothing more shocking than kids who take their own lives.

Remembering that trauma almost made me reconsider my plan, but the black urge inside me hectored me so hard there was no going back.

Tony had left a cassette in the tape deck. I cranked the volume up.

First up was Deep Purple: "Highway Star."

The perfect tune for a devilish deed.

Chapter 33

WHEN MY FINGERS WERE about twelve inches long, I knew it was time. I revved the engine. I had to do it before I was too fucked up! But the moment I gripped the steering wheel, a Hell clown squelched out from the center and spun his reeking head like a propellor and vanished before I could even scream.

Except for the snow gently ticking against the windshield, the night was quiet.

My breath came in painful gasps. I thought my heart might explode in my chest.

Do it before the car melts! Before your brain melts!

I ripped the Camaro out onto Steel Street. I skidded into the empty intersection and faced east on Flux. The escarpment edge was a kilometre away.

In my rearview mirror, The Blue Ball was dark and empty, its neon sign flickering. The gas station was quiet. The night shift cashier was likely asleep at the till.

The Village was dead.

Perfect. Soon I would be, too.

My right arm swelled up like a fiddler crab leg. I could feel my hair growing.

Suddenly, the Village seemed to be throbbing like a heart. Like *my* heart. How had I not noticed that before?

But more than that, I could see the streetlights for what they actually were! How had I not noticed the angels before? Their faces were warm and beautiful and serene, their silky hair garlanded with gold crowns. A gust of wind swayed their long, white robes. Their song was the sound of love.

But the demonic voices were louder. And I knew what they wanted me to do.

Indecision straightjacketed me.

Reality melted around me like burning celluloid.

No more pain. No more pain. Fuck you, Sophia! You did this to me! You!

I floored the gas pedal. Thrust sucked me back into the seat. Like Terrence and Robbie had, I flew down Flux Road, aiming for the Other Side.

My heart thumped a hissing countdown. Time elongated—the drugs. Everything was surreal and oozy.

I knew the demons were in the back seat but I couldn't bring myself to look.

I was going so fast I felt I was flying. But the edge of the escarpment seemed to be getting further and further away.

Faster. The road's idea.

Death. My death.

I heard a baby crying and discovered it was me!

I became aware of Donny and Norb running on either side of the car. They wanted me to stop but I knew I wouldn't. Norb's body was strangely round, and Donny's mouth took up most of his face.

"I'm sorry," I said to them, sadly. "I have to."

The inside of the car flashed red and blue.

In terror, I tightened my grip on the steering wheel. It squirmed like a snake.

A wrench smacked down on the steering wheel. Tony was in the passenger seat beside me, a smoke in his mouth, and a beer in his hand. He was so young! Just a kid, really.

With a gasp that sounded like a truck's air brakes, he was suddenly gone.

The neon Aurora pizza sign spun past the car like a flying saucer.

The demons in the back seat thrummed in my ear.

I passed a video billboard fifty stories high. Sheena was making passionate love with her new boyfriend. "See, I told you so," the billboard said to me. Damn it was smug.

I burned with jealousy.

Suddenly, it seemed like the car was frozen in time. The escarpment edge was so close I could almost see over it.

Dad, Mom and Amara were in their mourning clothes, on their way to my funeral. They were soaked to skin with their own tears.

Kill yourself you piece-of-shit son!

The hissing countdown grew louder.

Totally numb now. I was going to do it.

The road pulled me along.

The car flew faster and faster and faster. Two more hissing heartbeats to take-off. To pain-free.

Chapter 34

MONDAY, APRIL 5, 1:15 p.m.

I *felt* it.

After I'd left The Astoria, my friends had called everyone they knew in The Village to help rescue me. When Tony had told me that at the hospital, two hours later, I'd cried—in shame and gratitude.

Tony had told me he'd saved my life by driving his F150 pick-up truck in front of me to slow me down. He'd done a skillful job, but, still, the impact from hitting his back bumper at 150 km per hour had smashed my face against the steering wheel and my arm against the dash. It hadn't helped that I wasn't wearing a seat belt and the old Camaro didn't have air bags. He'd saved my life—ten metres from the edge of the escarpment.

An ambulance had rushed me to Henderson Hospital. Multiple staff kept telling me how lucky I was to be alive. My arm was in a cast and I had stitches in my cheek. There were going to be a lot of bruises.

The bloodwork revealed I'd overdosed on DMT, psilocybin, LSD, and tranquillizers. The doctor who told me this was blessedly judgement-free but also suggested counselling.

I couldn't believe I'd tried to kill myself. I never thought I'd be that guy. And the shame alone was enough to make me still want to kill myself, in theory anyway. Just thinking about that night now made me shudder. I never wanted to sink that low ever again.

When I apologized profusely to Tony for stealing and wrecking his car, he tore up my cheque and said he could easily fix it and would only charge me for parts. By the look on his junk-yard-dog face, I'd known better than to disagree. I insisted on paying for a new garage door and he agreed to that. He said he'd send me the bill. I was still waiting for it.

"Thanks Elise." I gave her a smile that made the fresh scars on my cheek twinge.

She handed me my coffee, eyeing me skeptically. "You sure you can manage this, with that sling? Make sure you get someone to hold the door for you. You know, you're not cut out for bad boy roles, Johnny. None of youse are." She thought I'd gotten hurt doing my own stunts in Dirk's movie. I was certainly not going to correct her.

"Oh, don't worry. Lesson learned."

I carried my care package—a BLT and an extra-large black coffee—outside into the warm sun and sat down on a plastic crate beside a dumpster. Today, I was at our other Tim Hortons, at the corner of Molson Boulevard and Flux Road. I'd been craving a little change-up to my routine. A real estate agent smirked above me, gold letters splashed on the huge billboard: "If I don't sell your home in thirty days, I'll buy it!" *Donny*, I thought, wryly, *you missed your calling, buddy*.

A steady stream of shoppers went in and out of the Canadian Tire and the Price Chopper in the plaza. In an unexpected warm spell, the sun winked in the windows and melted the plowed-up snow piles in the corners of the parking lot. A young woman wearing shorts leaned against the brown brick of Tim's and enjoyed a smoke. She was pushing her luck, but I couldn't blame her. I was ready for winter to be over, too.

Marvin the-sausage-man had parked his cart outside the auto service customer entrance. He had a steady line-up of customers. He liked to brag that he hadn't missed a day of work in thirty years.

My near-death experience had changed me. Determined to finally move forward in my life, I'd signed back up with Dr. Hotz. She had put me on Doxepin and it seemed to help my mood, although it did make me groggy.

She pushed me to be more social, so I'd swallowed my pride and played Dungeons and Dragons with Donny and Norb. It was cringe-y but embarrassing fun.

Whenever Donny went off the rails about a new idea or job or Norb drifted off into his fantasy world, I didn't feel the urge to offer a cutting response, and I was *glad* I didn't.

The cast had come off two days earlier. I was wearing the sling because the muscles in my arm were still a bit weak. I'd gone back to helping out at the Olympia, although I couldn't manage heavy trays, yet. My folks were ready to retire, finally, and they were actively looking for a buyer.

So, things were definitely looking up for me. Despite the six weeks when I was still too injured to teach using my arms—thank God my legs had survived the accident—four new dance students had signed up for an entire year and none of the regulars had quit. Lyra had found a new love interest, a used car salesman name Bobby Leslie. He never stopped smiling.

I touched the bandage covering the deep cut on my cheek. It was taking forever to heal up. After removing nineteen stitches, the doctor had said the scar should eventually fade.

A recent brain scan revealed that my brain hematoma had disappeared and, thankfully, so had my headaches.

I inhaled the last bite of my BLT. It tasted especially good to me today.

I heard the sound of footsteps and got a funny, jittery feeling in my stomach.

I looked up. A figure eclipsed the sun.

Sophia! Holy shit! I leapt up, scattering my food wrappers and upending my coffee. A jolt of pain shot up my arm and I held my breath.

She was pregnant!

And she was beautiful.

"Donny told me you'd likely be here," she said, her voice trembling. Then pain scrunched up her face. Tears rolled down her cheeks. She stared at my banged-up face in horror.

I felt paralyzed.

She spoke softly. "For the past two days I parked and waited for you to show. I'm so sorry to startle you, John, but I needed to see you. You deserve an explanation. You always did."

I bowed my head, embarrassed by my tears. *Shit!* Crying was the last thing I'd ever wanted to do, if we met again. *This isn't how this is supposed to go!*

She was blubbering, now. "I'm sorry, John. I'm just so sorry—for everything!"

Should I hug her? I found I couldn't. A weight unlike anything I'd ever experienced anchored me in place.

"Please," she said, snuffling, wiping her tears with a tissue. "Let me explain."

She motioned me towards her white BMW. Numbly, I followed her and sat in the passenger seat.

Her face was plump now, due to age and her pregnancy, but that made her even more beautiful. She barely fit behind the wheel. Her ankles were swollen. Her brunette hair had become frizzy, maybe because of her pregnancy. But her brown eyes stirred up my heart the way they always had, and that *hurt*. I didn't want to be affected by Sophia Andonis anymore.

All of a sudden, seventeen years of reunion fantasies evaporated, and I was confronted with the cold, hard fact that Sophia was a real person living a real life, *without me*. She was no longer the young woman I'd enshrined inside my head, *and* she was pregnant with another man's child. We were cautiously facing each other, like frightened cats.

"I can only imagine how important our meeting was to you, John, and I'm so sorry I bailed, but I was so guilt-ridden and terrified of your reaction I couldn't stop throwing up."

I still couldn't forgive her. Almost two decades of my own pain had made me grim.

She snuffled. I could have offered her a tissue from the box between the seats but I was still in grudge mode. She needed to feel my pain.

"I apologize for walking out on you without an explanation," she said. "I—"

"And divorcing me!" I shot back. "Don't forget about that!"

She nodded, then sobbed some more. My heart sank. I couldn't hate her. But I had every right to be hurt. And disappointed. And angry.

"Go ahead, Johnny," she cried, "tell me how badly I fucked you up. Take all day if you need to. I deserve it. It's the least a coward like me can do for you."

You're definitely a coward!

But no matter how much I'd planned to tear into her and tell her in exact punishing detail how she'd ruined me, I suddenly realized that what had wounded me most was not the loss of our amazing, paint-peeling sex, it was that I'd lost my *best friend*. How had I not seen that? My anger had made me stupid.

Suddenly, I didn't want to punish her.

Slowly, she lifted her head but she didn't quite meet my gaze. My heart begged to speak for me and I let it, for once.

"Don't hate yourself, Sophia. I don't hate you. You hurt me more than I can express. But I don't hate you. Okay?" My anger resurfaced, just for a moment.

I glanced at her swollen belly. "You obviously didn't come here to marry me again."

She ducked her head at my cutting tone.

"Congratulations, by the way," I sighed, trying to be a better man. She wasn't carrying *our* baby so just how happy was I supposed to feel?

"Thank you. Just so you know I have a fifteen-year-old daughter and a ten-year-old son."

That was a double gut-punch. After dumping me, she hadn't waited long to start a family. I did the math. *Two years!*

I took a deep breath, readying myself. "Let's hear it. All of it!"

Trembling, she turned as much as her round stomach would allow. Her voice was soft.

"I wasn't in love with you, John. Not really. I loved that you were Greek and I loved that my parents loved you, and I thought all that would be enough and eventually I'd feel what I was supposed to, but no matter how hard I tried, I couldn't fall in love with you. And I really, really tried." She burst into tears again. "And all our friends were getting married, and it seemed like the thing to do, and you were so very handsome, and—"

"Stop!" I roared, smacking the dashboard.

So there it was. The truth! From Sophia's mouth. *Be careful what you wish for—you just might get it, John!* Deep down I'd known. I was so stupid that way—I *had* to hear her say it!

When I saw her face, I reined in my anger and crossed my arms. I sank some more. This wasn't how this was supposed to go. She'd stolen my anger! And I still loved her. *Fuck.*

Maybe to show her how deeply she'd disappointed me, I stared out the window and slowly shook my head. It was time to say all the things I'd planned for so long, but for the life of me I couldn't remember any of them my brain was that foggy. *Don't screw this up!*

Step Number Six: Resolve issues with ex-wife so you can fall in love again.

Damn it! Why did healing have to involve so much frickin' *pain?*

The fog cleared just enough. "I've wasted my life thinking you'd made a mistake. I convinced myself you still loved me, that you'd gotten side-tracked by the allure of more money, a cushier lifestyle. I fantasized that you'd finally recognize that and do the right thing and come back to me."

Her face was a blotchy mess. "Dan wasn't rich," she said, "not at first, but he had aspirations. But that wasn't why I married him, John. I needed to really fall in love, and he turned out to be the one. Dan is the love of my life." She paused. "I'm sorry I wasn't in love with you, John. Please forgive me. I just can't take the guilt anymore."

"Forgive you?" I steeled myself. "Dan, who? And where did you meet this *Dan*?"

"Dan Hillman. He was a year ahead of us at Irondale. I had a serious crush on him, and, to be honest, it never let up."

"I don't remember a Dan Hillman." But high school was like that. There was always a guy you walked by in the hall for years but never knew his name or what grade he was in.

I handed her a tissue. The snuffing was getting on my nerves.

"Why didn't you tell me this when you divorced me? Do you know how much grief you could have saved me? For better or worse, I was your goddamn *husband*, and what about our wedding vows? Didn't they mean *anything* to you?" My heart was smashing my chest. "Were you having an affair with him? While we were married? I wasn't just some fucking boyfriend you could ditch! You knew I had a heart when you married me, and yet you torched it like some evil b—" I stopped short.

The tears were pouring down my cheeks.

Her voice grew shrill and wild and broken. "I didn't cheat on you John but I knew I would eventually. I was so pent up with the guilt I had a nervous breakdown. You were at work, I think. I was so distraught, I hid at my parents' house. They begged me to tell you the truth, but I knew how sensitive you were and how deeply you loved me and I just couldn't do it!" She was gasping. Snot and tears drizzled down her face. "If I were you, I'd hate every fucking inch of me."

Maybe part of me did hate her. But I was relieved she'd told the truth, as brutal and painful as it had been for me to hear. I softened, just a little.

"I'm so sorry for ruining your life!" she wailed. "Please forgive me, John!" She buried her face in her hands. She'd obviously suffered as much as I had. But was it up to me to absolve her of her guilt? Could I be that big of a man, after what she'd done?

I collected my thoughts. "Yeah, you did ruin my life, Sophia," I said quietly. "You're fucking right you did." I sighed. "But then so did I. I'm just as much to blame."

It wasn't my desire to make good on The Steps that changed me towards her in that moment. It was seeing the woman who had been the love of my life, tortured with guilt and regret, the way I'd been.

Her pain had come as a shock to me. I thought she'd felt nothing or had easily blocked me out. How wrong I'd been!

I'd always been terrified of forgiving Sophia, as if I'd be closing the casket at her funeral. I could never say goodbye to her because then she'd be dead to me. Or maybe that act of forgiveness would invalidate my pain. Would I have suffered all those years for nothing, if I forgave her now?

"I accept your apology," I said. Man, that hurt. My pride cringed. And just how long would my forgiveness last? Five seconds? A day? Week? A lifetime?

Sophia took me by surprise when she leaned her head against my shoulder. Heat grew in my belly. I was grateful for that moment of affection. I deserved to be loved. I really did. And so did she.

We shed our remaining tears together. She took my hand, and we squeezed on and off for about ten minutes, because that's what people who care for each other do: comfort each other, in love or lovingly, and either way was fine by me.

A lightbulb went off in in my head. "Here we are together and I don't know about you, but I feel peaceful. It feels good to see you again, even though we're not going to, you know, reunite or anything."

She nodded.

"After a divorce, it's difficult to stay friends, although I've read there are exceptions."

She sighed. "I dunno John."

"I'm guessing Dan would disapprove?"

She tilted her head. "Uh, hard to say."

"I wouldn't blame him if he did."

I slipped my hand out of hers and we sat back in our seats.

"Sophia?"

"Yes?"

"Do me a favour?"

"Okay?" she said, hesitantly.

"In our *minds*, let's be friends, and every morning let's telepathically wish each other a great day, that kind of thing." I felt sheepish, but I knew that I was on the right track.

She laughed. Her face brightened. "Sure, I can do that."

"But *will* you?"

She saw that I was serious. "I will. Why not?"

I pushed my luck. "What if you and Dan include me in your life? You can both come to my dance studio for a free lesson, bring your kids if you like, or maybe you can invite me to a family birthday party?" I leaned towards her, but not too close. "Sophia, your total absence in my life did a number on me. You were my best friend, and I really miss my best friend."

I waited for her reply. She considered my words carefully.

"You were my best friend, too, John. And we did have fun together."

"Yes," I said, hopefully. "We did. Listen, I'm not trying to win you back, I promise. You're in love and happily married. Forever and ever, Amen. I get it. It still hurts, but that's on *me* to fix, not you."

She briefly touched my shoulder with affection, then removed her hand. "You always were a deep thinker, John."

I sighed. "Yep, lucky me."

She went silent.

Things had gone better than I'd expected, so I knew to turn the conversation back toward lighter topics.

I asked her about her pregnancy and about Dan, who, it turns out, was a workaholic who ran a highly successful construction business and was away on business a lot. I was secretly glad he wasn't perfect. It made me feel a little better about myself.

"I'd better be going," she said after a while. She looked wrung out.

Knowing she was leaving panged me, but I took the high road. "Of course." I cleared my throat. "Will you think about what I said?"

"I definitely will."

I rested my hand on the door handle.

Gone was my anguish and pain and bitterness, and so was twenty-three-year-old Sophia Andonis. It was as if meeting her again had updated my ancient software. She was free to go now. I was glad I'd forgiven her. I was happy we'd met again. And I was happy knowing that she still cared for me enough to even consider my "telepathic friendship" proposal, although I wasn't so sure how realistic that was.

Now that I'd seen her in the flesh, a happily married, pregnant forty-year-old, it would be impossible to think of her any other way. Our meeting had been the wake-up call I'd seriously needed. I just wished it had happened much, much sooner.

"I can't believe I, uh, didn't say all the terrible things I'd been planned to say if we met again. To be honest, I'm shocked. I must be evolving."

She was a good woman, and she deserved to be in love with the right man. I knew then that maybe, just maybe, I could finally move on.

"Hey, look!"

I turned my head in the direction of her finger.

She gave me a peck on the cheek.

"You tricked me," I laughed. That little kiss had been healing. I slid out of the car.

As she turned her car towards Flux Road, we exchanged tentative waves.

And then she disappeared, zipping home to be with her kids and the love of her life.

It was over. Finally. After so many years!

Walking home, I actually felt happy. Lighter. *I love you, Sophia.*

I felt like dancing.

Chapter 35

MONDAY, MAY 2, 10:30 a.m.

I slipped into Jimmy's barber shop. Hank was in the sun-filled waiting area, reading a *Playboy* magazine with one eyebrow cocked. He practically lived here, it seemed.

Smoke curled out of the cig in Jimmy's mouth. "Ah, Johnny," he said, bits of ash falling onto his customer's head. "I knew you'd show up. Take a seat, lad. I'll be right with ya."

"Okay, Mr. Psychic," I mumbled, good-naturedly.

I plunked down beside Hank and opted for *Outdoors Canada*. It's not that I didn't approve of *Playboy*, it's just that I couldn't *read* the magazine with other people watching.

Five minutes later, Jimmy bid his customer farewell and had me sitting in his chair.

"Is Agnes working today?"

"She doesn't start until noon."

I was kind of relieved. I wanted our conversation to be private. "She working out okay?"

"Aye, *too* okay. She's charmed up the customers and now everyone wants her to cut their hair. Half the time I'm stuck sitting with my thumb up my arse, reading the girly magazines with old Hank. I'm starting to lose my touch."

Hank merely grunted and turned a page. His focus really was impressive.

"So, business is good then?"

"Aye, business is good." He cleared his throat. "Hardly recognized you wearing those old jeans, Johnny. Did ya suffer a blow to the heed?" He lit up another cig.

I laughed. "Jimmy, you were right when you said I over dress to compensate for my pain. You're a very insightful man."

"I said that?" He blew smoke. "I don't remember, to be honest."

"Yes, sir, you certainly did. Gumball Wisdom, remember?"

"Oh aye, Gumball Wisdom. Well, I do my best, son."

He wrapped a tissue around my collar, then firmed it in place with the blue cape he clipped behind my neck.

"So, you're just a regular Joe like the rest of us now?"

"Yep. Except when I'm Gene Kelly."

He scoffed and sized me up in the mirror. My scars were fading a little. "I heard what happened the night of Zoe's wedding. Are you going to be okay?"

"I am, Jimmy. I am. Thanks." I tried not to feel embarrassed, but I still felt shame.

"Everyone was really worried about you, son," he said, sizing up my shaggy curls. I was way overdue for a trim.

"I'm sorry I put everyone through that," I said, finally. "That was a real low point in my life." *Understatement of the century.*

"Ach, don't be sorry, Johnny. In the end, what doesn't kill you makes you stronger."

I checked to see if Hank was listening. He'd practically pressed his nose against the centerfold page. I hoped that it was because he'd forgotten his reading glasses and not for some other reason.

Jimmy studied me in the mirror. "Are you afraid I'm going to make a mess of your beautiful curls?"

"To be honest, Jimmy, yes, I am."

"Not too late to pack it down to Robertson's. They'll give you exactly what you want for five times my price."

"That won't be necessary. The Village has everything I need. Including your shoddy haircut."

"Hey, watch your tongue, Sonny Jim."

"Or?"

"Or, no more gumballs for Johnny." He wagged his comb at me, mock-scolding.

"Only kidding, Jimmy. I trust you."

"Ach, well, that was your first mistake."

By the time he'd finished cutting my hair, I didn't recognize the Greek man in the mirror.

Short hair! A sleek, sophisticated cut! I looked like a guy who could run a kick-ass dance studio.

"Change is good, Jimmy," I said, beaming.

Jimmy smiled. "Aye, son, can be."

Hank looked up. He was now holding the Outdoors Canada Magazine. I wondered if he realized they didn't do centerfolds.

Chapter 36

SATURDAY, MAY 14, 7 p.m.

Donny was right—dreams *can* come true! Dirk's movie, *All Along*, had been picked up by a Bollywood distributor! I was with the rest of the cast, strolling the red carpet before the premiere at The Royale Cinema in Brampton, Ontario. Exuberant fans of Dev and Sita begged for selfies with the two stars. The men in our party wore tuxes and the women were resplendent in gorgeous saris. Dirk was beside me, smiling a mile wide.

More press had shown up than I'd expected. Family and friends had spread the word and quite a lot of hype had built in Brampton, where there was a huge Indian-Canadian population. In fact, the flourishing local movie industry was being referred to as "Brollywood".

It was a relief to finally get inside, away from the cameras and the noise.

The cast and crew took their seats in the first five rows. Behind us were family and friends, who'd taken the opportunity to dress to the nines.

Archie Love had donned a tartan kilt, jacket and waistcoat. "Loud and Proud," he'd hooted on the red carpet when some of the ladies had giggled at his bare legs.

Beside me, Sheena gave a little gasp.

"Sorry!" I whispered. In my struggle with Imposter Syndrome, I'd been squeezing her hand a little too tightly.

"Don't worry, it's going to be great. I can't wait!" She gave me a reassuring grin.

When the lights went down, the crowd shrieked like banshees.

I have to say, it was a visually stunning movie. The music, the sets, the costumes, the close-ups—everything was so much more polished than I'd expected. I could see that Dev and Sita were on their way to big careers. They had real on-screen charisma.

With ten minutes remaining, my big scene finally arrived. My character, Achilles, was one of the last two challengers for Kiara's love. Up there on the silver screen, on a street set inspired by *Singin' in the Rain*, rained on by red Cupid arrows (courtesy of CGI magic), Dev and I literally flew down into the street scene and prepared to dance our hearts out, in an effort to win the heroine. Dirk's team had managed to make me look ten years younger. I breathed a huge sigh of relief. One of my biggest fears had been that I was going to look ridiculous amongst the young cast. Sita was stunning in a golden sari, with glowing light around her face. Her surly, suspicious grandmother stood beside her with her arms crossed.

I was channeling Gene Kelly, swinging on a light pole, CGI sparkles shooting out of my umbrella and magic pink rain falling. Costumes had put me in a purple suit and fedora. "Look at the state of him!" Archie had hollered, prompting laughter. Dev looked much more dignified in an electric blue *sherwani*, dancing an over-the-top version of the *Bharatanatyam* dance, each move making the air shimmer around him.

In our dance-off, Dev would try to top my moves by adding an Indian twist. Occasionally Dev would stumble, and then Sita would gaze at me adoringly, and her grandma would stare *real* daggers at me, to the audience's delight. But then Dev would spring back to his feet and do me one better.

At one point, Sita couldn't keep her eyes off me as I did the propellor roll. Grandma caught Sita swooning over me and beat her own head in horror. The audience howled with laughter. I had no idea how funny this was going to be!

I felt a surge of pride at the way I had danced—pretty damn good for an old guy!

Courtesy of movie magic, Dev and I were suddenly in tuxedo tailcoats, having a tap-off. The air was filled with sparkles. The routine was so aerobic that I was surprised I hadn't had a heart attack. Dev tapped his way up a set of stairs, then dove off the railing into a magnificent split leap. The audience had divided up into two factions by now, and the supporters of Gary Kumar cheered enthusiastically. When I followed with a *cabriole*, my Village crew responded with raucous shouts.

Then Dev knocked out three back flips in a row. The Brampton crowd went bananas for him.

Halfway into *my* third backflip, Grandma flung a Ninja star at me. It bounced off my forehead and I crashed into the floor. The audience screamed with laughter as CGI pain emojis floated around my head.

Dev seized the opportunity by tapping around me like a matador circling a dying bull. Grandma cackled like a demon and shook her fist triumphantly. The audience loved her. I wondered if Dirk had realized he was making a comedy.

The final part of our competition involved a trampoline built into the set floor. This was the routine that had left me the most sore after rehearsals. Dev and I stood opposite each other on first-floor balconies. Dev leapt first, his black sequined unitard sparkling, and bounced up to my balcony with impressive mid-air splits. He smirked at me and the audience applauded. I one-upped him with a back flip after my bounce. I landed across the way on the second-floor balcony and gave a saucy click of my heels.

Dev jumped again, back-flipped, landed on his stomach, and shot up three stories! From the balcony above me, he leaned down and patted me on the head. Fierce-faced, I leapt and bounced up an incredible four stories, striking a proposal pose in mid-air! A CGI ring twinkled in a little velvet jewelry box. The air around me pulsed with red hearts.

Achilles had stolen Kiara's breath away. She'd pressed her hands to her bosom. Her grandma's scowl filled the entire screen, rotten teeth and all, and she was screeching, screeching, screeching! The audience was practically rolling in the aisles.

In her rage, Grandma leapt up onto the trampoline, bounced, and struck a superman pose. She grabbed me around the waist and flung us up through the rain clouds into oblivion!

The sun came out. The clouds were gone, and so was I. Grandma floated down on the back of a flying peacock, her smile serene.

Kiara and Gary ran into each other's arms and kissed, long and hard. Turns out Gary had been the man Kiara had loved all along but it had taken a dance-off for her to realize it.

Grandma winked at the audience. *She'd* won!

The credits rolled.

I choked up, moved to tears. I'd pulled it off.

The movie theatre thundered with applause. The audience leapt to their feet.

We'd knocked it out of the park! The movie was spectacular! Dirk was on Cloud Nine. There was lots of hugging and back-slapping and heartfelt congratulations. For once, Mr. Love behaved himself. With an unlit cig in his mouth, he proclaimed to Dirk how much he'd always loved Gene Kelly.

Thanks to the reach of the Bollywood film industry, *All Along* became an instant hit in India. We'd all risked so much, and it had paid off, big time.

As strangers and friends congratulated me, I felt so emotional—something deep inside me had finally uncorked.

To show my gratitude, I treated my fellow Villagers and cast members to dinner at the Mandarin Chinese buffet. We had a jolly good time. The bill came to 2500 dollars, and I'd been more than happy to pay it, despite death threats from Mr.Valentini and Mr. Love and Dad. Eventually, I caved and accepted a hundred dollars from each of them, soothing their bruised egos.

Anyway, I made it all back, as it turned out, because six months later, I received a royalty cheque for ten grand! I was floored.

At road hockey, Machine Shop Psycho Scabbard had congratulated me. "Not bad for a Greek faggot!" he'd blurted. For Scabbard to compliment me was like winning the Powerball Lottery. And then just to show him how much I appreciated his back-handed compliment, I danced past him and scored a goal.

Then something even more unbelievable happened. It seemed the entire Hamilton Indian Canadian population had seen *All Along*. Suddenly, I was a hot item, and my dance studio was packed with women!

On June 1, after forty-six years, my parents sold the restaurant. With me out of the picture, they'd finally accepted that they were too old and tired to run it on their own. The restaurant had been their constant through life's ups and downs—raising kids, a daughter's marriage, a son's divorce, grandchildren, deaths of family members, health scares—but no longer were they the young married couple starting life in a new country, their life fully ahead of them, now most of it was behind.

To help ease their pain and create a fresh start, they'd taken a month-long vacation to Greece and had caught up with old friends and family they hadn't seen in years. After arriving back home, Ma had cried, "Hawaii or bust!" and at first Dad had waved her off, but then he'd winked at Amara and me and we knew he was going to the land of pineapples.

My friends regularly checked in on me. Before my life had bottomed out, their kindness had always wounded my pride, but after Tony saved my life, all that changed. Something deep inside me finally relaxed and let go.

Headshop Bob and I became *great* friends. Often, Norb and I would hang out with him on his lunchbreak in the back room where he kept the bongs, and over coffee we'd listen to the Grateful Dead while discussing psylocibin therapy, Jungian philosophy, the meaning of life, all things Hamilton and, Bob's favourite topic of all, *rock'n'roll*.

Bob was one of the most intelligent guys I'd ever met. Most of the time Norb was content to listen and nod, happy knowing I'd welcomed Bob into our fold.

The only thing I couldn't stand about Bob was his love of the Chicago Black Hawks hockey team. A Canadian rooting for an American hockey team? Seriously?

With Bob and Norb present, I tripped weekly in the comfort of my own home.

I saw crazy joker-faced entities, and sometimes they scared me, and sometimes they made me laugh, and sometimes weep. I always felt lighter after my sessions. Seventeen years wallowing in a hell-of-my-own-making had made me powerfully empathetic towards others going through the same thing. I began to see people differently. I understood their pain. And I didn't judge them. And that was good for their mental health and mine.

After two months, I stopped tripping—I knew that deep down the sessions had served their purpose, but to continue would have been foolish, or somehow detrimental.

But I don't regret a second of it. It was part of my healing journey. And, in the end, I was a better man because of it, but also knew that what worked for me might not work for someone else, nor should it.

On Sundays, Norb, Donny, Bob and I play slot cars at Tony's. Bob bought a Can-am car he calls The Flamethrower. He'd painted it so it resembled an acid-trip. On the car doors, he'd painted DMT (Dimethyltryptamine). Turns out Bob's quite an artist.

Tony was worried Angelina would get the wrong idea about drugs and question the meaning of DMT, so he asked Bob to tape over the letters when she was playing with us. He happily obliged.

Chapter 37

Outside St. Demetrius Greek Orthodox Church on Flux, far enough along the sidewalk so I wouldn't be recognized by the arriving congregants, Sheena and I stood, wearing our Easter Sunday best.

I'd worked my way up to doing this. A month earlier, I'd gone to the christening of Norb and Morag's beautiful baby boy, Hans. It'd been at a United Church, not a Greek one, so there wasn't anyone there from my past. Anyway, I'd *had* to go, since I was the godfather. I survived.

Today everything was blooming. On the church lawn, robins hopped about or sang from the gnarled branches of the old oak tree that had been there since I was a kid.

After my divorce I hadn't set foot here, I'd vowed I never would, yet here I was. And boy, did I feel like the prodigal son!

I watched the families mounting the steps to the church and steeled myself. An irrational part of me felt guilty for deserting them. *These people love you. Remember Zoe's wedding, when they were so happy to see you?*

"You can do this, John," Sheena said, taking my hands in hers. She was wearing a smart blue dress and her hair was soft and natural against her shoulders.

The past two Sundays, we'd stood in the exact same spot but I'd chickened out. I was afraid that if I didn't go in today, Sheena would see me as a coward. So I *had* to.

She turned me to face her. "John, I have a confession to make."

I felt an anxious pang. "A confession? Sure, of course." What could she possibly need to confess? I tried to lighten the mood. "Let me guess. You're not really Scottish?"

She shook her head. "Not funny, John."

I laughed weakly. "Sorry."

"Promise you won't get mad."

"I promise." I checked my watch. "Are you sure this can't wait until after church? The service is about to start."

"No, it can't. And now *is* the best time."

I'd never seen her so earnest. She released my hand. "My Da was Greek."

"Your Da was Greek?" I laughed out loud. "Yeah, right!"

She shook her head and pursed her lips. "Greek, John, and Mum was Scottish. They met on a cruise ship. And they fell in love." Her eyes widened. "I know you won't like this, but I'm half-Greek!"

I burst out laughing. All my bottled-up stress poured out of me. I doubled over with laughter. The irony was just the tonic I'd needed.

She rubbed my back, patiently waiting for me to regain control. When she handed me a tissue, I discovered I had a few tears to wipe.

When I came up for air, I felt lighter. Something old and tense and sick had finally been released.

"I *love* that you're half-Greek, Sheena," I said. "I love you. You're my forever love." I pulled her close.

"You sure? You said you'd never date a Greek girl again, remember?"

"More than sure." I bent down and kissed her for all I was worth.

After a while, I pulled away. We were both out of breath, pleasantly gasping.

She looked surprised.

"Sheena, hold my hand. I'm ready."

Her face lit up and we strode towards the church.

Inside, we were met with friendly, familiar faces, now older, like mine.

When we stepped into the Narthex, it felt as if every head turned. Thankfully, the organist didn't stop playing. But it wasn't my imagination—a hush had fallen over the congregation. John Pappas had returned to the fold.

Friendly, familiar faces smiled.

Tears stung my eyes as we fumbled into the back pew. Sheena handed me a tissue and squeezed my hand. I daubed my face.

And I realized I was home, again, finally I had transformed in the past year. I had a new fiancé, a forever love. *Thank you, God!*

In two months, Sheena and I would be married. Tony, Donny, and Norb would *all* be my best men. And what could go wrong would, of course, but that would be another story for another day.

Would you please leave a review?

DID YOU ENJOY *Johnny Goes Loco*? If so, would you be kind enough to leave a review, either with the retailer where you purchased this book or at Goodreads? Thank you!

Indie authors rely on the kind reviews of readers to get the word out to others.

Don't miss out!

Visit the website below and you can sign up to receive emails whenever Dave Walker publishes a new book. There's no charge and no obligation.

https://books2read.com/r/B-A-CGLW-HJCSG

BOOKS 2 READ

Connecting independent readers to independent writers.

About the Author

Dave lives with his writer wife, Anne L. Darling, in Hamilton, Ontario, Canada. The author may be reached at: davewalkerauthor@yahoo.com Read more at www.davewalkerauthor.com.